DINNER, DESSERT . . . AND MURDER

Savannah Reid was never happier then when those she loved were seated around her kitchen table, stuffing their faces with her good Southern home cooking. At that moment, four of her favorite people were finishing off a platter of fried chicken, a bowl of mashed potatoes, and a boat of cream gravy. Tammy Hart, her health-conscious assistant, was enjoying her usual salad.

As Savannah joined the table, Ryan Stone asked, "Do you have time for a little extra work, Savannah? I've been hired by a beauty pageant promoter to 'guard' some lovelies who are competing for the Miss Gold Coast crown."

"Miss Gold Coast?" Tammy asked, nearly choking on her salad. "What a disgrace . . . Evaluating women on the basis of physical attributes."

"Yeah," Dirk agreed. "Disgusting. Do they need an off-duty cop as a chaperone?"

Savannah scooped up a big forkful of pie dripping with caramel and pecan sauce. "I'll take it," she told Ryan. "Looking out for some girlie-girl beauty queens, making sure they don't stub their pretty toes and ruin their pedicures, maybe breaking up a few catfights over false eyelashes and hair mousse—how hard could it be? I mean . . . What could possibly happen at a beauty pageant?"

Books by G.A. McKevett

JUST DESSERTS

BITTER SWEETS

KILLER CALORIES

COOKED GOOSE

SUGAR AND SPITE

SOUR GRAPES

PEACHES AND SCREAMS

Published by Kensington Publishing Corporation

Sour Grapes

G.A.
McKevett

KENSINGTON BOOKS
Kensington Publishing Corp.
http://www.kensingtonbooks.com

KENSINGTON BOOKS are published by

Kensington Publishing Corp.
850 Third Avenue
New York, NY 10022

All Kensington Titles, Imprints, and Distributed Lines are
available at special quantity discounts for bulk purchases for
sales promotions, premiums, fund-raising, and educational or
institutional use. Special book excerpts or customized print-
ings can also be created to fit specific needs. For details, write
or phone the office of the Kensington special sales manager:
Kensington Publishing Corp., 850 Third Avenue, New York,
NY 10022, attn: Special Sales Department, Phone: 1-800-221-
2647.

Kensington and the K logo Reg. U.S. Pat. & TM Off.

First Hardcover Printing: February 2001
First Paperback Printing: December 2001
10 9 8 7 6 5 4 3 2 1

Printed in the United States of America

ACKNOWLEDGMENTS

An artist seldom receives the kind of freedom and encouragement that I have enjoyed with my editor, John Scognamiglio. Bless you, John, for your generous spirit. And for your guidance, and your patience, and your great titles, and your plot ideas, and . . .

Chapter

1

Standing at the counter of Burger Bonanza, the tantalizing aroma of stale cooking oil tickling her nostrils, the sight of sandwiches in greasy wrappers setting her taste buds atwitter, Savannah Reid considered herself lucky to be within reach of food . . . any food. It had been a long night.

"Sure you can afford this cornucopia of culinary delights, big boy?" she asked her buddy, Dirk Coulter, who stood beside her, studying the backlit menu on the wall—specifically, the price column—with the discriminating eye of a first-rate cheapskate.

"I can afford it if you don't get carried away," he grumbled. Spotting a poster that dangled on a string from the ceiling, he brightened. "Hey, they've got a special . . . a Junior Deluxe with fries and a drink for ninety-nine cents! Let's get a couple of those!"

"Let's don't. I'm starved, and that measly kiddy meal

wouldn't fill a chipmunk's cheeks," she said, her Southern drawl becoming more pronounced, as it always did when she was irritated and hungry. And Savannah was frequently one or the other.

She stepped up to the counter and motioned to the skinny girl in the baggy, red-and-blue polyester pantsuit. As the Burger Bonanza hostess sauntered to the cash register, Savannah noted the plastic name tag on the breast pocket of her shirt. "Good evening . . . ah . . . Jeanette. I would like to order a—"

"I ain't Jeanette," the girl said as she slid an enormous wad of gum from one side of her mouth to the other and chomped on it. "Whaddaya want? We're closin' in a couple o' minutes."

Savannah forced a weak smile and resisted the urge to relocate the gum to some other orifice . . . like the left nostril or right ear. Both of which bore multiple piercings. Beside her, Dirk snickered, and she elbowed him in the ribs. "Well, Miss Scrawny-Assed, Ill-Mannered Person Wearing Jeanette's Uniform, I want a double chili-cheeseburger with a superlarge fries and about a quart of Coke and—

"Hey, stop right there!" Dirk held up one hand in his best traffic-directing mode. "I'm not made of money, you know. Cops don't exactly knock down the bucks."

"I know. I was one. But private detectives don't make a killin' either. And I just spent half the night, keeping you company on a duller-than-dirt stakeout *for free.*"

"I thought the joy of hangin' out with me would be payment enough."

Savannah looked him up and down, taking in the tousled, thinning hair, the decrepit bomber jacket, the ratty T-shirt with a faded Harley-Davidson logo, the nearly kneeless jeans, and the smirk on a face that

showed the wear and tear of more than twenty years as a
street cop.

In a weak moment, she might have admitted that ·
she joined him on midnight stakeouts for the pleasure
of his company. They had been partners on the San
Carmelita police force for seven years, before she and
the department had experienced a parting of the
ways. And she missed Dirk. If nothing else, she missed
the daily opportunities to yank his chain; he was just so
"yankable."

She gave him one of her deep-dimpled smiles, then
sniffed. "Eh . . . get real, Fart Face. You promised me
food. Now, fork over for a double chili cheese and the
works before I pitch a fit."

Dirk groaned—a beaten man. He turned to the girl
behind the register. "Get her what she ordered, before
she decides she wants onion rings and a strawberry sun-
dae, too."

A few minutes later, they were sitting on miserably
hard booth seats, their feast spread across the table between them. Dirk was pouting, and the expression
looked ridiculous on a forty-plus guy wearing a Harley
shirt.

"Geez, you didn't have to go ahead and order the
rings and—"

"Oh, hush and stuff your jaws." She shoved the oil-
soaked bag of onion rings over to him and grabbed her
own burger from the tray. Chili ran from both sides of
the sandwich and dripped onto the wrapper as she bit
into it. The spicy sauce filled her senses, and she closed
her eyes as she chewed, savoring the moment. Ah . . .
food, nourishment, highly saturated fat calories. Once
again, all was right with the world.

For just a second, maybe two, her pleasure was

slightly dimmed by the thought that tomorrow morning, this burger would be riding around on her butt or elsewhere on her body, along with about thirty extra pounds of Winchell's Donuts, Ben & Jerry's Chunky Monkey, Yukon Gold potato chips—drowned in French onion dip—and chocolate-dunked, peanut butter cheesecake. But, as always, these depressing thoughts had a short shelf life in Savannah's mental archives.

Long ago, she had decided to live comfortably with those thirty pounds. She liked the extra sixteen that had settled on her chest. And she figured a pound or two on her face filled out any fortysomething wrinkles. A pound on each foot and another for both hands weren't something she worried about. That only left nine unwanted pounds, which she assumed had wound up on her rear, and since she carefully avoided wraparound dressing-room mirrors, she hardly ever saw her backside. Outta sight, outta mind—it was a motto to live by.

Yes . . . after a bit of rationalization, Savannah had conjured a healthy self-image. Nine unseen pounds certainly wasn't enough to cause her to take drastic measures . . . like dieting or jogging.

"You'd think," Dirk said around a mouthful of burger, "that for the prices they charge, they'd install a decent sound system in here." He nodded toward the speaker mounted on the wall behind a potted plant with brown, crispy leaves.

Savannah squirted a glob of ketchup onto her fries as she listened to the scratchy version of "Hotel California." "Glenn Frey sounds good no matter what," she said.

"Eh, you've just had a crush on him since he was on *Miami Vice* a million years ago," Dirk said, sounding slightly miffed. Although they had never been romantically linked, Dirk sulked when she said anything good about another guy. And Savannah had to admit that she bristled when he made "Cindy Crawford-hot-bod" comments. But she wasn't about to admit that those minor irritations were indicators of anything other than a long-standing, completely blasé friendship.

"Are you goin' out with me again tomorrow night?" he asked, reaching for her soda. "That guy's bound to show up at his mama's house sooner or later, and then I'll nab his ass and stick it back in jail where it belongs."

"Yeah, I'll hang out with you again. But only because I have a special feeling in my heart for kid beaters like that one. I think it's called loathing. Get your hands off my Coke. Buy your own."

"What are you talkin' about? It's all-you-can-drink. When it runs out, you just go fill it up again. Why should I pay for two?"

She snatched the Coke out of his hand and returned it to her side of the table. "Because I don't want to swap slobber with you."

"I wouldn't slobber in it. Geez, Van . . . for a chick you can be really gross sometimes. I—"

"Sh-h-h. Heads up," she said, looking over his shoulder toward the front of the dining room, where a motley entourage was filing in, wearing the baseball jackets and caps, and red-kerchief bandannas that identified them as members of one of Los Angeles's more vicious gangs.

"What is it?" Dirk asked, instantly serious. They had worked together so long that they read each other well, and even though a half smile was pasted on her face, her blue eyes registered definite concern.

"Looks like we've got some big-city gang activity," she

said, "right here in the sleepy little beach town, tourist trap called San Carmelita."

"How many?"

She turned back to him but watched them in her peripheral vision as they spread out across the front of the restaurant. "We've got five males and a female. The girl's walking up to the counter. Looks like she's going to order."

"And the others?"

"We've got one very big, older and very mean-looking dude standing in the doorway, eyeing the parking lot. He's wearing a black-leather raincoat."

"It ain't rained since April."

"Exactly. Oversize, and he's got one hand inside."

Dirk winced. "Oh, shit. That there's bad news. What do you figure he's carryin'?"

"Whatever he ripped off in his last burglary. Could be an Uzi."

"Do you think it's them?"

Savannah didn't have to ask who he meant; the same thought had occurred to her the moment the crew had entered. An APB had been issued about a group of teenage gangsters, led by a guy in his early twenties, who had been holding up fast-food joints on the coast of California, north of Los Angeles. They picked spots—like Burger Bonanza—that were near a freeway entrance and hit them late at night, just before closing, nabbing the day's receipts. As soon as they robbed the place, they headed down the highway and were lost in the traffic.

So far, they hadn't killed anyone, but during the last holdup they had shot a cashier and destroyed the kid's right arm. Definitely bad guys . . . quickly getting badder.

"Oh yeah," she said. "I'd bet they're our buddies. And us here with I-Ain't-Jeanette and the salad bar cleaner-upper . . ."

Her voice trailed away as one of the males, carrying an enormous boom box, walked by their table on his way to a booth in the back corner of the room. He sat down, facing forward, set the box on the table in front of him, and turned on what Savannah called "rap crap," drowning out Glenn Frey and causing Savannah to hate him with all her being.

"He's mad-doggin' me, big time," Dirk said. "Sizin' me up."

"Yeah, the guy at the door is checking us both out and keeping an eye peeled on the parking lot. What do you wanna do?"

"Bust 'em?"

"Yeah, right. Duh . . . six to two are pretty lousy odds. I don't mind getting you and me killed, but if anything happened to sweet little Ain't-Jeanette, I'd never forgive myself."

"I guess you're right. Maybe if I just whip out my badge, it'll scare 'em away."

Savannah raised one eyebrow. "Hey, that's a possibility. Not *you* pullin' it out, but *me*. Remember what we did to distract those yahoos in Chat-n-Chew Café a few years back?"

"Yeah, but there were only three of 'em, not a roomful."

Savannah saw two of the other guys take seats in the front corner booths. The girl sat down beside one of them, a soft drink in her hand. She gave Savannah an icy, bitter look that belied the softness of her youthful face.

Savannah's anxiety barometer rose a couple of notches;

she and Dirk were now effectively surrounded. "Well, we gotta do something fast," she said. "They've taken positions. It's going down."

She reached under the table and tapped him discreetly on the knee. "Pass me your badge."

"Ah, man . . . how come you get to be the cop?"

"'Cause I'm the girl, and they won't get as shook up if it's me. Now give me the tin."

Reluctantly, he slipped his hand inside his jacket, then handed her the badge under the table. "It's not tin; it's gold . . . and you'd better not get any bullet holes in it."

She glanced around warily as she slid the thin, leather folder inside her sweater. "I'll try not to." Then, louder, she added, "I'm gonna make a trip to the salad bar. Want anything?"

Out of the corner of her eye, she saw the leader of the entourage tense and lift his left hand slightly. The others froze, their eyes darting between him and the booth where she and Dirk were sitting.

Dirk used the opportunity to glance over his shoulder at the front of the restaurant, the salad bar, and the players in their drama. "Yeah," he said with studied nonchalance, "nab me some breadsticks."

"Breadsticks comin' up."

Slowly, she stood and strolled up to the stainless-steel bar with its fake stained-glass canopy. The teenage, male employee had just finished covering the last metal canister and loading it on a cart with the others. All that remained was melting ice, strewn with bits of lettuce and other veggie castaways. He didn't look happy to see her.

"I've got everything put away," he said. "We're closing, you know."

"No, I didn't know," she replied, walking up to him and standing as close as she could without arousing the suspicions of the gangsters nearest her, about twenty feet away. "And I want some chocolate pudding."

"We don't have no pudding," he said, swabbing at the stainless-steel edge of the bar with a soggy rag. "And even if we did, I told you, we're closing."

Savannah took a couple more steps toward him, until they were nearly nose to nose. "I said . . . I want pudding. And I know you've got some in the kitchen." She jabbed his chest with her forefinger for emphasis. "You get back there and fetch it for me. I'm suffering from PMS and I need my friggin' chocolate fix. You hear me?"

The kid's eyes bugged slightly. "Yeah, I guess so. I mean, I'll see if we've got some."

As he started to walk away she whispered, "Stay back there. Both of you." He looked confused. She raised her voice. "And if you come out here without that pudding, mister, you're takin' your life in your hands!"

She lingered at the salad bar, checking out a shriveled radish, floating in the watery ice, until she could see that the boy had taken the clerk by her elbow and led her into the back of the kitchen out of sight.

Like cigarettes burning holes in an old sofa's cushions, Savannah could feel the gangsters' eyes boring into her as they watched her every movement.

Her mind racing, mentally rehearsing her next sequence of maneuvers, she meandered back to the table where Dirk sat. A thought raced through her brain, *This is a dumb idea. You're gonna get yourself and Dirk killed.*

She quickly retorted with a silent, *Oh, yeah . . . can you think of anything better?*

Predictably, there was no reply, silent or otherwise.

What she had in mind probably wouldn't work. But she couldn't think of anything else, and she'd much prefer to be active than wait and react to a roomful of armed kids with hardened, criminal mind-sets.

"Did you get me those breadsticks?" Dirk asked, loudly, rudely as she reached the table. He, too, was "getting into character" for their little drama, sitting there in the booth looking grouchy. Fortunately, for Dirk, acting grouchy wasn't exactly a stretch.

"Nope, I didn't get your breadsticks," she told him, "or my pudding either. They've put everything away. You're outta luck."

Taking a deep breath and saying a quick prayer for safety that Granny Reid had taught her more than thirty years ago, she stood next to Dirk. She felt him tense and knew he, too, was ready.

Suddenly, she grabbed him and yanked him out of the booth and onto his feet. A half second later, she had plastered his face against the nearest wall. "All right, buddy," she told him, kicking his legs apart, "you spread 'em and don't make a move!"

She heard the gang members gasp collectively, and one of them said, "Hey, man . . . what the hell?"

Only then did she allow them to see the 9mm Beretta she had drawn from her shoulder holster. "I'm a cop," she told them, showing them Dirk's badge in her other hand, "and I'm arresting this man. Just stay where you are and be cool, and I won't let him hurt you."

She put the badge away, grabbed a pair of handcuffs from her slacks pocket and put them on his wrists. "And you," she said, giving him an elbow in the back for emphasis, "better not cause me any trouble, or I'll part your hair with a bullet. What little you've got, that is."

Dirk growled under his breath; he was more than a little sensitive about his thinning, not-so-luxurious mane. "Watch it," he said. "You'll pay later."

"Was that a threat?" she said, showing him the Beretta. "Did I hear you threaten me, you lowlife scum?"

One of the hoods and the girl got out of their seats and took a couple of steps toward Savannah. She watched them warily.

"So, what'd he do?" the girl asked.

The big guy at the door strolled over. "Yeah, whatcha bustin' him for?"

"Murder," Savannah said. "I've been after this guy for a long time." Turning back to Dirk, she said, "That'll teach you to go on a blind date that your ex-girlfriend arranged. She fixed you up with a homicide detective, Lame Brain. We both owe her one."

Savannah gave the gangsters her best deeply concerned, maternal look. "You guys oughta get outta here while you've got the chance. I've already called for backup, and in a minute this place is gonna be swarming with cops . . . reporters, too. Maybe even the *America's Most Wanted* crew. If I were you, I wouldn't want to be in the middle of a mess like that. Once they start asking you questions, they never let you go."

The older guy gave his troupe a curt nod, and they rushed the door, en masse. Only the girl lingered, gazing at Dirk with what looked a lot like groupie adoration.

"You've been on *America's Most Wanted?*" she asked him, batting her eyelashes. "Who'd you murder?"

"He's a serial killer," Savannah supplied. "Murdered at least a dozen teenage girls . . . about your age."

Dirk shot Savannah a look. He was frowning, but his eyes were sparkling.

"Really?" The girl was completely smitten. "Wow!"

"Yeah . . ." Savannah added, on a roll, "even ate parts of 'em. Cooked 'em up, right there in his kitchen along with some onions, turnips, and mustard greens."

Dirk turned his face to the wall and cleared his throat. His shoulders shook slightly.

"Latisha!" The leader was holding the door open. "Move your ass, bitch!"

"Hmm, smooth-talkin' laddie, treats his ladies nice," Savannah mused as she watched them hustle out the door. "Busting him would be almost as much fun as slapping cuffs on you, Babycakes."

"Speaking of cuffs," Dirk said when the last one had stepped outside, "these *are* loose enough for me to slip 'em off if I need to, right?"

"Of course. You don't think I'd bind those mighty fists of fury, do you? I might have needed you to duke it out with the big guy."

"Yeah, right. How much of a head start are we gonna give 'em?"

"Not much. We've gotta see which entrance they take when they get to the freeway, north or south. Let's get going."

Keeping her gun in hand and highly visible, she led her "prisoner" across the restaurant and out the door. The gangsters were piling into two late-model luxury cars. Apparently robbery paid better than private detecting, Savannah decided as she directed Dirk to her 1965 Mustang on the opposite side of the parking lot. Its China red paint glowed a sickly coral in the light of the yellow parking-lot lamps. The feeble illumination also made it difficult for her to read the license plate on one of the cars that was revving up and getting ready to leave.

"I've got the Lexus," she told Dirk, who was shuffling along in captured-cannibal-serial-killer style.

"Yeah, and I've got the Acura. You carryin' your cell phone?"

"It's in my car pocket."

"Your what? Oh, yeah, I forgot . . . that's Southern for glove box."

When they reached her Mustang, Savannah opened the passenger door and shoved Dirk inside, then slammed it closed. A quick glance at the car nearest them told her the gang was watching. Sitting in the backseat, the girl had her nose pressed against the window and was practically drooling on the glass. Savannah was amazed; females who were hopelessly smitten with Dirk were a rare commodity.

She hurried to her side of the car, slid into the driver's seat, and got the motor humming. Her Mustang might be ancient, but thanks to her skilled mechanic, Ray, it could burn the wind when she applied a heavy foot to the pedal.

Dirk had already slipped off the cuffs, had her cell phone out, and was dialing. He ducked, hiding his face beneath the dash, as the first gangster's car peeled past them.

"Hey, Jake," he shouted into the phone. Dirk had never grasped the concept that you don't have to scream into a cell phone to be heard. "Where are ya? Yeah, right now." He listened for a second. "Good, I got a hot one for you. How would you like to help bust the 'Burger Bandits.' I kid you not, my man. Get as much backup as you can muster . . . a chopper if possible . . . and head for the 101. I'll be tellin' you north or south in a minute or so."

Savannah waited until both cars full of suspects had

left the parking lot before following at a discreet distance. As she had anticipated, they were heading toward the freeway entrance ramps.

"Northbound," she said, a bit surprised at their choice. "I figured they'd be heading home to L.A. I guess we didn't put the fear of God in 'em after all."

Dirk conveyed the newest bulletin to Jake McMurtry. "They're probably on their way to Santa Barbara," he added. "There's plenty of burger joints to hit between here and there."

Savannah nudged him with her elbow. "Tell Jake we gotta take them before they leave the freeway. The next ten exits go into residential areas. And if they get to another restaurant, we'll be in the same situation we were before."

"Did you hear that, Jake?" Dirk barked into the phone. "Don't screw this up, man. We need lots of units, and everybody's gotta know they're armed . . . at least one Uzi. Don't want nobody dead, unless it's them."

Savannah winced. Dirk wasn't known for keeping his negative, even hostile, opinions to himself. Even after years of seeing the worst of humanity, Savannah chose to look for the good in people, although it wasn't always immediately obvious. Dirk didn't bother. Dirk's theory: Life stinks, the world stinks, and everybody in it stinks. And with an attitude like that, he daily collected enough evidence to prove his hypothesis.

"Damn it, Van," he said, "I wish we were in my car. Not having a radio stinks."

"Don't gripe. Your heap isn't even running right now. Is Jake calling it in?"

Dirk growled and nodded as he listened on the phone. "Yeah. I hear him. He's outta breath . . . must be trottin' out to his car. Jake eats too damned much pizza."

This, from a guy whose decrepit Buick was a repository for a year's worth of junk-food wrappers and fast-food sacks. Dirk hadn't seen his rear floorboards since he had bought the Skylark in 1969.

Savannah speeded up a bit, keeping the two sets of taillights ahead well in sight. Other than a couple of eighteen-wheelers, they and the gangsters had the Ventura Freeway all to themselves. Recalling the hard, cold look in the leader's eyes and the dead expressions on the other kids' faces, she felt a shiver of healthy fear. She would be glad when the cavalry reinforcements arrived.

Like a fairy godmother's wish come true, three cruisers magically appeared in her rearview mirror. "Good goin', Jake," she whispered. "They're he-e-e-re," she told Dirk. "You've got backup."

"Don't you mean 'we'?"

"No way. I'm just the chauffeur along for the ride. Shall I move closer?"

Dirk looked over his shoulder, observing the units that were quickly closing the gap. "Where the hell are you, Jake?" he shouted into the phone. "You want a piece of this or not?"

Turning back to Savannah, he said, "Jake's north of us . . . about ten miles. They're closing off the freeway, in case they run when we try to stop 'em."

The three SCPD cars pulled even with them, one on each side of the Mustang and the third behind. Savannah cursed her lack of a radio to communicate with them and rolled down her window. The officer riding in the passenger seat did the same.

"The Acura and the Lexus, right?" he shouted.

She stuck her head out the window, and the night air whipped her hair into her eyes and took her breath away. "Yeah," she said. "Three passengers in each. Gang-bangers . . . armed-robbery suspects."

Dirk leaned across her and yelled, "May have an Uzi. Watch yourself."

The officer nodded. "We'll surround them, light 'em up, and announce. You guys take the left rear."

Savannah gave him a nod. "Gotcha." She rolled the window back up and, in unison with the patrol cars, increased speed until they had closed the gap between them and their targets.

The robbers' cars were side by side, the Lexus in the middle lane, the Acura in the fast lane. It took less than five seconds for the police to take their positions, one unit to the right, one on the left shoulder, another behind the Lexus and the Mustang behind the Acura. Blue-and-red revolving lights began to flash. A siren gave a couple of short shrieks.

"Hey, Van . . . been a while since you've done this sort o' take-down," Dirk remarked.

Savannah could hear it in his voice, the adrenaline-pumped charge of the chase. Her own pulse was pounding in her ears, her mouth was dry, her palms wet. "Yeah, a long time," she said, her eyes on the car ahead—major tunnel vision.

"Cool, huh?"

She grinned . . . a little. "Yeah, *way* cool. If we don't get killed."

At that moment, the three patrol cars directed high-powered spotlights on the suspects' cars, lighting up the interiors so brightly, they could clearly see each occupant. The gangsters' heads were whipping right and left, as they sized up their situation: Grim.

"They look a little shook," Dirk said, a smirk on his face.

Savannah nodded. "Shook is good. Shook is how we want them."

A deep, authoritative voice boomed from a loud-speaker. "Drivers, this is the San Carmelita Police Department. Bring your vehicles to a slow, controlled stop. Now, drivers. Slow your vehicles and come to a complete stop."

Savannah glanced in her rearview mirror. Not a headlight in sight. Jake must have had the freeway closed behind them, too.

Not that it would matter. The kids weren't stopping.

"They're not even slowing down," she said.

"Did you really expect them to?"

She shrugged. "Yeah, but I also believe in the tooth fairy, and that I'm going to marry Mel Gibson someday, so . . ."

Suddenly, the robbers' cars shot forward. Dirk swore and Savannah pressed her gas pedal to the floor. Thanks to Ray the mechanic, she had no problem keeping up, even when they reached 90 mph. Neither did the cops, who maintained their positions on each side, lights still flashing, more sirens blaring.

"Morons," Dirk said, hanging on to the console and armrest. "Where do they think they're gonna go? Have you got plenty of gas, Van?"

"Over half a tank. We're in there for the long haul. Sit back and enjoy the ride."

"Not with a broad driving," he muttered under his breath.

"Would you prefer to get out and run alongside?"

"Just keep your eye on . . . Hey, what's goin' on?"

Savannah was wondering the same thing. The patrol

cars had suddenly pulled back. Way back. She and Dirk appeared to be the only ones continuing the chase.

"Do you see anything?" she shouted as she maintained speed and their position behind the Acura, while trying to look into the cars. "What . . . ? Are they shooting? Do you see guns?"

Dirk was leaning forward, gripping the dash. "I don't see anything." He looked back at the cruisers, who were still with them but far behind. "Why did they—?"

Savannah saw it lying across the road ahead of them. A bar of metal, shining silver in their headlights.

Now she knew, but it was too late to stop.

The Acura shot across the metal. So did the Lexus. And the Mustang.

"Shit, spike strip," Dirk said. "Hang on, Van."

She heard the fatal, popping sound of her tires as they disintegrated beneath her. The Mustang shuddered, pulled sharply to the right, then the left, and she felt as though she were driving through half-set cement. Just ahead, the Lexus and Acura fishtailed, slamming back fenders before the Acura spun off the road and into the median.

Even as Savannah fought to maintain control of her automobile, she saw half a dozen patrol cars, some from SCPD, some from the county sheriffs, and Jake Mc-Murtry's van.

They were converging on the suspects' vehicles before they even came to a complete stop. Behind them, she saw some cops scrambling to retract the spike strip. The units that had been pursuing along with her and Dirk were approaching, driving through the median.

She brought the car to a halt on the right shoulder as the acrid stench of scorched rubber filled the interior.

Dirk jumped out of the Mustang, gun drawn, and

ran to the suspects' vehicles. Savannah followed right behind him, coughing, her eyes and throat burning from the smoke of twelve ruined tires. By the time they had reached the cars, Jake and his fellow officers had unloaded the suspects and had all six of them spread, facedown, on the asphalt.

One by one, they were cuffed, searched, and had their rights read to them. As Savannah ran her hands over the girl's body, she found a .22 caliber pistol shoved in the waistband of her jeans and a switchblade taped to her ankle.

"Didn't your mama ever tell you that ladies don't play with those kinds of toys?" Savannah asked as she turned the girl around to face her.

Even in the dim light of the freeway lamps, Savannah saw the look of recognition, followed by astonishment and anger, cross the young face.

"Hey, bitch," she said, "what're you doin' bustin' us? Where's the cannibal dude?"

"Right over there, reading your main man his rights," Savannah replied.

"Reading him his . . . what? He's a cop? The cannibal's a stinkin' pig?"

Savannah chuckled. "Oink, oink."

The girl was dumbfounded, devastated. Savannah hadn't seen such a look since her brother had told her younger sister that there was no Santa Claus *or* Easter Bunny . . . all on the same day.

"Oh, man . . . a cop." She shook her head, slack-jawed and glassy-eyed. "I didn't think they let serial killers be cops. I mean, how screwed up is that?"

It was Savannah's turn to stare, confused. Stupidity never failed to amaze her.

"Sounds like there are a few other things your mama

didn't teach you." She slapped her on the back. "You'd better get your act together, darlin', 'cause you're not sharp enough to be a criminal."

Savannah handed her over to Jake, then strolled back to her Mustang and began to inspect her tires. Eventually, Dirk joined her.

"Sorry about that, kid."

Savannah reached down, picked up a strip of shredded rubber, and held it out to him. "Just how sorry are you, big boy?"

He shrugged and looked away. "You know, sorry. *Real* sorry."

"About a grand sorry, I'd say. They were steel-belted, custom red-walled radials "

"No way!" He bristled; she could practically see the hair rising on the back of his neck. "They were recaps! Thirty-buck-apiece recaps. I was with you when you bought 'em!"

"Oh, yeah . . . I forgot." She nodded toward the big, black, late-model Mercedes that had just arrived, bearing the auspicious person of their police chief, Norman Hillquist—the individual who held the dubious honor of being "Numero Uno" on Savannah's fairly lengthy "Shit List."

"But as far as he's concerned," she added, lowering her voice, "they were red-walled beauties."

Dirk grinned, eager as always to stick it to his boss. "You've got it. Let's see if we can get your car towed and bum a ride off Jake. It's the least he owes us."

"Of course. Couldn't expect you to spring for a cab."

As they walked over to Jake's van, Savannah glanced sideways at Dirk and saw that something was troubling him. Something heavy.

"What is it, buddy?" she asked, slipping her arm companionably through his. "What's bothering you?"

"I was just wondering . . ."

"Yeah?" She donned her most sympathetic, maternal, tell-me-all-about-it look.

"If I get the department to cough up the fancy tires . . ."

"Yeah?"

"You'll let me off the hook for the burger dinner that you didn't get to finish, right?"

Chapter

Savannah Reid, transplanted Georgian belle, was never happier than when those she loved were seated around her kitchen table, and she was stuffing their faces with good, Southern home cooking. And at that moment, four of her favorite people were finishing off a platter of fried chicken, a bowl of mashed potatoes, and a boat of cream gravy.

Well . . . three of them were eating the calorie-laden goodies. Savannah's health-conscious assistant, Tammy Hart, was enjoying her usual salad. At least, she said she was enjoying it, though Savannah couldn't grasp the concept of "savoring" lettuce.

"Tammy, you need to eat something," she told her, passing a golden drumstick under her nose. "You're so skinny now, you'd have to run around in a rainstorm just to get wet."

The petite blond reached down and patted her

nonexistent fanny. "Actually, I've got to watch it. I've put on a couple of pounds lately."

Savannah tossed the chicken leg onto Dirk's plate and tried not to burp. A couple of pounds . . . on that size zero butt. Please.

She had decided long ago to feel no envy, only deep sympathy, for this emaciated waif. Okay, so Tammy might look great in a bikini, but she would never know the deep, soulish thrill of eating a huge slice of cheesecake, double-dipped in chocolate and topped with raspberry liqueur.

The poor child wasn't svelte; she was tragically deprived.

Savannah turned her attention to the opposite end of the table, where the object of most of her sexual fantasies sat . . . Ryan Stone, tall, dark, gorgeous, suave, debonair, her dear friend and sometimes fellow private detector.

And next to Ryan sat the reason why those delicious fantasies would never become reality—John Gibson, Ryan's life partner, an older, silver-haired, completely sophisticated and charming British fellow. She very simply adored them both. Sadly, so did Tammy and every other female who crossed their paths.

On the other hand, Dirk—being a red-blooded, all-American, highly heterosexual and not particularly tolerant male—had only recently learned to appreciate their unique skills. As retired FBI agents, they had used their expertise to help both Dirk and Savannah solve some difficult cases. Savannah had noticed that, after they had pulled Dirk's butt out of the proverbial wringer a few times, he had dropped the "fairy" and "twinkle-toes" comments.

At the moment, he was making no comments at all, because he was quickly dispensing the chicken leg off to "drumstick heaven." Dirk was never particularly conversational in the presence of food. Especially free food.

"This meal was absolutely delightful, my dear," John said, dabbing at his silver mustache with his napkin. "I can't believe I've lived my entire life thus far without the pleasure of Dixieland cooking."

She walked over to the kitchen counter where she began to slice a fresh-from-the-oven apple pie. "Then you should come over more often and make up for lost time," she said. "We can't have you walking around with a cholesterol level less than three hundred."

She slid a piece, dripping with French vanilla ice cream and caramel sauce, under Ryan's nose and was rewarded with a breathtaking smile. "Savannah, you spoil us rotten. Please don't ever stop."

"Never. Besides, we've gotta celebrate Dirk's big bust here."

She saw him glance down at his chest, and she was thankful his mouth was too full for him to make the predictable, corny joke.

"Yes, congratulations, Sergeant Coulter," John said, lifting his teacup, which was brimming with his own special blend of Earl Grey. "A most impressive showing on your part . . . and Savannah's as well."

"Five wanted felons and nine guns," Ryan added. "Good haul."

Dirk grunted, and his face flushed slightly. He wasn't particularly adept at accepting praise . . . receiving so little of it.

"Mmm, yeah, thanks," he muttered. "Those damned

gangbangers . . . bunch o' punks. I'm tellin' you, when I see the kids today, I just wanna get myself neutered, if you know what I mean."

Savannah reached into a drawer and pulled out a can opener. "If you're serious, I can take care of that right now for you."

"Gimme some pie instead."

"Say, 'please.'"

"Oh, yeah . . . please."

She gave him a double-sized piece. Might as well, she figured, and save herself a trip; he was sure to ask for seconds.

As she joined them at the table, her own generous serving in hand, Ryan asked her, "How is your schedule now, Savannah? Do you have time for a little extra work?"

She perked up instantly. As a private detective, she often found herself on the "famine" side of the "feast or famine" wheel of fortune.

"Work? *Real* work . . . like for *real* money." She gave Dirk a loaded, sideways glance, which he conveniently ignored.

"Well, I don't know how much work will be involved," Ryan said between sips of coffee. "It's more like presenting a presence. I've been hired by a beauty-pageant promoter to 'guard' some lovelies who are competing for the Miss Gold Coast crown."

"Miss Gold Coast?" Tammy asked, nearly choking on her salad. "What a disgrace . . . evaluating women on the basis of physical attributes like a herd of cattle."

"Yeah," Dirk agreed. "Disgusting. Do they need an off-duty cop as a chaperone for those chickie-poos?"

"I heard they have one more position to fill, and they specifically asked for a female," Ryan said.

"Reverse sexual discrimination. That's what it is. A middle-aged, white guy can't get a break in this country anymore."

"Hush and eat your pie, Dirk," Savannah said, nudging him under the table with her foot. "Guarding a batch of beauties would be bad for your blood pressure."

She turned back to Ryan. "Is the pay good?"

"Listen to her," Tammy said, snickering. "Like she's picky these days. I balance her books . . . or try to. Believe me, if it pays minimum wage, she'll jump on it like a hound on a T-bone."

"A hound on a T-bone?" Savannah laughed. "You've been hanging out with me too long, New York girl. I'll have you eating grits and gravy before you can shake a lamb's tail."

Tammy gagged. "No way. No grits, no gravy, and certainly nothing to do with a sheep's back end."

Savannah scooped up a big forkful of pie, dripping with the caramel and pecan sauce. "I'll take it," she told Ryan. "Looking out for some girlie-girl beauty queens, making sure they don't stub their pretty toes and ruin their pedicures, maybe breaking up a few catfights over false eyelashes and hair mousse. How hard could it be? I mean . . . what could happen at a beauty pageant?"

The beauty queen sat at her dressing table, wearing a pink chenille bathrobe and hair curlers, staring at her reflection in the brightly lit, Hollywood mirror. The dozen bulbs around the mirror's edge illuminated every tiny blemish on her nearly perfect complexion, and she studied each one, frowning, as though it were a critical issue that demanded an immediate solution.

The walls and shelves of her bedroom were laden with the spoils of her victories in the pageant world. Trophies, some over three feet tall, cluttered every horizontal surface. Vertical surfaces were covered with photographs—beautiful pictures, professionally taken over the years—showing a little girl who had been groomed to look like a woman at the age of six.

The closet door stood open, and inside glimmered an array of sequined and rhinestone-studded evening gowns of every hue, jostling for space with feathered boas, a hundred pairs of glittering shoes, and miscellaneous faux fur accessories.

Having decided on a course of action, the girl at the dressing table chose a particular cream from the dozens of bottles before her and began to dab the lotion on her "trouble spots." From time to time, she glanced to her right at the lighted glass case that sat on its own special table and held her pride and joy . . . the Miss California Sunshine crown . . . in all of its cubic zirconia glory.

She was good at what she did.

Very good. And she knew it.

She looked across the room at the younger, far less attractive version of herself stretched out on the twin bed against the opposite wall.

"Go downstairs and get me a soda," she told her sister. "And make sure it's a cold one from the back of the fridge."

"Get it yourself."

"I said . . . get me a soda, now!"

The well-trained younger sibling stirred from her bed, grumbling under her breath, but obeying nevertheless, trudging across the bedroom in penguin-spangled, flannel pajamas.

In their little sorority, hierarchy had been established long ago, and it was too late to challenge authority now.

"Diet! Make sure it's diet!"

"Eh, screw you." The objection was mumbled low enough that it didn't constitute outright mutiny.

As soon as sister number two had left the room, the beauty queen picked up the telephone and punched in some numbers.

Her party answered almost immediately. Keeping her voice low, she said, "It's me. Yeah. Did you think it over . . . you know . . . what we talked about?"

She frowned, not liking what she heard.

"That won't do. That's not what I want. I *told* you what I want."

She listened again, but not for long. "No! I don't care what you say; it's gotta be the way I told you before."

More objections on the other end.

She shook her head, sending curlers tumbling, and stomped her bare foot. "No, no, no, no! You better listen, or you'll be sorry. A lot of people are gonna be sorry if you don't listen to me."

As the party on the other end continued to fill her ear with unpleasantries, the bedroom door opened and her sister appeared, diet cola in hand.

Time to end the conversation.

"You heard me," she said in her most ominous tone—a voice she would never allow a panel of pageant judges to hear. "I made it very clear to you what I expect, and this isn't negotiable. I want action . . . very soon. Understand?"

She slammed the phone down and snatched the soda out of her sister's hand. "What are you grinning at?" she snapped. "What's so damned funny?"

"You." The younger girl walked back to her bed, flopped across it, and began to chew her thumbnail. "*You* trying to get your way with people."

"I don't *try.*" She took a long swig of soda and smiled. "I *do* it."

"Yeah, well, you're gonna squeeze the wrong person one of these days, and you're gonna get it . . . something you *don't* want, that is."

Beauty set her soda aside, took another look at her Miss California Sunshine crown, and went back to dabbing pimples with lotion.

"No way," she said. "I'm a woman who knows what she wants . . . and how to get it. Every time. You just watch me, Squirt, and take a lesson from an expert."

The younger sister groaned and rolled over to face the wall, mumbling minor obscenities . . . just loud enough to express her disgust . . . but low enough not to incur Her Highness's royal wrath.

Yes, in this tiny kingdom . . . everyone knew her place.

An hour later, on the sidewalk across the street from the beauty queen's modest suburban home, a figure stood in the shadow of some oleander bushes, watching.

The upstairs bedroom light had been out for twenty minutes. Twenty-three, to be exact. But the watcher still waited. Thinking. Planning.

Having observed the house before, the person knew that four people lived there: mom, pop, the beauty con-

testant, and her younger sister, and knew which bedroom was hers . . . the little bitch on the phone . . . the
one making demands.

The watcher knew what had to be done. The only
questions remained, "When?" and "How?" Some things
had to be done properly. Carefully. And murder was
certainly one of those.

The first time the thought *murder* had crossed the
watcher's brain, it had been like an electric shock, ter-
rifying, repulsive, foreign. But with each subsequent
thought, the concept seemed less revolting, more possible, even necessary. The would-be victim had chosen
her own fate. The rest was a foregone conclusion.

But when?

Now wasn't the time. Not on a quiet, residential
street in a house full of people. Not without a plan . . . a
good, well-thought-out plan.

The pageant.

The Miss Gold Coast Pageant began in two days. An
event full of emotion, confusion, hundreds of people
running around in semiordered chaos.

Yes . . . what better backdrop could there be than a
beauty pageant . . . ? The perfect stage for murder.

Chapter

3

"**G**ood morning!" Tammy looked up from the computer keyboard and gave Savannah the dazzling, bright, cheerful smile that could be conjured only by a dyed-in-the-wool "morning person."

"Oh, shut up," Savannah grumbled as she trudged down the stairs in her fuzzy red slippers and her ratty old robe that was basically the same faded shade of navy blue as the circles beneath her eyes. "You know better than to 'good morning' me before I've had coffee. Especially when I've been up half the night."

To her great dismay, Tammy followed her into the kitchen, opening blinds and curtains, spreading sunshine—literally and figuratively—all along the way. "Half the night? Cool! Does that mean you and Dirk were stalking that child-abuser guy again?"

Savannah groaned and hauled the largest mug she

could find out of the cupboard. "We prefer to call it a 'stakeout', not 'stalking.'"

"What's the difference?"

After only the briefest consideration, Savannah said, "Very little, come to think of it. But good guys get paid to do it."

"*You* don't; Dirk does."

After filling the mug with coffee stronger and thicker than Mississippi mud, Savannah added a decadent amount of Half & Half. From the corner of her eye she saw Tammy cringe, so she poured in more—nothing quite like a health nut to bring out the defiant hedonist in her.

"Once in a great while," she said dryly, "I get paid for it. And Dirk's good to help us out when we're in a jam."

She took a big swig of the coffee and felt the life-fortifying caffeine make a beeline for her bloodstream. She could have sworn her heart fluttered and slowly began to beat. Low-level brain-activity waves started to bounce through her head.

Heading for the refrigerator, she said, "Speaking of jam . . . do we still have some of Granny Reid's black-berry preserves? Or did I use them on the biscuits when I fed the troops yesterday?"

Tammy's chin hiked a couple of notches. "I don't know. I don't eat fruit that has been ruined by processed sugar. My body is a sacred temple."

Savannah found the jam hiding behind the hot-fudge sauce. "Yeah, well . . . your 'sacred temple' could get run over and mashed flat by a bus tomorrow, and you'll wish you'd had a decent last meal before you de-parted this earth. Want some eggs and bacon?"

"Absolutely not."

"Grits, swimmin' in butter? Hot, flaky biscuits? Cream gravy?"

"Get real."

Savannah shrugged as she pulled the necessary ingredients for a full, Southern-style breakfast from the refrigerator and cupboard. "Suit yourself, girl. You don't know what you're missing."

Tammy grimaced and mumbled, "A heart attack, high blood pressure, stroke, diabetes, obesity—"

"Watch yourself, Miss Prissy Pot." Both hands full, she kicked the refrigerator door closed with her foot and dumped the stuff on the counter. "I could fire you for insubordination."

"Fire me from the almost job that you almost don't pay me for?"

"That's the one. Careers like yours are hard to come by . . . studying at the gum-soled feet of a master detective."

Tammy glanced down at Savannah's fuzzy red slippers, grinned, and slid onto a kitchen chair to watch as Savannah began her preparations. "So, Nancy Drew . . . did you and the Hardy boy get your bad guy last night?"

"We did. The moron sneaked into his mom's house about two in the morning to pick up some of his CDs and a favorite baseball cap. He's paying for the stuff with his freedom. Where he's at, he won't get to use any of it.

"The little girl he abused was ecstatic to hear we'd picked him up. She can go back to school now, play in the yard again, live like a normal kid"—Savannah sighed as she stretched some bacon strips across a hot skillet—"until her mom makes another trip to the local bar and brings home the next yahoo pervert."

Tammy winced. "Ouch, that's pretty cynical."

"Yeah, well . . . when you've been around that block a hundred times, you learn the lay o' the land."

The smell of frying meat filled the kitchen and, apparently, wafted to the sunporch in the back of the house, because two sleek black cats—big enough to pass as miniature panthers—came running into the kitchen. Both wore black, rhinestone-studded leather collars and expectant looks on their faces.

"Ah, Cleopatra, Diamante"—Tammy reached down to stroke them as they passed, tails held high, on their way to their food dishes—"all you guys have to do is lie in the sunshine and eat. Tough life being a cat."

"Feline Americans," Savannah corrected her.

"What?"

"You heard me. This is a politically correct household."

Tammy snorted. "Since when?"

The telephone rang, and Savannah grabbed it off the wall. "Moonlight Magnolia Detective Agency," she said, her voice Southern silk. "Good morning."

Tammy pointed to the kitchen clock, which showed a quarter past one.

Savannah grunted and began to flip the bacon in the skillet. "Er . . . make that afternoon," she said.

The female voice on the other end was just as sultry and even more distinctly down-Dixie. "Don't know if it's morning or afternoon, huh? Late night?"

Savannah smiled, instantly feeling better in all areas, even ones the caffeine hadn't reached. "Ah," she said, "if it isn't my chronologically gifted maternal crone calling from Georgia."

"What?" The voice sounded a mite cranky.

"We're being politically correct around here this

morning . . . or afternoon. We're proving how enlight-
ened and—"

"Oh, hogwash. I didn't call you to get an earful of
bullpucky."

Savannah chuckled. "So, why *did* you call me, Granny
Reid? Not that you have to have a reason, of course."

"I called to warn you."

"Warn me? Why? Did you have one of your prophetic
dreams about me or—"

"No, not this time. I'm letting you know that you're
gonna be getting some company, a visitor from
Georgia."

"You? Are you gonna come see me again, Gran?"

A mischievous snicker on the other end. "Not me. I
don't think California has recuperated from my last trip
out there."

"That's true. Mickey Mouse and Goofy still have
hangovers. So, if it's not you, who?"

"One of your beloved siblings."

Savannah sighed. With one brother, seven sisters, and
a gaggle of nieces and nephews, the nerve-wracking possibilities seemed limitless. "Not Vidalia and the twins . . .
both sets, that is . . ."

Glancing over at Tammy, Savannah saw her assistant
make a wry face that reflected her own thoughts on the
subject. Both recalled the previous invasion of sister
Vidalia's terrorist munchkins. The cats were traumatized for weeks afterward, their fur standing on end and
their ears turned inside out. And the major house re-
pairs were on hold, waiting for the governor of
California to declare San Carmelita a disaster zone and
release the relief funds.

"Not me and not Vidalia," Gran said. "It's your baby
sister, Atlanta, who hightailed it outta here first thing

this mornin' on a plane headed in your direction. I would've warned you sooner, but your mama just told me about it."

Savannah didn't have to utilize any special detecting skills to figure out why neither her mom nor Atlanta had phoned ahead to announce the visit. In spite of the fact that Shirley Reid had born nine children, naming them after cities in Georgia, mothering wasn't high on the list of her priorities. It fell well below square dancing, Jack Daniels, turquoise and silver jewelry, and her favorite stool—third from the end, right below the autographed picture of Elvis—at Sam's Honky Tonk.

Mama Reid would be happy to be rid of the temperamental teenager for a while.

Over the years, Big Sis Savannah and Gran had done most of the mothering of the Reid brood. *Why should anything change at this late date?* Savannah asked herself.

"You there, hon?" Gran said, her voice soft with concern.

"Right here, Gran." Savannah reached for a spoon to stir the grits that were bubbling on the stove. "I'm just shocked into silence. I mean, I'm always glad to entertain a family member, but . . . Atlanta. She's a bit of a . . . challenge . . . p. c. speaking, that is."

"Eh, forget the p. c. nonsense. She's a pain in the hind end, that one. Don't let her walk all over you, darlin'."

"That'll be the day."

Savannah thanked her grandmother and said goodbye. As she hung up the phone, Tammy said, "So, when exactly is that day? The day you aren't going to let your spoiled baby sister take advantage of you, that is."

"Today," she replied with a weary sigh. "There oughta be a law against getting news like that before breakfast, with only one cup of coffee in your bloodstream. And while they're making rules, there should be another one about kid sisters showing up unannounced and uninvited. They oughta be required to give you a thirty-day notice so that you can move."

She chug-a-lugged another cup of coffee, then added, "And I say that with the deepest affection for Atlanta and all of my adorable siblings."

Tammy nodded. "Gotcha. Don't you sometimes wonder if you're ever going to get them all raised?"

"Naw, I gave up on that dream long ago. They're perpetual juveniles. Dysfunctional to infinity."

Tammy studied Savannah thoughtfully as she continued her food preparations. "How about you?" she asked. "You had the same parents—or lack of parenting—that they had. Plus you had the additional burden of being the eldest and all those responsibilities. Why aren't you dysfunctional?"

Savannah laughed and broke an egg into the skillet. "What makes you think I'm not?"

"You're one of the most together ladies I know."

"That's pathetic, Tam. Obviously, you've had lousy role models. Besides, I don't have time to be dysfunctional. I can hardly function as it is."

The sound of a car's horn blasted, just outside the kitchen door. Savannah left the eggs frying to take a look at her driveway. "A Yellow cab," she said. "Gee, we must have company. Who do you suppose it is?"

As she turned down the heat under her breakfast and made her way out the kitchen door with Tammy behind her, Savannah felt a flood of contradictory emotions, ranging from warm and fuzzy, to seriously irked. The strongest was guilt . . . guilt that she wasn't happier to see her own flesh and blood arriving on her door-

step. But she slapped a pseudo-smile across her face
and hurried to the taxi, her furry slippers flapping on
the cement driveway.

The back door of the cab swung open and out came
a guitar case, followed by an enormous garment bag . . .
and a positively bony teenager who couldn't possibly
have been spawned in the gene pool with anyone re-
lated to Savannah.

Rather than the dark-haired, voluptuous beauty she
had been the last time Atlanta had visited, this girl was
painfully thin, with sunken cheeks and ribs showing beneath her midriff-cropped stretchy shirt. And her hair,
naturally the same dark chestnut as Savannah's, was a
platinum blond haypile, stacked on her head and held
with a dozen glittering, butterfly barrettes.

Savannah's heart sank and a queasy feeling hit her
stomach with a wallop. The kid was sick! The kid was
very sick, maybe even dying! Yes, that had to be it! She
had come to California to live out her final days, bask-
ing in the healing golden sunlight, listening to the eternal song of the ocean waves and—"

"Hey, Van, I'm here to compete in a beauty pageant!" the girl shouted, running toward her, guitar
case and garment bag fluttering in the breeze. "Isn't
that just the coolest thing?!"

"Uhhh . . . yeah . . . cool."

Atlanta gave her an enormous, enthusiastic hug,
whacking her on the back with the heavy case and tan-
gling her hair in the bag's zipper tab. "Are you glad to
see me? Are you surprised?"

"Very glad, sweetie . . . and surprised." Savannah
placed a kiss on each of her sister's gaunt cheeks and realized that she *was* glad to see her . . . and somewhat
amazed that she was so glad. The kid was a pain in the

rear end, as Gran had said, but she loved her. She loved all of them; how could she not?

Atlanta released Savannah and turned to give Tammy a peck on the cheek. "Hey there. You still workin' for my sister? I figured you would've flown the coop by now, no more than she pays you."

Tammy received the kiss gracefully and replied with a noncommittal grunt. Savannah was grateful, knowing that Tammy held no deep or abiding affection for any of her siblings who had appeared on her doorstep. Bringing their own bundles of troubles and idiosyncrasies with them, they hadn't exactly made good impressions on Savannah's California friends.

"Let's get you inside," Savannah said, as the driver exited the cab and began to unload the trunk. A frightening amount of luggage was being dumped on the driveway, and Savannah started to worry about her impromptu visitor's Estimated Time of Departure. Savannah didn't recall moving in that much clothing when she bought the house.

Picking up as many of the bags as she could handle, she started toward the door, but Atlanta blocked her way. "Oh, yeah . . . there's just one thing." She looked a wee bit embarrassed. "This guy drove me all the way from LAX, and I owe him $145. I was hoping you'd pay him; I'm a little short on cash, you know, after paying for my airline ticket and all."

Savannah thought of the meager amount recorded in her checkbook ledger.

Oh well, she didn't need electricity or water next month.

She sighed and trudged to the door, lugging the bags—that must have contained liquid lead—with her. "Let me get my purse," she said, adding under her breath, "and let me raid the cookie jar . . . and the piggy bank . . . and my lingerie drawer stash . . . and . . ."

"Oh, yeah, Savannah," Atlanta called after her with a merry tone that made Savannah consider sister-cide, "my driver's been a super nice guy; be sure to tip him really good, okay?"

Ten minutes later, the three women and the 237 pieces of luggage were inside, and the pouting cabby had been dispatched. The fifty-dollar tip had depressed, rather than impressed, him.

"Gee, Savannah, you're getting cheap in your old age," Atlanta told her as she helped herself to a bottle of Tammy's diet herb tea in the refrigerator. "I mean, that was downright embarrassing, you stiffing him like that."

Two of Savannah's three remaining nerves snapped. "Embarrassing? You were humiliated, were you? What if I hadn't been able to pay him at all? You'd be out there, washing, waxing, and vacuuming his cab right now, blushing up a storm."

Atlanta plopped down on a chair at the kitchen table and twisted the top off the bottle, a completely disgruntled look on her face. Tammy sat across from her, pretending to shuffle and sort a stack of papers. Her eyes twinkled; she found the Reid clan an unending source of entertainment.

"Just out of curiosity, why didn't you call me and let me know you were coming?" Savannah asked. "I could have picked you up at the airport and saved myself a couple of hundred bucks."

Atlanta's bottom lip protruded. "I wanted to see your

face when you realized I'd come to visit you. And, now I'm sorry I did, because you didn't seem all that happy to see me."

Maternal guilt pangs stabbed at Savannah's conscience . . . along with some accompanying anger. Why did she always lose with this kid? Whatever she did, it was never enough. She seemed destined to blow it somehow.

"To be honest, 'Lanta," she said, walking over and laying her hands on the girl's shoulders, "I was worried to see how much weight you've lost."

Atlanta beamed. "I know! Are you proud of me, or what?! I've got another twenty pounds or so to lose, but I'm getting there."

"Twenty pounds?" Savannah glanced across the table at Tammy, who appeared to be as shocked as she was. And if superthin, ultra-health-conscious Tammy was concerned . . .

"You don't need to lose anything, Atlanta," Tammy said. "You're very slender as you are. What sort of diet have you been on?"

Atlanta's defense shields rose as she took a long drink of the tea and avoided looking at either of them. "I've just been watching what I eat," she finally said. "Cutting out the junk food, you know, all that garbage you eat, Savannah. Which, by the way, I can see you've picked up a couple of pounds since I saw you last. Especially in your hips. But that's always been your problem area, hasn't it? I guess I take after Mom's side of the family, because I've never had a problem with my hips and . . ."

Wandering over to the stove, Savannah looked at her eggs, which now looked like yellow-and-white rubber with dried, brown ruffles around the edges. Her grits had congealed into a pasty glob. The distinct, bitter smell of burned biscuits was wafting from the oven.

And she couldn't even run over to the local IHOP for strawberry cheese blintzes; she had given the cabby her last dollar.

Suddenly, she felt older and more tired than dirt.

Picking up her coffee cup, she fortified it with a generous splash of Baileys Irish Cream, then said, "You two, eat . . . or don't eat, whatever you can find. Just make yourself at home, 'Lanta. I'm going back to bed for an hour or two. I had a rough night."

As she shuffled through the living room, she heard her sister's voice reaching out to her . . . , "Savannah, could you take up some of those bags? You know, since you're going up anyway."

Marion Lippincott had organized 289 beauty pageants in her career, and she was darned good at it. Accustomed to the chaotic flutter of belles and gowns, frantic stage mothers and frenzied coaches, florists and seamstresses, beauticians and musicians, nothing fazed "The Lip" . . . as she was not-so-fondly called . . . but never to her face.

Over the rims of those tortoiseshell glasses that perpetually perched on the end of her nose she had seen it all. And, about a hundred years ago, she had done it all. Though her once-auburn locks were now a short, silver bob, and her crowns and banners were packed away in a trunk at the foot of her bed, she knew the pageant world inside and out.

And although many of the people scurrying about the gallery of the Villa Rosa Winery considered this one of the most important events of their lives, to Lippincott it was just number 289. She figured she'd retire at 300. Enough was enough.

"Whose bright idea was it to have this at a winery?" sounded a whiny voice in her left ear. Marion glanced up from her notebook for a half second, long enough to recognize the speaker as a professional pageant mom and not someone who required diplomatic handling, like a sponsor.

"It was *my* idea," she replied curtly, "a damned bright one. I'm glad you agree. Has your Desiree registered yet?"

The mom sputtered, stammered, then shook her head.

"I suggest she do so, right away. M through Z is set up in the tasting room." She flipped open her notebook to the accommodations chart. "She'll be rooming with Eileen Freeport in 2F . . . up the stairs, on the right."

"With Eileen!? No, they hate each other. Remember, I wrote you three months ago and asked that she be with—"

"Room 2F. Registration, Mrs. Porter, registration." She snapped her fingers and the discontented Mrs. Porter disappeared.

Marion strode across the gallery, the hub of Villa Rosa's busy visitors' center. Situated on the Ventura Highway, north of Los Angeles, but south of Hearst Castle, Villa Rosa was a popular spot along the Southern California tourist trail. The gallery—which was round, its walls paneled with oak taken from ancient barrels—itself looked like the inside of an enormous vat. Evidence of Villa Rosa's prestigious past was everywhere in the antique winemaking memorabilia. There were photos of five generations of Villas, all of whom had been masters at their art, while glass cases held the ribbons, medals, and awards for excellence that had been bestowed upon them over the decades.

To the right lay the tasting room, a luxurious affair, much larger than the average California winery provided. To the left lay the guest lodge, a two-story house with twenty beautifully decorated rooms for overnight visitors. Straight ahead, through two sets of French doors, lay a courtyard, lush with palmettos, hanging gardens, a three-tiered fountain, and comfortable lounging furniture.

The Villa family loved their wines, but just as much, they enjoyed sharing their passion with others. And the visitors' center reflected that generations-old tradition of hospitality.

But Marion Lippincott had precious little time to appreciate such things with a pageant to run. Waving away several other mothers with equally distressed looks on their faces, she picked up the telephone which was resting atop an antique that had once been a winepress, but now functioned as a visitors' registration desk. After punching in a few numbers, she heard her activities coordinator on the other end.

"Gertrude, I spoke to Anthony Villa, and he needs a podium for his welcoming address this evening, just a microphone and stand for me. Have the plaques arrived yet? Well, get the engraver on the line and give him grief. And dessert for the closing ceremonies? Tell the chef we need a low-fat sorbet selection."

From the corner of her eye, she saw a spray of spring flowers approaching, with a deliveryperson's legs below and a face hidden among the tulips, daffodils, and hyacinths. The flowers spoke, "I'm with Fancy Bloomers. These are for one of your contestants . . . a Barbie Matthews."

"No, I don't want the cheesecake on the menu," Marion barked, "or the chocolate mousse. These girls are watching their weight and their complexions."

"Excuse me," said the deliveryperson, "a Barbie Matthews?"

Marion glanced down at her notebook. "She hasn't arrived yet."

"Then where should I leave these?"

She flipped the pages until she found the room chart. "Room 1D." She jabbed a finger toward the hallway that branched off the gallery to the left, then turned her attention back to the phone. "I have to check the registration tables, to see how it's going," she said. "Gert, I'm sure you can handle all of this, and when I check back with you in half an hour, you'll have only good news for me, right?"

She hung up the phone before receiving the affirmation. She didn't need it. Gertrude was a most-capable coordinator. And she possessed another virtue that made her even more valuable . . . she was positively terrified of Marion Lippincott.

And that was exactly the way The Lip liked it.

Room 1D. A first-floor room. That was good. *Perfect,* in fact.

The person with the flowers had brought along more than tulips. The jar of red gore was tucked inside a jacket pocket, just in case.

But no. The "delivery person" wasn't that lucky. The room was locked, and there was no choice but to leave the arrangement outside in the hallway next to the door.

Oh well. It was probably better this way. The old bat with the notebook might remember later, and there needed to be some time between the "delivery" and the "incident."

Tonight would be fine.

Counting the steps to the exit at the end of the hall, the person mentally rehearsed the return. Fifty-five steps. Feeling the jar, heavy inside the jacket pocket, its contents sloshing around, brought a smile. If the flowers didn't change her mind, Barbara Matthews was going to get an unpleasant surprise.

Chapter

4

Savannah began to relax and enjoy the drive as she guided the Mustang along the winding highway through San Carmelita's outskirts. Although the steering was a bit off, the car drifting to the right. The temporary tires that Dirk had provided, while they waited for the city to come through with the new radials, were mismatched, and she was pretty sure he hadn't paid the extra few bucks to have them balanced. Tightwad. She'd have to give him a verbal slapping-around.

Atlanta sat in the passenger's seat, for once having little to say. There were a few advantages to quarreling—blissful silence being one of them.

Having left the beaches and citrus groves behind, they gradually climbed tawny velvet hills, dotted with copses of dark oaks, into California's Gold Coast wine region. On either side of the highway, perfectly straight rows of vines, heavy with fruit, glistened in the sunlight. And the smell of sun-warmed grapes scented the air.

All along the highway, at the end of each row, a rosebush had been planted, each blooming in a different shade of crimson, pink, yellow, and coral—Villa Rosa's trademark. Local legend had it that the winery's founder had planted them for his wife, Rosa, and they had been maintained and replanted in her memory since.

"We're there," Savannah told her silent passenger. "This is Villa Rosa, the winery where your pageant is being held. They're one of the oldest, but fastest growing wineries in the area . . . and they never pass up a publicity opportunity."

"Humpf."

Ignoring the less than enthusiastic reply, Savannah continued. "How about that . . . both of us winding up there, you competing and me working security."

"Yeah, it sucks. It *major* sucks."

Savannah looked over at the petulant face and ignored the itch in her palm. It was an irritation she often felt when she badly wanted to slap somebody.

"Sorry, Twerp," she said, knowing how much the nickname irked the kid. "I didn't mean to sneeze on your ice cream, rain on your parade, et cetera."

"Yeah, sure. Once again, Big Sister is watching every move I make."

Savannah gritted her teeth as she turned down a private road, marked with ornate wrought-iron gates and a carved, gilded sign which read: VILLA ROSA.

"I'm not sure how I turned out to be the bad guy here," she said. "You were the one who signed up for this thing, saying you'd been living in San Carmelita for the past five years, using my address without asking me."

"I saw it on the Internet, okay?" Atlanta said, examining the nail cuticles of her left hand. "It sounded cool, so I signed up on-line. How was I supposed to know that you'd be stingy with your ol' address?"

"Come on, 'Lanta. I may not be everything you want me to be, but the one thing I'm not is 'stingy' where any of you kids are concerned."

They were approaching the Villa Rosa complex, a sprawling but lovely configuration of buildings that resembled an elegant Italian villa more than a highly successful commercial enterprise. Ordinarily, Savannah would be looking forward to spending the next few days in such luxurious surroundings, but . . .

"You're acting like I'm some sort of silly kid with a pipe dream," Atlanta moaned. "This is for my career, you know."

The only "career" Savannah was aware of was Atlanta's weekend job at the Dairy Queen, but she thought it best not to ask for clarification on the subject.

"There are going to be talent scouts at this pageant," the teenager continued. "And when they hear me sing, I'll probably get a contract offer right on the spot."

"I hope you're not expecting too much from this," Savannah said dryly. "They'll probably wait until an intermission to make that offer, rather than disrupt the pageant with a lot of contract signing there on stage."

"Don't be a smart-aleck. Of course they'll wait until later. But that's how a lot of female country singers got discovered, you know."

"No . . . I wasn't aware of that fact. Who exactly got her start that way?"

Atlanta hemmed and hawed for a moment, then shrugged. "I can't think of names right this minute, but take my word for it . . . a bunch of them . . . a *big* bunch."

"So, you don't care if you win the pageant or not, as long as you get *discovered.*"

"That's right. Although I'll probably win, too. And that would be pretty neat."

Savannah had to laugh. The Reid women possessed many virtues, but humility wasn't among them. The Fear of Failure gene didn't appear to be swimming around in their pool.

As she pulled the Mustang up to the front of the Villa Rosa visitors' center, she saw Ryan Stone standing beside the door, wearing a tuxedo that complemented his dark good looks—as if they needed enhancing.

"Ryan is here?" Atlanta nearly bolted out of her seat. Like most females between the age of eight and eighty, Atlanta was wildly smitten with the handsome hunk. On her subsequent visits to California, she had fallen madly in love with him, convinced that if only given the chance, she could permanently alter his sexual preference. "Oh, wow! You didn't tell me that Ryan was going to be here!"

"Yes, he's working security with me. But don't worry . . . like I told you before, we'll be sure to stay out of your way. I don't want you to feel smothered or—"

"Oh, hush up. You know what I meant. I don't care if you and Ryan hang around me . . . some."

"Especially Ryan?"

"Well, he *is* mighty easy on the eyes."

Savannah gave Ryan a wave as she headed into the parking lot. He waved back and flashed her a breath-taking smile that set her hormones aflutter.

"Oh, yeah . . . Ryan's easy to look at," she agreed. "This is gonna be fun. A nice, easy gig . . . hangin' out with the gorgeous and genteel Mr. Stone. The worst thing that's apt to happen is a couple of girls wrestling over a can of hair spray. We'll stay out of your way, so that you don't feel smothered."

She shot a sideways look at her baby sister.

Pouting . . . again.

"What if I don't like this girl they stuck me with . . . this Barbie Matthews?" Atlanta's lip was protruding even farther than Savannah thought was physically possible.

Hefting two suitcases under each arm, Savannah led the way from the gallery down the center hall of the adjoining guesthouse. "You don't have to like her. You're not marrying her; you're rooming with her. And it's only for a few days."

"But I thought we were going to get rooms of our own. That's what it said on the web page."

Halfway down the long hall, they found the door with the brass "1D." Savannah set two of the suitcases on the floor and gave it a "shave-and-a-haircut" knock.

"Yeah, whaddaya want?"

Savannah flinched. If the current occupant of 1D was as rude as she sounded, this pageant could be a long, dreary experience.

One glance at her younger sister told Savannah the kid was ready to do battle. A harbinger of evil to come.

Atlanta pushed the door open with a much harder shove than was necessary, and it flew open, slamming against the wall.

Inside was a cozy, delightfully feminine room, a vision of hand-carved antique furniture, rose-printed damask spreads on the twin beds, and wallpaper sprinkled with tiny pink-and-red rosebuds. Atop a marble-topped dressing table was a lush spray of spring flowers.

The only item that seemed out of place in this dainty room was a young lady who was stretched out on one of the beds, drinking diet cola from a can. Though the term "lady" might be used loosely, considering the skimpy leopard-print teddy she was not-quite-wearing and the fact that she had one leg raised and propped on a bookshelf on the wall.

The teenager had impossibly red hair—a color that could have been achieved only with a bottle of hair coloring that contained the word "fiery" on its label. Her makeup was the heaviest Savannah had seen on a young woman north of the Mason-Dixon line. Beneath all the carefully applied goop, her face might have been considered pretty, had it not been pulled into a nasty frown.

"Hey, what do you think you're doing?" she snapped, lowering her leg from the shelf and tucking it under her. "Nobody invited you in here."

Atlanta stormed into the room, tossed one of her suitcases onto the floor, and said, "I registered. They told me room '1D.' That's all the invitation I need, thank you very much."

"Oh goody, a So-o-o-outherner. What are you, a Georgia peach? Or are you just a Georgia pee-can?"

Savannah winced, expecting the fur to start flying any minute.

Atlanta bristled. "As a matter of fact I *am* from the proud state of Georgia . . . originally, that is. Have you got a problem with that?"

"No problem at all," she drawled in an exaggerated and—as far as Savannah was concerned—downright vulgar impression of a Southern accent. "Yeah, boy, howdy . . . I whup Dixie belles in pageants every day o' the week and twice on a Sunday."

Now she was asking for it.

Savannah decided that if Atlanta didn't thrash her, she would. She could always claim the girl had presented some sort of grave security risk, and anyone who knew the kid would probably be grateful that she had beaten her.

But, ever the consummate professional, Savannah repressed her homicidal tendencies and stepped between them. "Okay, okay, girls, this is no way to start off the weekend. You'll be pulling each other's hair out by the roots, and heaven knows, you need every lock you've got to achieve that pageant 'big hair' look."

She walked across the room to the vacant twin bed and started to lay the luggage on it. But Atlanta grabbed her arm. "Wait a second," she said. "Mrs. Lippincott told me that I was supposed to have the bed against the wall. I'm sure that's what she said."

Savannah could practically hear the bell sounding "Round Two." "Well, it doesn't really matter all that much which—"

"It matters to me!" Barbie snapped. "I got here first, so I get to pick which bed I want. And I want the one by the wall. So there." She painted a saccharine smile across her suspiciously full lips, which looked like they had been plumped with collagen or repeatedly stung by honeybees. "You don't mind do you, Little Miss Pee-can?"

Atlanta turned from her obnoxious roommate and faced her sister. "You do understand, don't you," she said with a deadly calm that scared Savannah, "that the next time she calls me that, I'm gonna beat the tar outta her. And if I do, it's for sure that neither one of us is gonna win 'Miss Congeniality' in this pageant."

"I understand completely," Savannah assured her. "In fact, you have my blessing. But, if you would, please wait until I'm out of the room before you stomp a mud-hole in her. As much as I'd like to watch, as Security, I'm supposed to stop that sort of violence if I see it happening."

"Security?" Barbie was instantly alert. "You're Security? I thought you were the Georgia peach's mommy."

"Oh, now you *are* askin' for a beatin'," Savannah said. "But I'm not going to give it to you. You see, I've sworn a sacred oath to make sure that you young things stay safe and sound this weekend. And that means: no boys in your rooms, no smoking, no drinking booze . . . basically, no fun of any kind *at all.*"

She walked over to the bed where Barbie lay, looking more glum by the moment. "And in your case, Ms. Matthews, rest assured I'm going to take my duties very, very seriously."

"Gee, thanks," she said dryly as she tossed her empty cola can onto the floor. "I *was* worried, but you've set my mind at ease."

Savannah leaned over, picked up the can, and sniffed it. Satisfied that it had held only soda, she tossed it into a wicker wastebasket.

She looked around at the marble-topped vanity with its gilded mirror, the ornately carved armoire, and the damask bedspreads. "Such a pretty room," she mused. "Y'all enjoy it now, and Atlanta . . . don't be getting any of Ms. Matthews's blood on the linens. You can just tell by lookin', they're expensive."

Chapter

5

Savannah found Ryan Stone standing near the door of the gallery, explaining the workings of the ancient press to a bevy of giggling beauties. When she beckoned him with a crooked finger, he excused himself to the girls and joined her beside the display case filled with awards.

"Sorry to take you away from all of that adoration," she said.

"Ah, that's quite all right." He bent his dark head down to hers and whispered, "Tell me something, Savannah; I wasn't raised with sisters. Do girls always giggle that much?"

"Not *that* much. That sort of ridiculous tittering is usually done only in the presence of a gorgeous hunk."

He actually blushed. That was one thing Savannah loved most about Ryan Stone—his humility. A Greek god who was actually down-to-earth. Who could resist such an enticing combination?

"Did you get Atlanta settled into her room okay?" he asked.

"Well, she's settled. Only time will tell how 'okay' it is. She isn't too crazy about her roommate, a little priss named Barbie Matthews. To be honest, I'm not exactly nuts about the kid myself."

Ryan raised one eyebrow. "Barbie Matthews? I just turned away one of her admirers at the doorway. He said he was her boyfriend and had to talk to her about some urgent matter. He didn't want to take 'no' for an answer. I ah . . . escorted . . . him to the front gate, but I wouldn't be surprised if he shows up again sometime this evening."

"What does he look like?"

"About six feet tall, long brown hair, black heavy-metal T-shirt and jeans, tattoos on both forearms—skulls and crossbones."

"Hmm . . . what mother wouldn't dream of a son-in-law like that? Is there anyone else we're looking out for?"

Ryan gave a discreet nod toward a group of people, who had congregated on the other side of the room beneath a plaque that bore Benjamin Franklin's quote: "Wine is constant proof that God loves us and loves to see us happy."

"See the guy in the Brioni suit, fiftyish, salt-and-pepper hair?" he said.

"Yeah, nice threads."

"True, but in his case, clothes can't turn a pig into a gentleman. I don't like the way he's looking at some of the girls. A definite Dirty Old Man Alert."

Savannah watched for a moment, and just as Ryan had said, the guy's eyes were following each girl who passed with less than wholesome interest.

"Who is he?"

"Name's Frank Addison, a neighboring vintner and one of the pageant's judges, if you can believe that."

"Oh, yeah, I'll believe about anything if it supports my supposition that human beings are mostly turkey butts . . . no disrespect to the turkeys."

A tall, elegant woman, wearing a black-silk evening sheath and a strand of lavender-jade beads left the group beneath the plaque and walked over to Savannah and Ryan. In one hand she held a glass of red wine, the other she used to tuck a wayward strand of fine, blond hair back into her perfect French twist.

As she approached them she offered her hand to Savannah. "Good evening, I'm Catherine Whitestone-Villa. And I'm so glad you're with us this evening."

Savannah glanced sideways at Ryan; he seemed as surprised as she was at this gracious greeting. Apparently Mrs. Whitestone-Villa thought they were honored guests.

"I'm Savannah Reid," she said, returning the firm handshake. The woman's fingers were a bit cool and damp, and Savannah assumed it was from holding the wineglass. "This is Ryan Stone," she added. "We're working Security for you this weekend."

"Oh, yes, I know." The lady smiled broadly, showing a mouthful of perfectly straight, dazzlingly white teeth. "I'm delighted that we have professionals like the two of you. We want everything to go well for the girls and all of our guests here at Villa Rosa. We've never hosted a beauty pageant before, you know. Some cross-country runs for breast-cancer research, canoe-racing on the lake for muscular dystrophy . . . that sort of thing. But never a beauty contest. This is so exciting!"

"I can't imagine that you lack for excitement here at Villa Rosa," Ryan said. "Your winery produces pure artistry in a bottle."

Her green eyes glistened with pride. "Ah, then you've sampled our wares?"

"I've enjoyed your wines for years. Your 1982 Cabernet Sauvignon and your 1983 Zinfandel Ruby were amazing."

She nodded approvingly. "You have a discriminating palate. Those were two of my husband's favorites."

Savannah recalled hearing that Anthony Villa's grandfather had emigrated from northern Italy to the United States and founded Villa Rosa. She also remembered that Anthony Villa had political aspirations. Was it a seat in the state senate?

One quick glance-over told Savannah that Catherine Whitestone-Villa was the perfect, politically correct wife for a politician.

"And is our future senator with us this evening?" Ryan asked.

"I believe he's still up at the house, reading bedtime stories to our two boys," she said. "But he'll be joining us later. He's giving the welcoming speech at dinner. He's quite a powerful speaker. Have you had the pleasure of hearing him yet?"

Savannah was quickly amending her initial evaluation of Mrs. Villa. Old Kate was just a little too perfect, a tad too correct. Listening to her talk about her beloved gave Savannah that same slightly nauseous feeling that she got when she polished off an entire box of assorted chocolates by herself at home on Saturday night.

"No, but we're looking forward to hearing him," Ryan replied, "although we won't be able to give him our undivided attention."

"Yeah," Savannah interjected, "nose to the grindstone and all that."

"Of course, you have work to do," Catherine said. "Please keep a close eye on our lovely young ladies. Most of them came without their parents, and I feel like a surrogate mother to them."

"Don't worry, Mother Hen." Savannah wondered if Mrs. Villa could hear that faint, sarcastic note in her voice.

The green eyes flashed, ever so slightly. She had definitely picked it up, but had obviously chosen to ignore it. Yes, Anthony Villa had a valuable asset in his politic wife.

"You must excuse me while I play hostess." Catherine shook hands with them both once again, and Savannah noticed that her palm was even colder and clammier than before.

A moment later, she was milling among the guests, whose numbers were swelling, filling the gallery and flowing over to the tasting room, where dinner was to be served.

Neither Savannah nor Ryan spoke for several moments after her departure, as they watched her in silence.

Finally, Savannah said, "Do you like her?"

"Not really."

"Me either. She seemed a bit worried, don't you think? As though she might be expecting some sort of trouble."

"I thought so myself. Definitely concerned about something."

Savannah crossed her arms over her chest and continued to watch the lady thoughtfully. "What sort of wine was she drinking?"

"I believe it was a Merlot."

"You don't chill Merlot, do you?"

He gave her a sly little grin. "Nope, you don't."

She nodded. "I didn't think so."

Atlanta sat on the bed, putting the finishing touches on her makeup, attempting to see what she was doing in the tiny, handheld mirror she had brought with her, while trying to ignore her roommate, who was hogging the well-lit dressing table. They had reached an uneasy truce. The only details of their unspoken agreement: Don't look at each other, say a word to each other, or in any way acknowledge the other's existence.

This was especially difficult for Atlanta, whose mouth seldom stopped running for any reason, even self-preservation.

The only sounds were the clatter of makeup paraphernalia, and Barbie's frequent cell-phone conversations. It seemed her phone was constantly buzzing, or she was continually calling someone.

Atlanta eavesdropped with interest; Barbie had a fascinating social life. Better still, she seemed to be pissing a lot of people off. Every exchange appeared to be some sort of confrontation.

When the phone rang again, Barbie swore, threw down her mascara, and grabbed it, knocking over a bottle of foundation in the process. She ignored the "Tawny Taupe" puddle that spread across the dressing table's marble top.

"How the hell am I supposed to get ready for dinner?" She stabbed at the "on" button and put the phone to her ear. "Yeah, who is it? I told you not to call me anymore! Are you stupid or what?!"

Atlanta continued to apply her blush, but her ears were practically standing out on stems.

"Big deal!" Barbie continued. "Some cheap flowers. What did you do, pick them out of your mother's backyard? Geez, you're such a freakin' loser. I hate you, you know that? I freakin' *hate* you."

Atlanta glanced over at the flower arrangement that was obviously from a professional shop, and had set someone back a hundred dollars or more. *Backyard flowers my eye,* she thought. *Some guy is treating her better than she deserves.*

Barbie clicked off the phone and began dabbing at the spilled foundation with a handful of tissues.

Eagerly, Atlanta waited for the next scene of the Barbara Matthew's soap opera to begin. It didn't take long.

Barbie tossed the soiled tissues in the general direction of the garbage can, then whirled around on her seat. "Aren't you about done with your face there, Georgia?"

"What's it to you?" Atlanta replied. "I'm not escorting you to dinner, so why should you care when I'm ready?"

"I need a little private time in *my* room, if that's okay with you. Or even if it's not."

Slowly, methodically, Atlanta began to replace her makeup items in her cosmetic bag. While she wouldn't admit that she was deliberately irritating her roommate, the old metaphor, "As slow as molasses in January" did float through her mind.

"Sorry," Atlanta said, sounding completely remorse-free. "I'm not even dressed yet. I'll do well to make it to dinner on time; I'm almost always late for everything. It's part of my charm."

"What charm?" Barbie grumbled as she picked up the phone again and punched in some numbers.

As Atlanta casually strolled around the room, collecting her lingerie, dress, and shoes from her assorted suitcases, she didn't even bother to pretend that she wasn't listening.

Barbie's party answered right away. "Yeah, it's me," she said. "What's up?"

Atlanta sat back down on the bed and began to carefully check her stockings for runs. She could see Barbie's reflection in the mirror, and one look was enough to see that Ms. Matthews was unhappy with what she heard on the other end.

"Well, did you . . . you know . . . have that little talk?" She paused, tapping her fingernails on the table impatiently. "Yeah, and so? That is *not* what I want to hear! That is *so* not what I want to hear!" She glanced at Atlanta in the mirror and lowered her voice a notch. "This . . . situation . . . is getting worse, not better. We know who's going to be the sorriest in the end, and it ain't gonna be me. Fix it, dammit! You *caused* it; you *fix* it!"

She clicked off the phone and hurled it across the room onto her bed.

Atlanta realized she was standing there with her mouth hanging open, so she snapped it shut. Barbie shot her a look that was so cold and full of hate it gave Atlanta the shivers. Where did she get off being so angry?

"Plumbing problems at home," she said. "Damned basement's flooded."

Atlanta nodded. "Yeah, sure. Happens all the time. Ours floods every morning, at nine sharp, like clockwork."

Barbie mumbled a nonreply and returned to her toiletries.

As appealing as the prospect was—of continuing to irritate the heck out of her roommate—Atlanta decided that she had enjoyed as much of Barbie's scintillating company as she could stand. Besides, in spite of what she had said, Atlanta prided herself on usually being prompt, or at least, not scandalously late.

So she quickly wriggled into the simple, white-linen dress she had brought for the occasion, slipped on sandal, strap-around-the-ankle pumps, single-stud, rhinestone earrings, and a delicate tennis bracelet.

Barbie turned to give her a once-over. "Is *that* what you're wearing, Geor-gia?"

For half a second Atlanta felt a twinge of self-doubt. But just in time, the Reid Super Self-Confidence kicked in. She twisted slightly, until the side slit of her skirt showed a shapely expanse of thigh. "Yeah, eat your heart out, Miss Barbie." She sauntered over to the door and jerked it open. "Later," she said as stepped outside and slammed it closed behind her.

"Ah . . . a breath of fresh air . . . ," she said as she strolled down the hallway toward the gallery, with a distinct Reid sashay to her walk.

Chapter

6

The moment Savannah stepped into Villa Rosa's tasting room, she looked around, caught her breath, and grabbed the sleeve of Ryan's tuxedo.

"Whoa! Get a load of this place!" she said, "I want a living room that looks exactly like this."

Ryan laughed. "I suppose you do."

Savannah gazed about, awestruck, taking in the enormous room with its twenty-five-foot-high, open-beamed ceiling, its old oak wainscoting, its mile-long, brightly polished, mahogany bar, and its massive stone fireplace. The carpeting beneath her feet was the deep, ruby shade of a fine Bordeaux, and when she stepped on it, she felt like she was sinking in to her ankles.

"Yeah, right," she said, giving Ryan a nudge with her elbow. "Easy for you to say. You *have* a living room like this. *Just* like this."

He grinned down at her. "Not *just* like this. You can't

stand up in my stone fireplace, and I don't have twenty dining tables, or forty beautiful girls and their friends and families sitting around them."

"You would, if you just crooked your finger. But then, what would you do with forty beautiful girls?"

"Precisely. And I couldn't stand to hear that much giggling. That's one thing I've always liked about John; he hardly ever giggles."

Savannah sniffed the air, fragrant with the aroma of roasted meat, herbs, and wine sauces. China, silver, and crystal gleamed in the candlelight, spread across snowy, linen-draped tables.

The "Welcome Dinner" was semiformal, and gentlemen, looking wonderfully elegant in their tuxedos, escorted the beauty contestants, their mothers, sisters, and friends, who were decked out in evening dresses made of luscious fabrics in every pastel and jewel tone imaginable.

As usual, when hobnobbing with the rich and famous, Savannah felt a bit underdressed. Her "little black dress" was a good one, and the strand of pearls around her neck had been her Granny Reid's. But her one-and-a-half-inch, practical pumps were $15.99, and she had even waited to buy those until she'd found a 10 percent off coupon from Spend Less.

Savannah wasn't fooling anybody . . . least of all herself. She was hardy, peasant stock without a drop of aristocratic blood in her veins. But, considering Granny Reid was only two generations away, she considered herself fortunate. Royalty or not, she was of noble blood.

"Mmm . . . that dinner sure smells good," she said. "I wonder what it is." The ruined breakfast that she hadn't eaten had worn off long ago, leaving her weak with hunger.

"Whatever it is," Ryan said, "I'm sure that Mrs. Lippincott made certain it has no calories. She's scary, that one. Reminds me of a Marine drill sergeant I once knew."

Savannah looked around the room until she saw the lady in question. A pale lavender, satin gown hadn't softened Marion Lippincott's stern appearance one bit. Although she had exchanged her sensible loafers for two-inch heels, she still had a daunting, deliberate stride as she patrolled the room like a Coast Guard cruiser—everyone snapping to attention in her wake.

"Eh, she's not so bad," Savannah said. "It takes a tough old bird like her to run a gig like this. And it looks like she's doing a good job. Everything's going smoothly."

"So far, so good," Ryan agreed. "Time to do the rounds?"

Savannah nodded. "I'll mill around the room here," she said. "Then I'll check the upstairs hall of the guest-house."

"I'll go back to the gallery, make sure nobody's trying to crash the party, and then I'll walk the lower hall."

Ryan disappeared, and Savannah slowly circled the room, acquainting herself with all the new faces. And pretty faces they were, too.

She had to admit that the big sister in her was coming to fore as she sized up each of the contestants. She couldn't help comparing them to her own baby sister. She also couldn't fight the abiding conviction that the kid had them all beat—hands down.

The vast variety of pulchritude was interesting: fresh-

faced sweeties, model types with gaunt, chiseled features, and a few girls who appeared to have become
women before their time, their eyes reflecting a bit too
much worldly knowledge for their young ages.

Savannah recognized a few guests as socially prominent San Carmelitans, whom she had dealt with on
other occasions. Catherine Whitestone-Villa was sitting
at the head table next to a handsome, silver-haired
gentleman. From the way she was hanging on his arm
and gazing at him adoringly, Savannah surmised this
was Catherine's beloved husband, Anthony, the wanna-
be state senator. He appeared less comfortable with the
social scene than his effervescent wife. He had a slightly
"hunted" look, as though he would much prefer to be
somewhere far away from the formal, stuffy crowd.

Strange, for someone seeking public office, Savannah mused.
He'd better get used to it.

A number of people clustered around the head
table, clamoring for the Villas' attention, but they
seemed more interested in the quiet conversation they
were sharing with each other.

It was only when Mrs. Lippincott strode over to their
table that Anthony disengaged himself from Catherine
and stood, shaking Marion's hand vigorously.

She pointed to the podium on the slightly elevated,
temporary stage that had been assembled at the far end
of the room. Anthony Villa nodded his approval and
shook her hand again.

Savannah smiled to herself. Yes, she could definitely
take some lessons on People Management and Manip-
ulation from the formidable Mrs. Lippincott. Even the
seemingly shy Anthony Villa was eager to do her bidding.

As an army of waiters and waitresses dressed in stiffly

starched black-and-white uniforms invaded the room, Savannah decided to take her leave. She hadn't been invited to join the guests for dinner, so what was the point of tormenting herself? She'd score something in the kitchen after hours . . . and what the heck, she'd get a double portion of dessert to reward herself for delayed gratification.

When Savannah reached the top of the guesthouse stairs and looked down the hallway, she was surprised the difference thirty minutes could make. Half an hour ago, on her last round, the floor had been teeming with tittering teenagers, racing up and down the corridor in all stages of dress and undress, rollers in their hair, curling irons in their hands.

Now the hall was empty—its silence almost eerie.

She strolled along the passageway, her pumps making no sound as she stepped on the carpet that was nearly as plush as that of the tasting room, only this rug bore a classic pattern—a green trellis on a background of antique gold with grape leaves bordering both edges.

The walls were covered with the same wainscoting of old oak, while the upper half was stucco-textured in old-world mission style. The ceilings here were also open-beamed, and at the end of the hall was a large window with leaded glass. An outside light cast its glow through the golden glass, giving the hallway a pleasant, Midas-touch ambience.

Savannah was more than halfway down the hall when she noticed that one of the doors—2C—was ajar. She heard voices, females voices, coming from within the room.

Normally she wouldn't have bothered eavesdropping on what was probably a frivolous conversation. But something in the tone—an almost ominous, very serious note to the voices—caught her attention. Silently, she took a few steps closer and listened.

"Don't worry about it," one of the girls said. "Now I wish I'd never even told you about it."

"Well, you *did* tell me, and I *am* worried. I'm *really* worried. And if you were half as smart as you think you are, you'd be worried, too."

Savannah heard rustling in the room and got ready to step away from the door if necessary, but the girls continued talking.

"I told you, I thought about it for a long time. It's gonna work out just the way I planned. Everything's set, you'll see."

"I don't know. I've got a bad feeling about this. I think you should tell your folks. That's what I'd do if I were you."

"*My folks!* You've gotta be kidding. They're the last people I want to know about this . . . at least until it's all settled. Then I'll tell them, and they'll be cool about it."

"And if they aren't?"

"They won't have anything to say about it, will they?"

"You'd better be careful. You could get hurt."

"Naw, if anybody gets hurt, it isn't going to be me. Guaranteed."

Again Savannah heard activity inside the room. "Come on," one of the girls said. "We've gotta get downstairs before Mrs. Lippincott misses us."

"You go ahead. I've got one more quick phone call to make, then I'll be down."

Savannah had time to take a couple of steps backward before the girl emerged from the room and closed the door behind her. She was lovely, petite, with glossy black hair cascading in waves to her waist. She had big, golden-brown eyes that grew even wider when she saw Savannah standing there.

"Oh," she said. "Who . . . who are you?"

"My name is Savannah Reid. I'm working Security for the pageant. Just making my rounds. And you are . . . ?"

"Francie Gorton. I'm one of the contestants."

"Nice to meet you, Francie. Is everything all right?"

The girl gave a furtive glance at the closed door. "Ah, yeah . . . I . . . everything's fine, I guess."

Savannah put on her best soft, big-sister face. "You don't sound too sure to me."

"Yes, I'm sure. But I have to get down to dinner now. I'm late."

The girl started to pass Savannah in the hallway, but Savannah stepped in front of her, reached out, and laid her hand on her shoulder. "Is there anything I can do? If there's a problem, maybe I can help."

Francie glanced at the door again, and for a second Savannah thought she might be about to open up and confide in her. She obviously needed to; her eyes were full of fear, and she was visibly shaking.

"No, really. You can't help. I mean . . . it's not my thing."

Savannah pointed to the closed door. "Is it *her* thing? Does your friend need my help?"

The girl shook her head, and for a moment, sadness replaced the fear in her eyes. "No, Barbie knows everything. If you don't believe that, just ask her. She never needs anybody's help. Now, if you'll excuse me, I really have to go downstairs."

Savannah released her. "Yes, of course you do. If you change your mind, and you want someone to talk to, I'll be around. Okay?"

"Yes, thank you very much. You're nice . . . for a Security person. No offense."

Savannah smiled. "Gee, thanks. I'll take that as high praise. Have a nice dinner, and good luck with the pageant."

As Savannah watched her hurry away, she could hear the low murmur of the other girl's voice on the opposite side of the door. When she had first heard the voice, she'd thought she recognized it: Barbie Matthews, all right. That level of conceit and cockiness was distinctive, even in an adolescent.

She couldn't understand any of the specific words the girl was saying, but she sounded angry, even furious.

So, what else was new with Barbie Matthews?

For a moment Savannah considered knocking on the door and questioning the kid. But instinctively she knew that Ms. Barbie would be far less cooperative than her uncooperative girlfriend had been, so it was pointless.

She walked away, easing the queasy feeling in her stomach by promising herself to keep a close eye on Barbie Matthews for the rest of the pageant.

The problem was: She just wasn't sure exactly what to watch for.

Was she protecting Barbie from someone who might want to hurt her? Or was she protecting someone in particular—or everyone at the pageant—from the temperamental Ms. Matthews?

Chapter
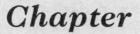

By the time Savannah returned to the gallery she found it virtually empty, except for a few Villa Rosa staff members who were scurrying through, their arms laden with everything from trays of dishes, to flower arrangements and stacks of linens.

Even Ryan was gone. She assumed he was patrolling the downstairs hallway of the guesthouse, or checking the grounds.

Villa Rosa's visitors had migrated to the tasting room, and Savannah could tell by the clatter of dishes and silverware that dinner was well under way. The smell of food was driving her crazy. Right now she would even settle for one of Dirk's bargain kids' burgers and a greasy bag of cold fries.

When she entered the tasting room, she found a semidark, discreet spot against the wall to the left of the main door, where she stood for over half an hour, keeping an eye on things but maintaining a low profile.

Other than the fact that she was starving, she had to admit, this was a pretty easy way to make a buck. She'd have to thank Ryan again for recommending her. It had been ages since she'd had a gig this laid-back.

If she could only get her paws on one of those plates of herb-roasted chicken. . . .

Barbie Matthews was feeling better than she had for weeks; finally, things were starting to go her way. The plan she had crafted so carefully was beginning to unfold.

Winning beauty pageants was fine, but Barbie had so much more in mind for her future. After all, what was the point of being beautiful if you didn't use it fully to your advantage?

As she hurried through the now-vacant upstairs corridor of the guesthouse, she felt her pulse pounding with excitement. When she had made the phone call and demanded the meeting, she hadn't really expected the other party to agree. But, to her shock and delight, the person had, and she was on her way to a meeting that would change her boring, mundane life forever.

Once downstairs, she stuck her head around the corner and glanced around the gallery. The only activity she saw was the bustling of waiters and waitresses, who seemed preoccupied with their own activities.

Head held high, her purse tucked under her arm, Barbie walked briskly through the gallery and out the front door, trying to appear as nonchalant as possible—for a young woman whose life was about to change dramatically.

Outside, the cool, damp night air was filled with the

fragrance of fruit on the vine . . . and the evening was full of delicious possibilities.

Wouldn't everyone be surprised?

Sometimes Barbie felt that those around her hadn't given her the proper respect she was due. A lot of people claimed to be special, but she really *was*. Though sometimes that gift was less of a blessing and more of a burden.

It wasn't easy, being the prettiest and brightest person in a room at any given time and not being recognized as such. But those days were over. After tonight, everyone would see her in a whole new light. She would receive the special attention she had always craved.

She glanced around, trying to get her bearings, but—although gifted in all the really important ways—she had never developed a sense of direction, and everything looked different than it had earlier in the daylight.

This far out in the country, the night was darker than in town, and only a few round-globed, antique streetlamps illuminated the grounds.

To her right was the small building that housed the Villa Rosa gift shop, straight ahead lay the road that led to the main gates and the highway, and to her left was the parking lot.

She headed in that direction, as she had been instructed on the phone. She had been told to go to the far side of the parking lot, where she would be met by her visitor near the swimming-pool area.

Her heart began to pound even harder, and she shivered with anticipation. She had won! Of course, she had always known she would, but now that victory was within reach, it was far sweeter than she had even imagined.

A cold, wet breeze swept over her, chilling her back, which was bare, her dress being particularly low-cut. She had just left the terra-cotta-tiled walkway and stepped onto the parking-lot asphalt, when the cell phone inside her purse buzzed against her ribs.

"Not now!" she said as she fumbled inside her purse and brought out the phone. Aggravated though she was, she was afraid not to answer it. Her party might be calling to inform her of a change of plans.

"Yeah? Who is it?" She paused beside an old, bright red Mustang and tapped her foot impatiently.

"Your mother," said a voice just as impatiently. "Where are you? Your father and I are sitting here at this banquet table, waiting for you to show up. I sent your sister to find you twenty minutes ago."

"Great . . . that's just what I need . . . the Squirt on my tail."

"And your friend, Francie, is here. She said you were on your way down from her room half an hour ago."

"I'm not coming."

"What do you mean you aren't coming? If your family shows up at these functions to show their support for you, the least you could do is make an appearance."

Barbie sighed and rolled her eyes. Once again . . . no respect.

"I don't feel good, Mom, and I *sure* don't feel like eating the garbage that they're serving. I'm just going to stay here in my room."

"What's the matter? Are you throwing up again? I'll bring you something to settle your stomach."

"No! I don't want to see you. I don't want to see *anybody.* Just leave me alone. If you guys are bored, go home. I never asked you to come anyway."

She punched the "talk" button before her mom

could get in that irritating last word that she always insisted on having. Mom was quite the controller in the family, leading Dad and Louise around by the nose. Barbie was the only one with enough guts to put her in her place.

Barbie smiled broadly. Yes, when Mommy Dearest found out what was going on, she was probably going to be the most surprised of all. Everything wasn't as in control as she had thought.

Smoothing her hair and licking her lips, Barbie continued across the lot. She peered into the darkness on either side of her, but saw no one—only rows of parked cars. The night here seemed even cooler than before, and she had to clench her teeth to keep them from chattering.

Out here, alone in the dark, her mental vision of her bright future dimmed just a little. For a moment, Barbie felt a trickle of fear run from her tailbone up her back to the base of her skull.

Something wasn't quite right.

She had felt this way once before . . . when she was six years old. She had stretched out her hand to pet the neighbor's German shepherd. Looking into his eyes, she had felt the same sensation that she felt now. The dog had bitten her. Hard. It had taken seven stitches in the hospital emergency room to close the wound. She still had the scar to remind her, the only blemish on an otherwise perfect body.

Having reached the edge of the lot and the appointed spot near the pool and patio area, there was nothing else for her to do but wait. And Barbie wasn't good at waiting, especially when she was feeling a bit weird and freaky. She gripped the cell phone tightly and felt a little less vulnerable.

"You'd better show," she said under her breath. "And you'd better get here pretty soon, too. I'm not going to wait all night . . . not even for you."

Just as she was deciding that she had, indeed, been stood up, Barbie heard footsteps approaching from behind her. She turned around, a smile of greeting on her carefully glossed lips. But the smile quickly faded when she saw her visitor's face.

"You? What are *you* doing here?" Rage swept through Barbara Matthews, hot and searing, replacing cold caution. "No, no, no! You aren't going to screw this up for me. You're *not!* I swear, I'll kill you first."

The dark figure laughed, and the harsh, hard sound of it would have terrified a more timid—or sensible— soul than Barbie Matthews.

But Barbie's terror came a moment later when she saw the glint of a gun pointed straight at her head.

"You have two choices," the person told her. "Number one: You don't follow my instructions, and I kill you here and now. Number two: You be a good girl, do everything I tell you to do—when I tell you to do it— and I'll kill you later. It's up to you. What's it gonna be?"

Barbie could almost feel that German shepherd's fangs sinking into her tender hand. The danger she had seen in the dog's eyes was exactly what she could hear in this person's voice. She was in trouble . . . big trouble.

And she wanted to live, even if it was only for a few more minutes or hours. Barbie Matthews, Miss California Sunshine, swallowed her pride and nearly choked on it.

"What you want me to do?"

"Turn around . . . and put your hands behind your back."

For one of the few times in her life, Barbie did exactly as she was told.

"Now see there; isn't that easy?" said the person with the gun. "Even an airhead like you can do it."

While Savannah wasn't jazzed about the idea of her little sister strutting her stuff in what she considered a glorified meat market, she had to admit that she was pretty proud of the kid.

From her posted position against the wall, Savannah could see Atlanta across the room, sitting at a table with some other girls, laughing and chatting as though they had known each other for years. With familial satisfaction, Savannah noted that Atlanta was, by far, the most attractive one at the table, despite the fact that she was dressed less expensively than the average attendee.

Savannah wished that Atlanta had asked her for something more appropriate to wear, but she quickly dismissed the idea as ridiculous . . . as if anything in her closet would fit that teeny-tiny body.

She watched to see if Atlanta was actually eating anything off the plate set in front of her. While she had her fork in her hand and appeared to be moving food from one place to another, she didn't actually seem to be sticking any of it in her mouth, chewing, and swallowing.

A look around the room at the other girls did little to put Savannah's mind at ease. Most of the young ladies appeared to be doing the same thing . . . pretending to eat. And most of them were just as slender as Atlanta, some even more so.

Savannah could remember being that thin . . . but she had to stretch her memory back . . . *way* back . . . to junior high school. Though not as skinny as these girls, she had been teased mercilessly, called Beanpole, Toothpick, and Ostrich Legs.

At that time, voluptuous curves were "in." And she was basically curveless, until the hormones kicked in . . . about tenth grade. Suddenly, those distinctly feminine attributes appeared, burgeoning forth with a vengeance. And for about a week, Savannah had been hot stuff on campus.

But then, suddenly, "stacked" was "out" and models in miniskirts with figures similar to those of prepubescent boys were "in."

In one week, Savannah had gone from Beanpole to Major Babe to Fatso.

Life sucked.

But she had learned a valuable lesson: You can't rate yourself by society's fickle standards.

She had decided, then and there, to love her flesh . . . every gorgeous, soft, feminine inch and ounce of it. And, with all her heart, she wished she could give that precious gift of self-love to every young woman in the room. Unfortunately, it wasn't something you could transfuse.

Clicking back into professional-bodyguard mode, she surveyed the room again, looking specifically for Barbie Matthews. But she didn't see her. Apparently the girl hadn't come down yet. Her friend, Francie, had taken a seat at Atlanta's table, and there was an empty chair beside her. Savannah assumed she was saving it for Barbie.

The girl still looked worried and preoccupied, not joining in the lively conversation at the table.

The welcoming speeches had begun with Mrs. Lippincott onstage, introducing the various luminaries in their midst. Savannah watched her with interest, noting her expertise and ease at the microphone. If beauty-pageant experience imparted this sort of social grace to its participants, perhaps it could be a positive thing for the contestants after all. Such skills would be useful in many of life's venues.

If only Savannah could get over the unpleasant feeling that these girls were being evaluated on the sum of their external parts, rather than the intrinsic value of their souls.

When Mrs. Lippincott began to introduce the girls, and they filed across this stage, one by one, speaking a quick hello into the microphone, Savannah's uneasiness increased. Across the audience, she saw expressions on some of the men's faces that reflected genuine appreciation for the girls' youthful beauty, and even some worshipful adoration.

That was all fine and good.

What she didn't like were the eyes that racked up and down each girl, while their owners engaged in their own little private, out-of-body experiences . . . fantasies that probably would have offended, if not horrified, the girls on the stage. And most of those wearing that sort of look were old enough to be the girls' fathers . . . in some cases, their grandfathers.

One of the worst offenders was the guy that Ryan had warned her about earlier, one of the judges, Frank Addison. Sitting at a front table, he had an excellent view, which he was taking full advantage of.

When Atlanta's name was called, and she glided across the stage to speak her "hello" into the microphone, Savannah couldn't help noticing the lecherous attention he was paying to her baby sister.

"Roll up that tongue of yours and stick it back in

your mouth, you old perv," she whispered. "And screw your eyes back into their sockets while you're at it."

When Atlanta left the stage, instead of returning to her table, she exited the room by way of a side door. Savannah had seen a number of the girls coming in and out through that door. It appeared to be the shortest route to the ladies' room.

Alarm bells went off in her head as she watched Frank Addison rise from his seat and stroll nonchalantly through the same door behind Atlanta. It took Savannah only a few seconds to get across the room and out the door.

"Oh, no you don't," she muttered as she followed him, rapidly closing the distance. "Don't you even think about what you're thinking about . . . not with any of my girls, you peckerhead, and *especially* not with that one!"

Barbie Matthews knew with more certainty than she had ever known anything before, that she was about to be murdered; the only question remaining was, "How?"

She had done everything she had been told to do. She had allowed her hands to be taped so tightly that her fingers had almost immediately gone numb. She had submitted to having a wide piece of the silver tape stretched across her mouth, which itched terribly and tore her lips, besides making it difficult for her to breathe. She could taste her own stomach juices, bitter in her mouth, and she was afraid she would vomit and choke.

For just a moment Barbie thought of how many times she had used self-induced vomiting to keep her weight down. How ironic if she actually died that way, after hearing all the warnings about how dangerous the practice was and dismissing them as alarmist hogwash.

Her captor had forced her to walk to the back of one of the cars that was parked at the edge of a lot, and now the person was opening the trunk. The gun was still pointed at her face.

"Get inside. Now . . . move it!"

So, she wasn't going to be killed here at this location. Barbie mentally clutched at the hope that a car ride might provide her with an opportunity to escape. Obediently, she climbed into the trunk. It was harder to do than she would have thought, with her hands taped behind her and her legs weak and shaky from fear.

But she managed to crawl in, scraping her shin painfully, and lie down as she was instructed.

Crunched into a fetal ball, on her side, she could smell the moist, mustiness of the trunk, the rubber of the spare tire, and the gasoline residue on the outside of a metal can beside her head.

But those odors were only faint impressions. Barbie had far more pressing issues than unpleasant smells to worry about. Something in the manner of the person standing over her, leaning into the trunk, told her that something was about to happen. Something very bad.

Maybe she was going to be killed right there and then, after all.

Briefly, she wondered what it would feel like . . . a bullet passing through her flesh. She had heard that sometimes people were shot and they didn't even realize it. Maybe it wouldn't hurt too badly.

As though from far away at the end of the long, dark hallway, she could hear her tormentor saying, "You're nothing but a cockroach. You know that, don't you? A girl like you, who doesn't care who she hurts, who she uses—you're nothing but a damned cockroach."

Barbie had a thousand things she wanted to say in her own defense, a thousand things she wanted to tell her captor, having to do with their illegitimate birth, incestuous relationships, and their most unpleasant, eternal destination. Most of all, she wanted to say that she was special . . . far too special to be treated this way.

But now, for the first time in her life, when she wanted most to speak, Barbie Matthews was speechless—because of the tape across her mouth.

Her tormenter was rummaging around in the trunk near Barbie's feet. "You know how they kill cockroaches?" the voice asked.

Mash them? Barbie thought. Oh, god, was that how she was going to be killed? Squashed flat like a bug on a sidewalk?

Was she going to be crushed here in this car?

"I'll tell you how they kill cockroaches." The person actually sounded happy, as if enjoying the situation. The thought made her even more sick to her stomach. She had known it would be risky—this plan of hers. But if you didn't take the occasional risk, you got nowhere. And Barbie had grown tired of being nowhere.

But in her wildest fantasies, she'd never thought of this as an ending to her story.

She tried to see what was going on as the person continued to fumble with something in the trunk. But Barbie was facing the front of the car and could see nothing but faint outlines in the darkness.

"Here's how they kill vermin like you," the person said.

Barbie closed her eyes and winced, expecting . . . she didn't know what.

Then she heard a pop, followed by a spewing sound. And she smelled a strong, acrid, chemical odor, that stung her nostrils and made her eyes burn.

"Bug bombs." That's how to get rid of cockroaches like you."

Something hard was tossed into the trunk, and Barbie felt it hit her leg. Something moist sprayed against her calf, and the bitter smell was suddenly much, much worse.

"You blew it this time, Barbie baby. You fucked with the wrong person, one time too many. And now you're going to die for it."

The trunk lid slammed closed, leaving Barbie in complete darkness. As the deadly vapor filled the small enclosure, she thought she must be breathing pure fire into her lungs.

She tried to scream. The tape ripped the tender skin on her lips, but it wouldn't come off.

She twisted her wrists until they were sticky with blood, but the bindings held fast.

She rolled over onto her back, pulled her knees up to her face, and kicked as hard as she could at the top of the trunk. But as much pain as the movements caused her, the metal didn't budge.

"Help me! Please, please, help me!" she screamed behind the tape. But there was no one to hear her muffled cries.

After what seemed like an eternity, the terrible pain in her lungs seemed to lessen just a little. Moment by moment, Barbie's panic gradually began to subside, and she stopped her futile thrashing.

It wasn't so bad.

Maybe she didn't need to fight it. Maybe she didn't need to escape.

This darkness. The comforting, warm darkness, closing all around her . . . it wasn't so bad.

In the fuzzy recesses of what remained of her mental functions, Barbie Matthews was mildly surprised.

Who would have thought it?

This dying . . . it wasn't so bad, after all.

Chapter
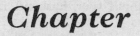

Just as Savannah had surmised, Atlanta was heading into the ladies' room. And her wanna-be stalker, Frank Addison, was making a production of lighting a cigarette and studying a piece of impressionistic art on a nearby wall.

As Savannah waited and watched, half-hidden behind a giant potted palm, several females came out of the rest room, including contestants, their mothers, and some of the Villa Rosa staff, as well as Catherine Whitestone-Villa.

When Catherine passed the palm on her way back to the tasting room, she spotted Savannah. A look of concern crossed her face, and she walked over to her. "Is everything all right, Savannah?" she asked. "You seem . . . upset."

Savannah glanced over at Addison, who was still pretending to be absorbed by the painting. "Oh, sure.

Everything's just peachy. You go on back to your dinner, Mrs. Villa. I think your husband is beginning his speech."

"Oh, yes!" Her face brightened. "I don't want to miss that. He counts on me to be in the audience." She lowered her voice and whispered, "Tony's actually a little bit stage-shy, if you can imagine that. Isn't it sweet?"

"Oh . . . sweet . . . very sweet, indeed."

As Catherine walked away Savannah resisted the urge to gag. Maybe she wouldn't want dessert, after all—not even one helping, let alone two.

But her nausea quickly changed to cold-blooded fury when Atlanta came out of the bathroom and was immediately intercepted by the horny Frank Addison. Although Savannah couldn't hear what he was saying, it was easy to catch the drift of his conversation as he dug into his Brioni jacket pocket, produced a business card, and tucked it into Atlanta's hand.

Savannah was there in half a dozen strides. She was just in time to hear him say, ". . . anytime . . . love to hear from you . . . many things to talk about. . . ."

She wasn't sure who was the more surprised, Frank or Atlanta, when she snatched the card out of the girl's hand. She gave Atlanta a quick, businesslike smile, and said, "I'll take that, and you can go back to your dinner, Miss Reid."

"But . . . but this . . . gentleman and I are talking," Atlanta sputtered.

"This *gentleman* and I have business to discuss, and you need to return to your table, Miss Reid . . . immediately." She gave the girl a slight push toward the door, and Atlanta walked away, glaring at her older sister over her shoulder.

"Dang, I'm gonna pay, big-time, for this," Savannah

muttered. She turned to Frank Addison, who by now was more angry than surprised. "What did you think you were doing there, Mr. Addison? I'm sure someone told you it's against the rules for the judges to consort with our pretty contestants."

His face turned so red that his nose flushed purple. She half expected him to have a stroke right there in front of her but decided that was too much to hope for.

"Consort? Who's consorting?" he said. "The young lady dropped a piece of paper, and I picked it up and gave it to her," he said with a sniff that was, no doubt, intended to sound indignant, but Savannah decided he probably just had allergies. "Boy, that's what you get for trying to be a gentleman. You do a good deed, and somebody thinks you're up to no good."

Savannah cast a withering glance down at the zipper area of his trousers. "Oh yes, I can see that your 'no good' is up. And that's what bothers me. I saw the way you were looking at the contestants when they were traipsing across the stage. And I saw you follow that particular lady to the bathroom and wait for her to come out. And I saw you hand her your business card. And I heard what you told her about getting together later, so don't try to bullshit me, Mr. Addison. I know exactly what you're trying to pick up . . . and it ain't no piece of paper for a lady."

He said nothing, but Savannah noticed that his purple nose turned three shades darker, and his gray eyes burned with an anger so intense that she quickly realized: This man was more than your run-of-the-mill pervert; he was potentially very dangerous.

So, it was even more important to make her message unmistakably clear.

Savannah stepped closer to him, and since he wasn't

a particularly tall man, and she was wearing pumps, they were standing eye to eye. "Let me put it this way, Mr. Addison," she said, her voice ominous in its lack of inflection. "In the future, when you look at our pretty little girls, you better put all those wicked, nasty thoughts right out of your mind, 'cause they're gonna get you in *big* trouble with me.

"You see, I'm working Security at this pageant . . ." Just for effect, she lifted her skirt a few inches to reveal the holster and pistol she had strapped to her thigh. "So, I'm looking out for *all* the girls. But that one girl you were trying to hit on—well, let's just say you've got good taste but rotten luck—she's my little sister. And I'm very protective of my family members."

"I'm sure you are," he replied in a tone that was far too casual for her liking. He still hadn't gotten the message.

"If you know what's good for you, Mr. Addison," she said, moving even closer until her nose was almost touching his, "you'd better behave yourself at this here pageant. Because if you don't, I'm gonna get hold of a great big knife and lop off your tallywhacker. Then I'll feed it to you on a hot dog bun with mustard, relish, and extra onions. Do you understand me, sir?"

He didn't answer but gave her a curt nod. She could tell, by the fine sweat breaking out on his upper lip and the shortness of his breath, that her unladylike, but graphic description had produced the desired effect.

She started to turn away, then reconsidered. "Oh, yes, by the way . . . when it comes judgment time, you're not to hold this conversation between you and me against Miss Atlanta Reid. And you don't need to give her any special consideration because of it either. You rate her like you would anyone else, and you and I will get along just fine."

She left Frank Addison standing there with his inflated blood pressure and deflated ego and returned to the tasting room, where dinner festivities were coming to a close. Anthony Villa had finished his speech, the dessert dishes were being cleared away, and the rich aroma of coffee filled the room.

Glancing over at Atlanta's table, Savannah quickly noted two facts: Barbie Matthews still had not made her appearance, and Savannah's younger sister was positively livid, her eyes shooting blue lasers across the room at Savannah.

"Ah, the joys of sisterhood," Savannah said with a sigh. "Oh, well, it just goes to show you: No good deed goes unpunished."

Savannah had expected a certain amount of hostility the next time she conversed with her youngest sibling. But nothing had prepared her for the storm that descended upon her head when she crossed the path of Hurricane Atlanta in the gallery half an hour later.

"Get away from me! I am not speaking to you!" Atlanta said with a Vivian Leigh toss of her head. "In fact, I'm considering never speaking to you again. Not for as long as I live. Not for as long as *you* live. Not for as long as—"

"Okay, okay, I get your drift." Savannah sighed and ran her fingers wearily through her hair. Her "do" had long since died, along with her hopes of wringing any enjoyment from this assignment.

She glanced across the gallery and saw Mrs. Lippincott, surrounded by a circle of tired staff. Ryan was with them, looking as fresh and debonair as he had at the beginning of the evening. *Dang his hide,* she thought.

She lowered her voice, not wanting an audience for this little domestic squabble. "I understand that you're very upset with me, 'Lanta," she said. "So, what else is new? Older sisters are a lot like parents; they seldom, if ever, do anything right . . . at least according to the younger kids in a family."

"But you were rude to a judge! A judge, Savannah! And he was being so nice to me. He probably would have given me really high marks, if you hadn't stuck your big, fat nose into things."

Savannah reached out, put her hand on Atlanta's forearm, and gave her a cautionary squeeze. "Sh-h-h . . . keep your voice down. Let's go into your room to discuss this."

Atlanta shook her hand away. "There's nothing to discuss. We aren't speaking, remember?"

"So, I guess I should have just let you go on talking to that sleazebag. He was going to hit on you, do you know that?"

Atlanta's face lit up. "Really? Really, do you think he likes me that much?"

Savannah resisted the urge to strangle her. "No-o-o, I'm quite sure he doesn't like you. He doesn't even know you. He's only interested in banging you, and he doesn't have to like you for that."

Atlanta's nostrils flared, and for half a second Savannah expected flames to shoot out of her nose. "What's the matter, sissy?" she said bitterly. "Do you want him for yourself? You've got a thing for him? Is that it?"

"Don't be ridiculous. I—"

"I think that's exactly what it is. I think my big sister is sexually frustrated and—"

"Atlanta, that's enough." Savannah gave the teenager the same look that Gran had given the Reid children about three seconds before her righteous wrath exacted its toll on their backsides. "For your information, young lady, the only frustration I'm feeling at this minute is the overwhelming desire to bend you over my knee and paddle your hind end."

"This conversation is over," Atlanta said in a tone that was less self-assured than her words.

"Yes, it is. We've already said way too much for a couple of sisters who aren't speaking to each other."

Savannah felt a flood of sadness sweep over her as she watched her sibling walk away. Did all families have these problems, she wondered, or were the Reids specially blessed in that regard?

She didn't have to think that one over for very long. Having been a police officer for years, she knew all too well the kinds of problems that some families had— problems that sometimes ended in tragedy.

This little disagreement was nothing. Really.

So, why did it hurt so much?

Savannah felt someone's presence behind her, and when she turned around she saw Mrs. Lippincott standing there, watching. She had left Ryan and the staff members and walked over to Savannah's side of the gallery. Savannah wondered how much she had overheard.

"Is everything all right, Savannah?" she asked.

Savannah considered brushing her off with a flip answer, then at the last second decided to be honest. "Not exactly. I've certainly lived more peaceful lifetimes . . . but I'm fairly certain I lived them as an only child."

Mrs. Lippincott smiled. "I understand. I have three younger sisters of my own."

Several of the contestants walked through the gallery, snickering, giggling, excited and as happy as only a group of carefree teenagers could be. As they passed Savannah and Mrs. Lippincott, the older woman watched them with a look akin to resentment on her face.

"What a waste," she said. "All that beauty, health, and energy squandered on the young. They have no idea how fleeting all of those gifts are. If they did, they would enjoy this period of their lives so much more."

Savannah nodded. "How true."

"Don't you envy them . . . their youth?"

Savannah thought for a moment. "Not really. Along with the beauty and energy goes a lot of inexperience and naïveté. I wouldn't be that young and stupid again for anything in the world. Those life lessons were too hard-earned to be given away."

Marion Lippincott quirked one eyebrow. Savannah got the distinct impression that she wasn't accustomed to being contradicted. "Oh? May I ask how old you are, Savannah?"

"I'm in my early forties."

"Ah . . . that explains it. Check back with me in around twenty years, and we'll see how you feel about the subject then."

Savannah chuckled. "You may be right. By the way, Mrs. Lippincott, I was going to ask you about one of your girls . . . a Barbara or Barbie—"

A horrible, terrified scream cut through the room.

Savannah swallowed her words and nearly her heart. The sound had come from the direction of the guest-house, the same direction that Atlanta had walked just moments ago. And somewhere in the recesses of her mind, Savannah knew—with sickening conviction—that it was her little sister who had screamed.

"Oh, my God. . . . ," she whispered. But she was already running, with Ryan at her side, her gun in her hand . . . and Mrs. Lippincott trailing somewhere behind.

Savannah and Ryan nearly collided with Atlanta, who was racing down the hall, running away from her room. Thankful to see the kid in one piece, Savannah holstered her Beretta and held out her arms. Atlanta flew into them, sobbing.

"What is it, sweetheart?" Savannah asked, trying to peel her sister off so that she could check her for injuries. "What's wrong?"

"Was it you who screamed, Atlanta?" Ryan asked. He still had his gun drawn, but was holding it behind his thigh and out of sight.

Atlanta nodded vigorously and tried to squeak out a couple of words, but she was crying too hard.

Mrs. Lippincott came running up behind them, followed by half a dozen of the staff members. Excited and alarmed, they were all trying to talk at once.

"What happened?" Mrs. Lippincott demanded. "What's going on here, and why are you crying, Ms. Reid?"

Savannah held up one hand in a manner that clearly said, "Back off."

"Wait there please," she said. "Let us take care of this for the moment."

Mrs. Lippincott seemed to get the message, and she took a couple of steps backward. "Okay, okay," she said to the staff, "quiet down. Everybody be calm while they figure this out."

Savannah put her hands on Atlanta's shoulders and gently shook her. "Come on, honey, and take a couple of deep breaths. Do it. In. Out. That's it. Now tell me what's wrong."

Atlanta shivered, turned, and pointed to the door of her room, which was half-open. "In there," she said, "on the bed."

Ryan hurried on down the hall, reaching the room just before Savannah. They positioned themselves on either side of the door, nodded to each other, and Ryan shoved it the rest of the way open with his foot, his gun lifted and ready.

After a quick glance, they charged into the room. Expecting the worst—whenever that might be—Savannah had also drawn her Beretta. But the room was vacant.

"What is that?" Savannah said. "What's the problem that—"

She didn't need an answer from Ryan; by then she could clearly see the problem for herself.

There on the bed next to the window—Atlanta's bed—was a large pool of red ugliness.

"Blood," Ryan said simply.

Savannah nodded and moved closer. When she was

about a yard from the bed she could smell it, the thick, coppery stench, that was instinctively repulsive and set one's nerves on edge.

"There's a lot of it," Ryan commented.

"Yes, definitely not caused by nicking your legs with a dull shaver."

Savannah heard Mrs. Lippincott at the door and turned around to see her entering the room. "Stop! Stop right there. Don't come in here."

"But I have every right to—"

"No! Nobody comes in here," she said with an air of authority that wasn't to be denied . . . even by the formidable Mrs. Lippincott. "Everyone stays out until we see what we have here. This may be a crime scene, and we don't want it contaminated more than it already is."

The two lamps in the bedroom weren't particularly bright, but they gave enough light for Savannah to see that there was more than just blood on the bed. The stain itself was three to four feet across and in the center of it was a fist-sized hunk of some sort of bloody, fleshy tissue.

"What do you suppose that is?" she asked Ryan in a voice too low for those in the door to hear.

He shook his head. "I don't know. I don't think I want to know."

"Have you got your flashlight?" Savannah said.

Ryan handed her a small, but powerful penlight. She shined the beam into the center of the gore. In the doorway she heard Atlanta gasp. She felt she should offer her some words of comfort, but under the circumstances, none came to mind.

Ryan moved closer to her, and after looking at the mass a while whispered, "A fetus?"

"That's what I thought," she said, "but I don't know

for sure." She pointed to the wall over the bed, just beneath the window, where a word had been scrawled in blood on the rose-covered paper. "What do you make of that?"

He squinted at the writing. "T-U-L-S? Tuls?"

Savannah cocked her head sideways. "No, I don't think so."

"Some of the letters are backward," Ryan observed. "I guess that means our offender is dyslexic or—"

"It's upside down. It's been written upside down. It says S-L-U-T. Not very friendly."

"Not friendly at all. Who do you suppose wrote it?"

"It was Barbie," Atlanta said from the doorway. "It was that rude bitch, Barbie—excuse me, Mrs. Lippincott—who did that to my bed. We had a fight earlier and—"

Savannah hurried over to her sister and grabbed her firmly by the forearm. "That's enough, Atlanta. You had a shock, honey. And I think you need to sit down somewhere and collect yourself." She turned back to Ryan. "Do you have your cell phone on you?"

He nodded.

"Why don't you call Dirk and get him over here?"

"Good idea," he said.

"Who is that?" Mrs. Lippincott asked. "Who's Dirk?"

"Detective Sergeant Dirk Coulter," Savannah said. "He's with the San Carmelita Police Department. We have to report this and have it checked out."

Savannah looked back to the bed with its gory stain and at the offensive word on the wall. "Tell Dirk that he should probably have Dr. Liu come out, too." she told Ryan.

He was already dialing.

"And who's this Dr. Lou?" Mrs. Lippincott wanted to know. "Is he your family physician?"

"No," Savannah said. "Dr. Jennifer Liu is the San Carmelita medical examiner . . . the coroner."

Chapter
10

Since Ryan had offered to guard the door to Atlanta's room until Dirk arrived, Savannah decided to take her sister a comfortable distance away from the unpleasant scene. Believing that some fresh air would help, she led her out into the courtyard, where they found a wrought-iron park bench near the fountain with thick, inviting cushions.

Savannah had also chosen a spot where she could see the front door and would know the instant Dirk or Dr. Liu arrived.

"Are you okay, kiddo?" she asked her, putting her arm around her shoulders. The girl was still shaking, but she had stopped crying, and that was a good sign.

"Why do you think Barbie did that?" Atlanta asked. "I mean, I know we didn't like each other. We were giving each other a hard time, but it wasn't all that bad. Why would she put that horrible stuff on my bed?"

Savannah had a couple of theories running around in her head. And Barbie vandalizing Atlanta's bed was only one of them. She wondered whether it would be wise to share the possibilities with Atlanta . . . especially if the other scenarios might be more frightening than the first.

"How could she hate me that much? It's such a crazy thing to do," Atlanta continued. "And where would she get so much blood?"

Savannah decided to plunge ahead, even if it might make things worse. "We don't know for sure that Barbie was the one who did it. And we don't know if it was meant to scare you or her. There's a lot we don't know yet, so just hang in there, honey, until we find out what's going on."

Through the glass French doors Savannah could see a bustle of activity in the gallery. Mrs. Catherine Whitestone-Villa had said good night and excused herself earlier in the evening, to return to her home, a lovely Spanish-style hacienda on the hill behind the center. But apparently someone had alerted her to the problem in the guesthouse, and she was on the scene, running around in quite a dither.

For a moment Savannah wondered why Anthony Villa hadn't returned with his wife. But then she remembered the mention of children being tucked into bed and decided that Anthony had probably remained behind for their sake.

"Atlanta, sweetie," Savannah said, torn between family loyalty and duty, "if you're feeling better, I should probably talk to Mrs. Villa for a minute, just to fill her in on what's happened."

Atlanta nodded. "Sure, I'm okay."

She didn't sound nearly as certain as her words.

Savannah could tell she was trying to be brave, and she respected her for it. Most people twice Atlanta's age would have freaked out under the circumstances.

Savannah stood. "Would you like to sit here for a while, or would you rather come with me?"

Atlanta jumped to her feet. So much for wanting to be rid of her interfering older sister.

The moment they stepped into the gallery Catherine ran over to them. She had changed from her evening wear to a designer jogging suit that looked like it had never been taken on a run. Her white tennis shoes were spotless, and her French twist still perfect. Her already fair complexion was even more pale, and she appeared terribly upset.

"Oh, Savannah, I'm so relieved to see you." She clasped her hands to her chest dramatically. "What on earth is going on around here? Somebody said that one of the girls had something dreadful put on her bed." She turned to Atlanta. "I believe they said it was you, Miss Reid."

Atlanta glanced at Savannah, who gave her a warning, "keep quiet" look. She shrugged and studied the ranch-pegged hardwood floor.

"Well, yes, that's true," Savannah offered. "Although we aren't sure yet how it got there or exactly what it is."

"I was told it's blood," Catherine said. "You don't think one of our girls has been hurt, do you?"

"I certainly hope not. We've called the police and—"

"The police? Was that really necessary? I mean, if word of this gets out . . ."

"Yes?"

Mrs. Villa actually looked embarrassed, as though ashamed to be caught worrying about anything so frivolous as her vineyard's reputation, when one of her young guests might have recently shed some of her life's blood on one of her bedspreads.

"You . . . you know . . . how this sort of thing gets all blown out of proportion," she said. "People *love* a morbid story, and I can just see it all over the newspapers by tomorrow morning."

Savannah pasted a sympathetic look on her face. "Of course I understand. But certainly none of *us* would call the press. And the police officer who's coming is a personal friend of mine. We were partners together on the force for years. I'm sure we can trust him to be discreet."

Mrs. Villa seemed immensely relieved. "Oh, thank goodness." She glanced around and lowered her voice. "After all, this event was meant to generate positive publicity . . . what with my husband running for the senate. And, of course, we did it to help the girls with their scholarships, and all that."

"Of course . . . all that."

Catherine paused, giving Savannah a searching look, as if trying to decide whether or not she was being mocked. Savannah decided to let her wonder.

"I just feel so terrible about this." She toyed with the drawstring of her jogging pants. "Is there any way I can help?"

"Actually, yes," Savannah said. "If you can ask your staff—anyone you can spare—to help us. Ryan Stone and Mrs. Lippincott are organizing a search for one of the young ladies who appears to be missing."

"Missing? Oh my! Now you *are* scaring me!"

"Please don't be overly concerned at this point," Savannah said with far more assurance than she felt. "This may be nothing more than a cruel, tasteless joke. We'll know more soon."

"Do keep me informed. I want to know *everything*. I'll go speak to Mrs. Lippincott now about that extra help."

"Thank you. You're most gracious."

As Savannah and Atlanta watched Catherine Whitestone-Villa hurry away, Atlanta leaned close to Savannah's ear and said, "Do you like her?"

"Of course I do. She's my employer. And when you're a private detective who gets a job once in a blue moon . . . you like anyone who offers you a paycheck. So what if she's shallow, a bit dense, and a snob? That doesn't make her altogether a bad person, does it?"

Atlanta gave her a half smile. "Pretty close, I'd say."

Savannah pressed her finger to her lips. "Sh-h-h, now would be a good time to keep your opinions to yourself. Which reminds me, I don't want you to tell anyone here about your disagreement with Barbie. *Nobody*. Got that?"

Atlanta's eyes grew wider, and she gave a paranoid glance around. "Why? Do you think somebody hurt her? You do! And you're afraid that they'll think I'm the one who did it. That's it, isn't it?"

"You know that old phrase: What you say can and will be used against you? Well, that's as true for innocent people as it is for guilty ones. So please, Atlanta, for right now say as little as possible to everybody here. Trust me on this one; okay, sweetie?"

"Okay." In a spontaneous gesture that went straight to Savannah's heart, Atlanta threw her arms around her neck and gave her a suffocating hug. "Thanks, Van. Thanks for everything. I'm sorry about what I said earlier, about you being sexually frustrated and all that. Even if you are, I shouldn't have brought it up like that."

"No problem." Savannah returned the hug, squeezing her tightly around the waist and trying not to think about how bony her ribs felt. "All forgiven. All forgotten. All gone."

"Really?"

"Really, really."

The front door of the gallery flew open, and Dirk entered, looking even more rumpled and grumpier than usual. Savannah gave Atlanta a comforting pat on the shoulder and said, "Hang tight, kiddo. I've gotta have—"

"I know, I know . . . a few words with Dirk, fill him in on what's going on." Atlanta sighed, once again dissatisfied with her lot in life. "I need a Diet Coke. I think I'll go to the kitchen and see if they have some."

Savannah tried to think of a delicate way to express her concern, but she couldn't, so she said it straight. "Be sure that you're around people. Don't go anywhere that you're going to be alone. Understand?"

She saw the fear intensify on Atlanta's face and hated to see her sister so scared. But, on the other hand, fear could be a good thing; it made you more careful. And under the circumstances, caution was definitely in order.

A few minutes later, she was showing Dirk the stain on the bed and trying to explain the finer points of Barbie Matthews's psyche.

"She's a raving bitch. A spoiled brat. And she's up to no good, I'm sure of that. Ah . . . if she's alive, that is."

Dirk played his flashlight over the soiled bedspread. "Yeah, I hear ya. This is a pretty gross mess all right." He lowered his voice. "If this goop came out of her, she's probably not feeling too good right now. You know anybody with the urge to kill her?"

"You mean, besides me and Atlanta?" She shook her

head. "I don't really know the girl, only talked to her a few minutes."

"And that was enough to make you hate her?"

"Absolutely. I'm sure you'd agree if you'd had the displeasure of making her acquaintance."

Dirk glanced around the room at the scattered clothes, makeup, jewelry, hair dryers, and towels. "But this was Atlanta's bed, not the other kid's, right?" he asked.

"Yes, but this one had been assigned to Barbie. She bullied Atlanta into changing with her. So we don't know whose benefit it was done for." Savannah pointed to the writing on the wall. "Why do you suppose they wrote that upside down? It's not easy, writing while standing on your head."

Dirk walked closer to the bed and shined his flashlight along the window sill. "The lighting really sucks in here. Can we turn those lamps up?"

"No," she told him. "I think they were going for cozy ambience when they decorated, not crime-scene processing. What are you looking for?"

"With a little luck, bloody fingerprints," he replied. "I think the reason the word was written upside down is because the person who dumped the blood . . . and the other guck . . . on the bed was outside, leaning in through the window."

Savannah thought that one over for a second and grunted her approval of his theory. "Good. Yeah, that makes sense. And hey, look, the screen is off."

"How much do you want to bet it's layin' on the ground outside?"

"Let's go look."

"Naw, you stay here and wait for Dr. Liu. Me and Ryan'll check outside."

Savannah didn't have long to wait. No sooner had Dirk left than Catherine Villa appeared, escorting Dr. Jennifer Liu.

"This lady says she's the county medical examiner," Catherine said, her voice shaky. "She says you sent for her."

"I did. Don't worry, Mrs. Villa, it's just . . . in case . . . really, don't worry."

"Don't worry? You call the coroner to come to my property, and you tell me not to worry?"

Savannah grabbed Dr. Liu by the arm and pulled her into the room. "Excuse me," she said to Catherine, "but we have to do a little work in here. I think I'll close this for now. See you later."

She slammed the door in Catherine's extremely concerned face and turned to Dr. Liu.

Medical examiner Dr. Jennifer Liu looked like anything but what she was. Tiny, petite, deceptively fragile in appearance, she hardly seemed like someone who cut up dead bodies for a living. But she claimed to love her work and frequently regaled crowds at cocktail parties and the local Irish pubs with her vast repertoire of "stiff" jokes.

"Don't worry? You told her not to worry?" Dr. Liu asked. "Somebody somewhere had *better* be worried, if I was called out in the middle of a very hot date."

Savannah looked her up and down, noting the black-leather pants, the four-inch high-heeled boots, and the black, sequined, angora sweater. It must have been a very hot date, indeed.

"Oh yes, I'm worried. I'm very worried." She pointed to the bed.

Jennifer took a look. "Yuck."

"Yuck? I didn't know that word was in a medical examiner's vocabulary," Savannah said.

"Sure it is. I get grossed out as quickly as anybody." She set the case she was carrying on the floor and walked closer to the bed.

"Then how do you do what you do?"

The M.E. produced a flashlight and leaned over the stain, studying it closely. "Easy," she said. "My curiosity is greater than my yuck-factor."

Savannah allowed her a couple of minutes to think and scrutinize the area, until her own curiosity got the best of her. "Well, what do you think? Any ideas about what that fleshy stuff is there in the middle?"

Dr. Liu opened her case and removed several items: a large cotton swab, a glass vial, and a small bottle of fluid.

"I have an idea what it is," she said. "Or at least what it isn't. Hang on a minute and let me check."

With one of the swabs she collected some of the blood that lay, congealing, near the unidentified tissue, and stuck it into the glass vial. She unscrewed the lid of the bottle and poured a small amount of the fluid into the vial. After swirling it around for a moment, she held it up to the light and nodded. "Yes, that's what I thought."

"What? What did you thought . . . er . . . think. What the hell is it?"

Dr. Liu sealed the vial with a stopper and began to write on its identification label. "It's blood, but it isn't human. And neither are those." She pointed to the glob in the center.

"Not human?" Savannah released a sigh of relief. "Well, what kind is it?"

Dr. Liu laughed. "You detectives don't expect much of us medical examiners, do you? I can't tell. These field tests aren't that sophisticated. Although once I get back in the lab, I'll be able to identify the source."

She placed the vial in a small, padded pouch and zipped it closed. Then she removed a Polaroid camera from her case and took a couple of photos of the bed, the wall and its writing, the window and surrounding area.

"Those organs are too small to be human," she said. "I don't even think they're mammal. If I'm not mistaken, I think that mass on the right is a gizzard. Probably from a chicken."

Savannah looked closely at the area she was indicating. "It does look that way, doesn't it? I remember Granny Reid used to fry up a batch of those when we couldn't afford wings and drumsticks."

Dr. Liu gave her a funny look, and she quickly added, "Hey, they weren't so bad. Anything's good if you slap enough gravy on it."

"Ah-h huh. Whatever you say."

"I say, 'Thank God, this isn't a homicide scene.' It must be somebody's idea of a sick joke. But when I think of how scared my baby sister was, I want to shove these chicken guts up their nose sideways."

"I understand completely. I'll take these back to the lab and identify them for sure. And then if you find your culprit, you can have them back and do just that."

Dr. Liu finished scraping the entrails into another evidence container. Then she knelt on the floor, packed everything away, and snapped her case closed. Standing, she brushed off the knees of her leather pants.

"So, you don't mind if I go back to my hot date? I left

him in a Tahitian bar, sipping daiquiris from a pineapple. If I'm lucky, he'll still be there when I get back."

Savannah grinned and slapped her on the back. "Don't worry, Doc. He'll be there. As good as you look tonight . . . believe me . . . he'll be there."

"He'd better be," she said as she opened the door. "If he isn't, you owe me a ten-pound box of Godiva."

"You've got it. Have a good time."

Savannah saw that Catherine Villa was still there, standing in the hall outside the doorway with that distraught look on her face.

"Mrs. Villa, good news," Savannah said, motioning her to come closer. Then she added under her breath, "If you consider having chicken blood and guts on your bedspread good news." She patted the woman's shoulder comfortingly and said, "Now I'm not nearly so worried about Barbie Matthews, and you shouldn't be either. She's probably ju-u-ust fine."

Chapter

11

As Savannah stood in the shower and allowed the hot water to flow over her weary body, she wished that she could just melt and slide down the drain along with the shampoo suds.

She was sure that she had been this exhausted and discouraged at some point in her life, but at the moment she couldn't remember when.

The night hours spent looking for Barbie Matthews in every nook and crook of Villa Rosa had rendered absolutely zip, and in spite of what Savannah had been telling everyone associated with the winery and the beauty pageant, she *was* worried about the missing teenager. She was worried sick.

Having missed an entire day's worth of food, and a whole night of sleep, Savannah had already decided that when they found the kid, she had better be dead, or *she* would kill her for having caused such a ruckus.

But she was afraid someone might have beaten her to it, or at least done the girl some major harm.

Stepping out of the shower and drying off with one of Villa Rosa's lush towels, she silently thanked Catherine Villa for furnishing her guests with quality appointments. One nice thing about most snobs, Savannah had noticed: They tended to have good taste in clothing, furnishings, and cocktail-party guests.

She pulled her robe around her and stepped into the room where her younger sister lay sleeping on a twin bed. This second-story room was similar to the one downstairs that Atlanta had shared with Barbie, only a bit larger and more lavishly furnished. Catherine had offered it to Savannah, making it clear that she hoped she would remain on the property until Barbie had been found. And Savannah had insisted that Atlanta sleep there, where she could keep an eye on her.

"Van? What are you doing?" Atlanta asked, stirring beneath the covers. One foot emerged, then a hand and finally a tousled, platinum blond head.

"Getting ready to go to work."

"Work? Have you been to bed yet?"

"No, but I'm not a contestant; I don't need that much beauty sleep."

Atlanta yawned, stretched, and opened one eye. "Did you guys find Barbie?"

"No. That's why I'm heading back out. It's dawn now, and we're going to check the grounds again. Hopefully, we'll find something we missed, now that it's daylight."

"Dawn?" Her other eye blinked and opened. "It's *dawn?* No wonder I'm still dog-tired. You can get up with the chickens if you want to, but I'm lyin' here and relaxin' for a couple more hours at least."

"How lovely for you," Savannah replied dryly as she

slipped into a silk tank, linen slacks, and loafers. "Catch a few winks for me, and don't let *anybody* in here except members of the Moonlight Magnolia gang. Do you hear me?"

There was no reply.

Savannah strapped on her shoulder holster and Beretta and pulled a light jacket on over it. "You've gotta rise and shine, at least long enough to bolt this door behind me."

A grunt was all she heard from beneath the rumpled covers.

"Shake a leg, gal. You're holding me up here."

Finally, Atlanta rolled out of bed, a drowsy figure in pajamas with big, yellow roosters crowing on bright red flannel. She followed Savannah to the door, where she accepted a kiss on the cheek from her older sister.

"Be careful, Atlanta. Stay in here by yourself with the door locked or out there in a crowd of people. Okay?"

"Okay. Okay. Okay. Don't worry, *Mom.*"

"It's my job. Throw the bolt and then go back to bed, Sleeping Snoozie."

In the twenty-five minutes it had taken Savannah to run upstairs and shower, reinforcements had arrived. As she entered the gallery she saw Ryan standing near the door, talking to Dirk, Tammy, and John.

Tammy was holding a small, pink, paper bag in her hand, that Savannah didn't dare to hope was . . .

"Tammy, you darlin' girl! Did you bring me donuts from the Patty Cake Bakery?"

Smiling, Tammy held out the bag to her and gave her a hug. "Better than that. I bought you two chocolate-covered, custard-filled Long Johns and an apple fritter."

"I love you. I truly do. I'll give you a nickel-an-hour raise."

"Gee, after a month or so, I'll be reimbursed for the donuts."

Savannah attacked the bag with a fury born of acute starvation. And while she was filling her face with creamy custard and chocolate, Dirk presented her with a super-sized Styrofoam cup of coffee.

"Ah, Dirk. Bless your little heart. You dropped by the Java Nut House and bummed them out of a free coffee. You shouldn't have."

"An extra big one, too."

"What a guy! When you panhandle, you beg for only the best. You're a class act, Coulter."

Dirk beamed, and Savannah wondered whether the fact that insults frequently flew over his head made the game more fun or a source of frustration. She decided it was a bit of both.

Savannah looked over at Ryan and noticed, for the first time, that he looked almost as tired as she felt. His usual, outdoorsy tan was more pale than golden, and he, too, had dark circles under his bloodshot eyes. Apparently, he had gotten the same amount of sleep that she had . . . none. And Savannah knew how seriously Ryan took his work, especially when it involved young people and their safety.

In a fit of self-sacrifice, she offered him her precious apple fritter.

Realizing the depth of her generosity, he gave her a warm smile and shook his head. "No thanks. You need it more than I do; John brought me fresh bagels with lox, cream cheese, and capers."

Savannah sighed. "Ahhh, lox and bagels . . . John

Gibson, would you do me the honor of being my husband?"

John took her hand and lifted it to his lips, tickling her with his mustache as he kissed her knuckles that were dusted with powdered sugar. "My dear Savannah, I assure you . . . should I decide to take a bride, you would be the first lady on my short and exclusive list."

Ryan laughed, Tammy giggled, and Dirk snorted, but for once he kept his comments to himself. "So," he said, "what's the game plan?"

"We're here to help," John told him. "Put us to work wherever you like."

Tammy began to practically hop up and down in her well-worn running shoes, so eager that Savannah had to resist the temptation to do her bodily harm; it was that "morning person" thing again. "I've already talked to Mrs. Lippincott," she said. "And she specifically asked me if I would go along with some of the girls who want to take a morning jog around the property, look at the vineyards and all that."

"That's good, and I need to call Barbie's parents again," Savannah said. "When I spoke to them last night on the phone, her mother didn't seem terribly concerned that her daughter was missing. I got the idea this disappearing act might be Barbie's standard MO."

"Did you tell Mrs. Matthews about the blood on the bed?" Ryan asked.

"I just told her that the room had been vandalized. She didn't ask for details, so I didn't elaborate."

Dirk grabbed Savannah's coffee and took a long drink of it. "Yeah, you don't want the old lady thinking that her daughter got nabbed by some voodoo cult. She'll start worryin' that the kid might be stretched out naked on some sacrificial altar somewhere with her throat cut, a big, upside-down pentacle painted on her chest in blood."

Savannah nearly choked on her fritter. "Well, thank you very much, Detective Coulter, for that lovely visual. Personally, the worst I had imagined was the girl lying, raped and murdered, out among the grapevines."

Wearily, Ryan ran his fingers through his hair. Savannah was fairly sure it was the first time she had ever seen it mussed. She hated to think what her own dripping-wet mop must look like. "So, this is what we're going to do," he said. "Savannah, you call the parents. Tammy, take the girls for their run. John and I will search the grounds again. Now that it's light out, maybe we'll see something we missed earlier."

"I'll go with you," Dirk said, returning Savannah's coffee and snatching one of the Long Johns out of her bag. "I wanna check that parking lot again. It was so dark out there last night, you couldn't see squat."

As Savannah watched the team disperse, she felt a wave of sadness. Mostly, she felt that way because with every hour that passed, the hope grew dimmer that this disappearance would have a happy outcome. And partly because Dirk was walking away with the rest of her breakfast. Two pastries and half a cup of coffee just didn't contain enough chemical stimuli to make up for a day's fasting and a night without sleep. She decided to hit the kitchen on her way to the telephone. What the heck—the Matthews clan wouldn't want to be awakened this early anyway.

"I think you might want to come out to Villa Rosa," Savannah had told Mrs. Matthews on the telephone. "I really do. We'd like to ask you and your husband a few questions about Barbie's . . . habits . . . and we don't want to interrupt our search here."

This time, Mom Matthews had seemed more concerned and assured Savannah that she and Pop Matthews and Sis Matthews were on their way.

And they were—promptly. Less than twenty minutes after Savannah called them, they came screeching up to the front door of the complex in their late-model Volvo and ran inside.

Savannah had been on her way up to Francie's room, to see if the girl was awake yet, but she was intercepted in the gallery.

"Where's my daughter?" Mrs. Matthews demanded. "I was told you had excellent security here. How could you morons lose one of the girls?"

Savannah checked the family out with a quick once-over. Middle-aged dad was deeply tanned, muscular, and dressed in a stained T-shirt and jeans decorated with splotches of paint and bits of dried cement. A builder of some sort, no doubt.

Dressed in a calico-print dress with a white-lace collar and white sandals, Mom looked as though the extent of her physical labor might be lifting the gavel at a PTA meeting. From the bossy, take-charge look on her face, Savannah was sure she would be president. She could also see where Barbie had gotten her penchant for heavy makeup and "big" hair.

Younger sister would have been perfect for a talk-show makeover. The opposite of her mother and sister, the dowdy teenager appeared to give no time or effort to vanity. Her unwashed hair had been pulled back into a scrunchy, her baggy jeans and oversize sweatshirt hung limply off her shapeless body, and her thick-lensed glasses would have been improved by a simple cleaning.

Savannah instantly pigeonholed them into three uncomplimentary slots: Mom the Hen, Dad the Pecked, and Sister the Ugly Duckling.

In her personal life, Savannah tried to avoid snap judgments of individuals. People were complicated creatures, far too complex to be evaluated in a matter of minutes.

But, as a street cop Savannah had learned that survival itself depended upon making evaluations in seconds. And, while she was always willing to change her original opinion of a person—given evidence to the contrary—experience had taught her to trust those valuable first impressions.

Although she would have preferred to give this woman a karate chop, Savannah decided to ignore the insult. Exercising restraint was an excellent way to build character, and she figured it was a good time to chalk up some spiritual brownie points. Besides, she needed the bucks and didn't want to get fired from the gig.

"Mrs. Matthews," Savannah said, "I wouldn't necessarily say that your daughter is lost. She probably knows exactly where she is; the problem is, *we* don't know. And we're doing everything we can to find her."

"Then you'd better do more," Mrs. Matthews said. "If anything's happened to my baby girl, we're going to sue you people for all you're worth—you, and that Lippincott gal, and Villa Rosa."

"I have no doubt that you would do precisely that, Mrs. Matthews," Savannah replied. "But hopefully, we'll find Barbie soon, safe and sound, and all that nasty suing business won't be necessary. Because, if you intend to sue me for all I'm worth, I'm sorry to say, you won't get much . . . two lazy cats who eat as much as a couple of great Danes. That's about the sum of my assets."

No abusive reply was forthcoming, so Savannah softened her tone. "Come along with me," she said. "They have a lovely courtyard out here with tables where we can sit, and maybe you can tell me a few things about your daughter."

"Talk? Answer questions?" Mrs. Matthews's densely ratted, stiffly sprayed hair seemed to bristle, like a hunting hound who had caught a whiff of a raccoon. "We don't need to waste time talking, and the only question you need to answer is, 'Where is my daughter?'"

"I understand, Mrs. Matthews, that you're upset," Savannah replied. "I'm sure I would be, too, in your situation. But the best thing you can do for Barbie right now is to spend a few minutes with me, telling me about her daily life, her habits, her friends, et cetera."

Mr. Matthews laid a large, work-callused hand on his wife's shoulder. "Come on, Mother," he said. "Let's do what she says . . . for Barbie."

Chapter

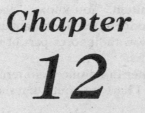

12

Savannah sat on one side of the table, taking notes on a small pad, and on the other side sat the three Matthewses, a united front of uncooperation.

So far she had received only the briefest answers to her questions—most of those supplied by the husband.

"Has Barbie been dating anyone special lately?" she asked. There, that should be simple enough to prompt a straightforward answer.

But no . . .

"Yes, she was," said Mr. Matthews.

"No, she was not!" His wife's jaw tightened and her nostrils twitched.

Savannah looked from one to the other. "Well? Was she, or not?"

Mrs. Matthews shot her husband a "shut up!" look, and he did so, staring down at his hands that were clenched together on the tabletop.

"Barbie *had* been seeing this punk kid from the east end," she admitted. "You know . . . the east end . . . ?"

Savannah nodded. Yes, she caught the woman's drift. The east end was the poorer part of town, the "other side of the tracks."

"But I told her in no uncertain terms to break it off with him. And I have no doubt that she did exactly as I told her."

From the corner of her eye Savannah saw the sister, who she had been told was named Louise, turn her head away from her mother and suppress a little grin. "Is that true, Louise? Did your sister stop seeing the boy, like your mother told her to do?"

The moment she asked the question, Savannah realized she had gotten the teenager in trouble. Mom poked her in the ribs with her elbow. "She did, didn't she?" Mrs. Matthews asked. But it was more of a statement than an inquiry. Obviously, it was beyond the woman's mental grasp—the concept that she had been disobeyed.

The girl shrugged, and mumbled, "Yeah, sure."

"And what's the name of this boy . . . ," Savannah asked, "the one she had stopped seeing on your orders."

"His name is Trent Gorton," the father supplied. "He's not really a bad kid, he just—"

"He wasn't right for Barbie," Mom snapped. "That's all that needs to be said. They just weren't right for each other, and I made that clear to my daughter."

Savannah scribbled for moment and thought. "Do you know how he took it . . . when she told him it was off?"

"No, I don't. We didn't discuss it." Mrs. Matthews glanced down at her wedding ring and noticed a fingerprint smudge on the surface of the impressive diamond. With the lace end of her sleeve she wiped it away. "Is that all?" she asked. "If it is, I want to start looking around for my daughter."

"Just two more questions." Savannah glanced down in her notepad. "When was the last time you had any sort of contract with your daughter?"

"It was during dinner last night," Mr. Matthews said. "We were here at the welcoming ceremony, but Barbie didn't come down for dinner. Mother called her on her cell phone, but she said she wasn't feeling good, that she was going to stay in her room for the rest of evening."

"That was about what time?"

"Between seven and seven-thirty."

"Okay, there's one more question I have to ask you," Savannah said. "Has Barbie ever run away before?"

"Absolutely not!" Mrs. Matthews's jaw was starting to lock again. "My girls are better trained than that. They know very well that if they did something stupid like that, they'd come running home a lot faster than they left, with me right behind them."

Again, Savannah saw the younger sister glance away, a smirk on her face and an unpleasant glimmer in her eye.

"Okay . . . thank you very much." Savannah rose from the table, signifying the end of the interview. "I can understand your desire to help in the search," she said. "But you might consider returning home . . . just in case Barbie should try to contact you there."

"No! We're staying right here until our daughter has been found." Mrs. Matthews replied, jumping up from the bench.

But her husband rose and again placed his large, rough hand on her shoulder. "I think Ms. Reid is right,

Mother. Barb might even be home when we get there. You never know what she's going to do."

To Savannah's surprise Mrs. Matthews nodded and took her husband's arm. "All right. We'll go on home, but you'll call us the moment you hear anything," she said.

It was a command not a question, but Savannah decided to furnish a gracious answer anyway. "Of course we will. And try not to worry."

The parents walked away, Mrs. Matthews still clinging to her husband's arm. But the younger sister lagged behind several yards.

Taking her cue, Savannah stepped up to her. "Yes?" she asked, keeping her voice low.

"My sister's a brat," Louise whispered. "A stupid, spoiled brat. She sleeps with everybody and runs away all the time. I think something bad's happened to her. And she probably deserved it."

Mrs. Matthews glanced over her shoulder and gave her younger daughter a warning look. Savannah dropped back and allowed the teenager to catch up with her parents.

Hm-m-m, Savannah thought as she watched the little family walk away. Maybe she needed to revise her opinion of Sister Louise. Perhaps she wasn't an ugly duckling after all. Considering the intelligent gleam in her eye and the smile on her face when she had expressed her opinion that her sister might be in trouble, Savannah decided that Little Louise might be more rat than duck.

Once again Savannah attempted to go upstairs and question Francie, but, just as before, she was intercepted in the gallery. This time it was Catherine White-stone-Villa who demanded her attention.

Villa Rosa's first lady came running up to her, her pale cheeks flushed as though she had raced all the way from the house on the hill. She had changed into a simple white-cotton sheath that complimented her slender figure and her blond hair was coiled into a bun at the back of her neck and held with a tortoiseshell comb.

But Catherine Villa looked tired. Apparently, it had been a long night for everyone.

"Have you found her yet?" the lady asked. "Please, tell me you have."

"No, I'm sorry." Savannah hated being the bearer of bad tidings—especially when she felt responsible for the news. This had happened on her watch . . . and that made it her responsibility.

Catherine passed her hand over her eyes and pressed her fingertips to her temples for a moment, as though she had a headache. "I was afraid of that," she said. "I just saw her parents and sister leaving. They looked so upset. Did you tell them everything?"

"Almost. I didn't mention the blood on the bed. Since it wasn't human, I thought I would keep it from them for a while. They're worried enough already."

Catherine sighed. "I just feel so sorry for them. I'm a mother myself, and I can't imagine how I'd feel if one of my boys was missing. Are the police here?"

Savannah nodded. "Detective Coulter has been here all night, as we have. And two more members of my agency arrived this morning to help us. How about your employees? Are they still searching?"

"Of course. And we won't tell them to stop until she's found. But what if she isn't even on our property? After all, she's a teenage girl. Maybe she left with a boy or just ran away."

"It could be something like that," Savannah said. "It could be any one of a hundred things. We'll just have to wait and see." She glanced around. "Where is Mr. Villa this morning? I haven't seen him since last night's dinner."

"Anthony is working," Catherine replied, a note of resentment in her voice. "With harvest coming and his campaign gearing up, he's working day and night. I don't want him bothered by this unfortunate circumstance. So, if you just deal with me directly, Savannah, I'd be grateful."

"Certainly." Savannah gave a tight smile. "We ladies have to look out for our menfolk, don't we?"

"Far more than they realize. Without us they're really quite helpless."

Savannah thought about the men in her life, their courage, resourcefulness, and that endearing streak of protectiveness that they all showed toward the people they loved. And Savannah considered herself fortunate to be one of those privileged to be inside their circles of protection.

"Helpless?" she said thoughtfully. "I suppose some are. But I certainly wouldn't say *most.*"

Catherine gave a delicate, aristocratic sniff. "Well, I suppose in your line of work you meet more macho types. The males I know can't function without a woman dictating their every move."

Savannah looked into her eyes and saw a coldness that made her feel a bit sorry for those men within Catherine's circle. "Please excuse me, Mrs. Villa, I really must get busy."

"Of course. I don't want to keep you from your work. I—"

The front door opened, and Dirk hurried into the gallery, followed by Ryan and John. Savannah could tell from the looks on their faces that something was wrong.

"What is it?" she asked. "What did you find?"

She rushed over to Dirk and met them in the middle of the gallery. Dirk held out something that was wrapped loosely in a couple of tissues. Carefully she folded back the corners and looked inside. A tangled mess of crushed, gray plastic and wires confused her eyes at first. Then she realized what she was seeing. "A phone, a cell phone?"

"We found it at the far end of the parking lot," Ryan said.

"It appears someone ran it down there on the tarmac with a vehicle," John added.

Savannah nodded. "Yeah, it's as flat as any roadkill I've ever seen. That's for sure."

Catherine elbowed her way between them and looked at the mangled equipment in Dirk's hand. "So, what does that mean?" she asked. "Do you think it has anything to do with the Matthews girl?"

Savannah thought of what the family had said about Mrs. Matthews speaking to her daughter last evening on the cell phone . . . their last contract with her. "Yes," she said, "I'm afraid it might."

Once again their conversation was interrupted by new arrivals. But this time it was Tammy who burst through the door. She had a wild, frightened look on her face, as though she was being chased by a pack of rabid coyotes.

Again Savannah felt the queasiness she frequently got

in her stomach just before she was going to hear bad
news. It was similar to the sensation of being aboard a jet
that had just hit an air pocket.

"We . . . we found . . . her. Barbie Matthews," Tammy
gasped, bending double and sucking large gulps of air.
Sweat dripped from her face onto the oak plank floor.

Catherine Villa gave a small, shuddering cry, then
said, "Is she . . . is she all right?"

"No." Tammy grabbed her sides and grimaced.
Savannah could tell she was in a lot of pain from having
sprinted heaven-only-knew how far. She could also pre-
dict her assistant's answer. Tammy was a pretty level-
headed girl, and she wasn't easily upset or frightened.

"Calm down, sweetie." Savannah reached for her
friend and pulled her over to a bench against the wall.
"Sit down and catch your breath."

Savannah could hear her own pulse pounding in her
ears as she waited for what seemed like forever for
Tammy to collect herself.

Finally, Tammy looked up at them, and tears filled
her eyes. "No," she said. "Barbie's not all right. While
we were out jogging . . . along the cliffs by the river . . .
we found her. She's hanging halfway down a forty-foot
embankment. She's not moving. I'm pretty sure she's
dead."

Savannah was pretty sure that Barbie Matthews was
dead, too. They had been standing on the edge of the
cliff, looking down at her body, for several minutes, and
the girl hadn't stirred. Calling out her name had produced no response either.

Savannah hated tragic endings—especially when it
involved a young person. As always in these circum-

stances she mentally rehearsed what she was going to say to the parents, and even though she didn't like Mrs. Matthews very much, she wasn't looking forward to giving her such terrible news.

Savannah had insisted that Catherine Villa stay behind, and John had volunteered to remain with her and calm her down. Tammy, Savannah, Dirk, and Ryan jumped into Savannah's Mustang, and Tammy directed them to the spot, a little more than two miles from the complex. On the way they passed Tammy's jogging buddies, a frightened group of wide-eyed beauties, running in the opposite direction, toward the winery's center. Tammy had beaten them by several minutes.

Farther down the road, Tammy pointed out a copse of oak trees growing near the edge of a cliff, overlooking the Santa Rosita River. Savannah parked near the grove, and they all got out of the Mustang and hurried over to the cliff's edge.

That's when they had seen her, hanging about twenty feet below them, her clothing caught on a dried sage bush, growing out of the side of the embankment. She was facing downward, away from them, so they couldn't see if her eyes were open or closed, but the only movement they observed was the fabric of her torn dress rippling in the soft morning breeze.

"I called Search and Rescue," Ryan said, replacing his cell phone in his jacket pocket. He took another look at the still figure dangling from the cliff's face. "I guess I should have told them it will be more of a search and recovery."

"She could still be alive," Tammy said hopefully. "Maybe she's just unconscious."

"Yeah, and the Dodgers could win the World Series next year," Dirk said.

Savannah smacked him on the shoulder. "Hey, it never hurts to hold a good thought."

"All the positive thinking in the world ain't gonna help that kid," Dirk said. "I guess she meant to end it all, and looks like she did . . . even though she didn't make it all the way to the bottom."

"What makes you so sure it was suicide?" Ryan asked. "Maybe someone pushed her over."

Dirk looked around the dry, dusty ground. "Don't see no drag marks. No scuffle marks."

"But the girls and I were running and walking all over this area," Tammy said, "before one of them spotted the body. I'm afraid we would have messed up any tracks that were here."

"Did you run any farther down the road?" Savannah asked.

"No, this is as far as we came. And I told them not to touch anything or do anything except run straight back to the center. Then I took off running. I couldn't wait for them to catch up."

"You did good, Tam."

Savannah listened as Dirk called Dr. Liu and informed her of their discovery. Her team would be arriving soon, along with the Search and Rescue crew.

Walking along the edge of the precipice, Savannah looked for something . . . anything . . . and found nothing. Then she saw it: a large, round impression in the dirt, nearly two feet across.

The indentation was almost directly over the place where Barbara Matthews was hanging on the cliff face below.

She tossed her key ring to Tammy. "Get my binoculars," she said. "They're in that black case in my trunk."

While Tammy did as she was told, Dirk and Ryan

joined Savannah at the cliff and peered along with her over the edge.

"What you see?" Dirk asked, squinting down at the body.

"What is it, Savannah?" Ryan strained to see as well.

"I'm not sure. Just a second."

Tammy returned with the binoculars, and Savannah used them to study a large object at the base of the cliff.

"That's what I thought," she said, handing the binoculars to Dirk. "Check out that big rock down there at the bottom. See it? The one right by the water's edge."

Dirk adjusted the focus on the binoculars, then nodded. "Yeah, okay, I see it. So what? There's a bunch of rocks down there. A million of 'em."

He passed the binoculars to Ryan, who also took a look.

"Can you see that circle of dirt stuck on one side?" Savannah asked Ryan.

"Yes, I see it there on the left."

Savannah pointed to the impression in the ground. "It's about the same size as that," she said. "There was a big rain a couple of nights ago. That's why the river is so swollen right now. The rain should have washed the dirt off that stone, like it has all the other rocks down there. That stone has fallen since the rains."

"Or somebody pushed it over the edge," Tammy added.

"Exactly."

"Why do you suppose they would shove a big heavy rock like that one over the edge?" Dirk said.

They thought for a moment; it came to them all at once.

"Somebody threw her over," Savannah said, echoing what the others were thinking. "And they intended for her body to go all the way to the bottom, maybe even be swept away by the river."

"But she got caught on that bush," Dirk said. "Bummer."

"Yes," Ryan said, "and they pushed the rock over the edge hoping it would dislodge her body."

They all stood there quietly, thinking, the only sound that of the river flowing below.

"Gross," Tammy said softly.

"Yeah," Savannah replied. "Really gross."

Chapter

13

The county fire department's Search and Rescue team wasted no time rappelling down the face of the cliff to reach their patient. But once there, it took only a moment for them to confirm everyone's worst suspicions: Barbara Matthews was now within reach, but far beyond help.

The Moonlight Magnolia gang stood by and watched as the litter, with her body strapped to it, was lifted from below.

"I just feel so sick," Savannah said.

"Man, I know what you mean," Dirk replied. He pulled his hand out his jeans pocket and rubbed his stomach. "That donut thing that Fluff Head brought us didn't sit too well without some real breakfast to go with it."

"That Tammy brought *us*? Those donuts were mine,

and if the one you ate gave you an upset stomach, you deserve it. I'm talking about this situation here, Mr. Sensitivity. I mean, the kid was a booger, but I hate it that this happened to her."

"Yeah, especially while you were on duty, so to speak."

Savannah shot him poisoned look. "That's strike two. Another comment like that, and I'm outta here."

"No you're not. You're hanging out, just like I am, to see if she got shot, perforated, or mutilated. And there's the lady who's gonna tell us."

He nodded toward a long white station wagon that was coming up the road, raising clouds of dust behind it. On the driver's door was the official seal of the medical examiner.

"I'm never going to get Dr. Liu paid off at this rate," Savannah said.

"Paid off?"

"Yeah. I keep bribing her with her boxes of Godiva chocolates in exchange for all these favors."

Dirk glanced over at the litter with Barbie's rigid body on it. The girl had been "setup" while bent double. "You don't have to pay Dr. Liu to handle this one," he said. "She has to look at all the 'unnatural' deaths, and this one definitely qualifies."

Minutes later, they were all gathered in a circle around the stretcher while Jennifer Liu made her initial field inspection of the body.

"There's no obvious cause of death," she said "but I don't want to undress her until I get her into the autopsy suite."

"Then maybe she did jump, after all," Dirk replied. "We were thinking that she was pushed, or maybe—"

"No, I don't think she jumped." Jennifer Liu reached down and with her fingertips gently brushed the girl's hair back from her face. "Not unless she jumped while trying to escape from the person who had her."

Savannah looked into Jennifer's dark eyes and saw that even the jaded doctor who had performed hundreds of autopsies was touched by this one. They all were affected emotionally when it was a kid.

"What do you mean?" Savannah asked. "How do you know someone *had* her?"

"Her hands were bound with tape," Jennifer said, "and her mouth, too."

"How do you know?" Tammy stepped closer, then leaned over studying the victim's lips and wrists.

"See there, across her face . . . that red rectangle around her mouth?"

They all nodded in unison.

"There was a wide piece of tape over her mouth, and you can see where it ripped off some of the skin from her lips when it was pulled away."

Savannah winced. "That must have hurt."

"Actually, I don't think it did. From the lack of bleeding, I suspect she was already dead when the tape was removed."

"And how about her hands?" Ryan asked. "Were her bindings removed postmortem, too?"

"I don't know for sure about that. I may be able to tell later."

"But you do believe there was tape around her wrists, as well as over her mouth?" Savannah asked.

Jennifer nodded. "You can see bald areas there along the backs of her wrists where the hair was pulled out when they took it off."

Savannah squatted beside the litter and looked closely. The doctor was right; the fine, blond fuzz on the girl's arm did end abruptly in a straight line just above both wrists. And the flesh there was also irritated, like that around her mouth.

Dr. Liu delicately lifted the hem of the girl's skirt and glanced beneath it. "Her underwear is still in place," she said. "That's a good sign . . . I guess."

Those in the circle exchanged a few relieved glances. The situation was tragic already. It was a small blessing if the killer had not added sexual insult to injury.

"Okay, boys and girls," Dr. Liu said, "you're going to have to stand back now and let my assistants do their thing."

The Magnolia gang moved out of the way as the crime-scene technicians took over, placing small sacks over each of the girl's hands, then loading her into a body bag.

Savannah always got a bit of the chill when she saw one of those blue bags, the ones with locks on their zippers. Those were for situations that required extra security because the individuals had died under unusual circumstances. Every time she saw one of those bags being zipped closed and locked, Savannah whispered a quick prayer that she would never see anyone she loved being zipped into a body bag . . . especially a blue one.

As the technicians were moving the corpse into the coroner's station wagon, Savannah left the rest of the group and walked farther down the road away from the scene. In one area the dirt was softer, looser than the rest, and she could see tire marks in the soil that were more than a yard long.

She knelt beside the most clearly defined section

and studied it. The tread size was substantial, not as big as a truck's, but wide for a car. She stood and motioned to Dirk. "Hey, buddy. Come check this out."

The technicians were pouring a plaster cast of the tire track, and Savannah and Dirk were observing the process, when Catherine Villa drove up in a green Jeep Cherokee. She stopped short at the yellow tape barrier, jumped out, and ran straight to Savannah.

"Oh, my god! I can't believe it. That poor girl!" She glanced around the scene, at the coroner's wagon, at the Search and Rescue team members who were packing their equipment into their van. "Where is she? I mean, where is the body?"

"They've already recovered her remains from the hillside," Savannah told her. "Dr. Liu has her in the wagon now, and she'll be taking her away in just a few minutes."

"But what do you think happened to her? Do you suppose she went for a walk out here in the dark and fell off the cliff?"

Savannah considered telling her about the tape bindings, but under these circumstances she had often found that the less said the better.

"We don't know exactly what happened to her yet, Mrs. Villa. The doctor will perform an autopsy on the body and that should give us some answers."

"This is just so terrible. We've never had anything like this happen around here. I'm sure as soon as the press hears about this, they'll be all over . . . and with Tony's candidacy. Oh, dear, this is just such an awful time to have something like this happen."

Savannah took a deep breath and gathered what little of her patience remained. "Yes, Mrs. Villa, it's perfectly dreadful. But then, there's no convenient time for someone to be murdered."

Catherine hesitated a long time before answering. She, too, appeared to be marshaling every ounce of courtesy that she could muster. "I realize, Savannah, that my comments may sound somewhat insensitive to your ears. But Tony and I have worked hard and long for him to win this senate seat. We've invested everything we have, financially, emotionally, so you'll just have to forgive me if I seem to be overreacting to this situation."

"Murder is always serious, tragic business," Savannah said. "It would be difficult for anyone to overreact to a young woman losing her life this way."

"*Murder?* Is that what you said? You actually think someone *killed* that girl?"

Catherine Whitestone-Villa was turning so pale that Savannah was seriously considering the best way to catch her when she fainted.

"It may be a homicide," Savannah said, "and maybe not. We'll see, once Dr. Liu has completed the autopsy."

"This is so awful! I wish we had never sponsored this pageant. Then none of this would have happened."

"Well, as I said, we'll know more later. So there's no need to speculate at this point."

Catherine shook her head, disbelief and shock registering in every aristocratic line of her face. "And what are they doing over there . . . on the ground?" she asked.

"They're taking a plaster cast of a tire mark there in the dirt."

"It's true then—the police are treating this as a homicide?"

"Not necessarily. They're just making sure to cover all the bases. By the way," Savannah said, "can you tell me where this road leads?"

"It winds, north to south, across the back of the vineyards along the eastern edge of our property, then turns west and intersects the main highway, several miles south of our front gates."

"Who uses this road?"

"We all do: our friends and family, the workers, delivery people, everybody. Why?"

"Just asking . . . trying to get a mental picture."

Catherine Villa's eyes narrowed. "No, you're not just asking. If you think someone at Villa Rosa hurt that girl, you're wrong. I know every person who works for me, and they are wonderful people. We've had many of our cellar workers and even seasonal workers for years. Many of them worked for Tony's father, and some even for his grandfather. None of them would ever do anything like this."

"I never said any of them did."

"If someone murdered one of the beauty contestants, it was somebody she brought with her, someone who came to Villa Rosa because she was here. I'm absolutely certain of that. Do you understand me, Savannah?"

Savannah sighed and felt the fatigue of the past twenty-four hours sweep over her. "I understand that *you* are absolutely certain, Mrs. Villa. On the other hand, I can't say that I'm sure about anything . . . except . . . that if I don't get some sleep pretty soon, I'm going to fall down dead in my tracks, and they're going to be carrying *me* out of here in a body bag."

*   *   *

An hour later, when Savannah returned to Villa Rosa's visitors' center, she passed through the courtyard and found Marion Lippincott standing beside the fountain, surrounded by a huddle of excited, frightened women. Savannah recognized the tiny lady with lavender-blue tinted hair and a stack of notebooks under her arm as Gertrude, Mrs. Lippincott's assistant. Savannah had met her only briefly before all the trouble with Barbie Matthews had begun and had decided that Gertrude was motivated primarily by fear of her boss.

Considering the fierce expression on Marion Lippincott's face, Savannah could hardly blame Gertrude. On "The Lip's" bad side was not a place anyone would want to be.

Savannah hoped to sneak through the courtyard unnoticed. But no such luck.

"Ms. Reid, we need a moment of your time. Now," Mrs. Lippincott called out, projecting like a mezzo-soprano singing to the last row.

Reluctantly, Savannah obeyed, steeling herself for a battle that she really did not want to fight in her depleted condition.

"These ladies are our volunteer hostesses," Mrs. Lippincott said with an expansive wave of her hand, introducing the lot. "We're discussing the best way to break this unfortunate news to the girls. With your vast experience, I was hoping you might give us some suggestions."

Savannah could hear the snide undertone; it was hard to miss. Obviously, Marion considered her partly, if not completely, responsible for the tragedy.

Savannah could feel the other women's eyes on her.

She could sense their fear and genuine concern. Some of these ladies were the contestants' mothers. And with everyone on edge, this wasn't the time to duke it out with Marion Lippincott, verbally or otherwise.

"I'm sorry, but psychology is a bit outside my field of expertise," she said as kindly as she could. "My only suggestion would be that you contact County Mental Health Services and ask their advice. Perhaps they could send professional grief counselors."

To her surprise, Savannah's words seemed to satisfy Mrs. Lippincott, and some of the hostility was absent from her voice when she replied, "Thank you. That's an excellent idea. Gertrude, get on that right now."

As Gertrude hurried away, Savannah thought it might be a good time to attempt an escape.

"If you'll excuse me now, we're really busy."

"Yes, of course," Mrs. Lippincott said. "But when you get some time I'd like to speak to you privately."

"Can you tell me where the girls are now?"

"Anthony Villa has taken them on a tour of the vineyards, the fermentation room, and the aging room. They left over an hour ago, so they should be returning anytime."

"Was Francie Gorton with them and my sister Atlanta?"

Mrs. Lippincott studied Savannah intently for a moment over her tortoiseshell frames before replying. "Yes, they were both with the tour group. They were instructed to go to their rooms the moment they returned. Lunch will be served beside the pool at noon sharp. I hope you can join us."

An invitation to lunch . . . now that was a pleasant

stroke of luck. At the very thought of food, Savannah's morale rose a few degrees.

"Thank you. I'll try to make it," she said. Then turning to the other women, she added, "And I'm so sorry that all of this has happened. But believe me, we're doing everything we can to make sure that the rest of the girls remain safe, and that everyone's questions are answered as soon as possible concerning the details of the tragedy."

If Savannah had learned anything, it was when to make a speedy exit. It only took her a matter of seconds to leave the group behind, cross the courtyard, and bolt through the French doors leading into the gallery. Alone in the dark, cool interior, surrounded by the pictures and artifacts of the ages-old art of wine making, Savannah closed her eyes for a moment and willed her troubled spirit to be quiet.

Her next step was to question Francie Gorton, but the interview would have to wait a few more minutes, until the girls returned from their tour of the winery.

She thought of Dirk, who had the difficult task of informing the Matthews family of their loss. For once, she was actually relieved that he was the cop and she the private detective.

Tammy and Ryan were still at the cliff, watching as Dr. Liu's technicians processed the scene. And although she felt guilty even considering the option, Savannah knew that the most practical thing to do at the moment was go upstairs to her room and lie down, take advantage of this five- or ten-minute break to rest and collect her thoughts.

It was as she was climbing the stairs, one weary step in time, that she remembered her famous last words,

"How hard could it be? I mean . . . what could happen at a beauty pageant?"

Someday she would learn to keep her big mouth shut . . . or so she kept saying.

Chapter
14

"Savannah, Savannah, hey . . . wake up!"

"Wha . . . what?"

Floating deep in the warm, black ocean of blissful sleep, Savannah felt a rough hand, reaching for her, pulling her, dragging her to surface.

"Come on, Van. Wake up."

"No. Go away. Leave me alone."

The hand shook her again, even harder. "Savannah, you have to wake up."

Shoving the offending hand aside, she sat up in the bed and rubbed her hands over her eyes that still burned with fatigue. In the semidarkness of the room she could see the outline of the cursed creature who had disrupted her sleep . . . Atlanta.

"Why?" she moaned. "Why did you wake me up?"

"You were snoring."

"What?!"

Atlanta walked over to her own bed, tossed her purse

aside, and kicked off her shoes. "I said, you were snoring. Remember, you told me to wake you up if you were snoring, so that you could break the habit, in case you ever got married someday and actually slept with a man."

"I told you that years ago, when we were sleeping in the same bed with Vidalia and Marietta. What the hell does that have to do with right now?"

Atlanta yawned, stretched, and sat down on her bed. "I thought I'd take a quick nap before lunch. Some of the judges will be there, and I wanna look good. That tour of the vineyards and winery about plumb wore me out. And how can you expect me to get a wink o' sleep with you lyin' there, sawin' logs?"

Cold fury flooded Savannah's bloodstream with enough adrenaline to jolt her fully awake. Grabbing her pillow, she jumped out of bed, ran across the room, and began to beat Atlanta with it as hard she could . . . which wasn't very hard, considering it was a fine, goose-down pillow and ridiculously soft.

"Hey! What was that for?" Atlanta yelled when she finally stopped.

"Think about it again in about ten years. By then, maybe you'll be older and wiser and less self-centered, and you'll realize how lucky you are that I didn't use a hatchet instead." She sighed, exhausted from her outburst. "Shit. What time is it, anyway?"

Atlanta got up, walked over to the window, and opened the curtains, allowing a nauseating amount of golden California sunshine to stream into the room. She glanced at her watch. "It's ten-thirty-eight. What time did you lie down?"

"Ten thirty-four."

"Well, no wonder you're cranky."

Savannah walked into the bathroom and glanced around for a clean cloth to wash her face and perhaps revive her sagging spirits, not to mention her sagging chinline. There had been four fresh cloths on the counter when she had left earlier. They all lay in a damp, rumpled pile on the floor. *Er-r-r-r . . . teenage sisters,* she thought. *They should all be put on ice and not thawed out until they're thirty.*

She opened the cupboard under the sink to check for any extra linens, but instead, found the space overflowing with "Atlanta Stuff." Amid the jumble of hair rollers, makeup, and curling-wand cord, she saw two small boxes. Both alike. One of them was open, its contents half gone.

"'Lanta," she said, reaching for the boxes. "Come here, darlin'."

Atlanta stuck her head around the corner. "Yeah? What?"

Savannah held out the boxes. "Are these yours?"

Atlanta snatched the laxatives out of her hand and held them against her chest. "So, what? Don't you ever get stopped up once in a while?"

"Once in a blue moon. But a bowl of bran flakes usually does the trick, and it's a lot healthier than that stuff."

"Well, bully for you. I need a little more help."

"So, increase the fiber in your diet."

"Yeah, right . . . this from the Donut Queen."

Savannah walked out of the bathroom and pulled her sister over into the light by the window so that she could get a good look at her. Her skin looked terrible, dry and lined like that of a person who was much older.

Her face wasn't just thin, it was gaunt. And in the bright light, Savannah could see that she had used a lot of concealer to cover the dark circles under her eyes.

Savannah reached out, grabbed her sister by both shoulders and made her face her squarely. "Atlanta, are you using laxatives to purge? Do you take those things to keep your weight down? Tell me the truth, dammit. This is important."

She tried to pull away, but Savannah held her tightly. "No. It's just that sometimes . . . I get bloated, you know. Like water weight. And if I take a water pill and some of those, I can drop a couple of pounds right away, and then I look better."

"Look better? You're gorgeous! A little scrawny at the moment, but you're a beautiful girl. Why would you mess with your health like that? Don't you know, you're not just washing away body fluids, you're losing minerals and lots of good stuff that you need to function? You'll wind up in the hospital if you don't watch out."

Atlanta put on her most sullen face and pressed her lips together until they nearly disappeared. Savannah knew the look: The kid wasn't talking.

"Honey, tell me the truth . . . are you puking, too?" No reply.

"Are you inducing vomiting? Is that part of your routine, too?"

"No."

Savannah didn't know whether to believe her or not. She felt as though her own stomach was doing a flip-flop. This was bad. This was potentially very, very bad.

Finally, when she received no further response, she released the girl and walked back to the bed, where she sat down . . . hard . . . her legs weak beneath her.

"All right. If you don't want to discuss it now, we

SOUR GRAPES   165

won't. But this subject isn't closed. This is a serious matter, whether you think so or not . . . far more important
than whether or not you can fit into a size six swimsuit."

"Size six?!" Well, at least she was talking. "What
makes you think I'm that big? I'm a four!"

"And you're a big girl—five feet eight and large-
boned. It's ridiculous for you to be that thin. You're
starving yourself to death."

"I'm not going to discuss this with you anymore." She
walked over to her own bed and threw herself across it.
"Let's talk about something else."

A bell went off in the back of Savannah's brain, an
alarm that jerked her back to the reality that she had
been struggling with before she had lain down for her
all-too-short nap.

Barbie Matthews.

"Oh, man . . ." she said, "this is like waking up from a
bad dream and finding out that everything's okay . . .
only in reverse."

"You didn't ask me about my tour," Atlanta said, hap-
pily rattling on, obviously relieved to have the subject of
her habits put aside for the moment. "It was really cool.
Mr. Villa took us through the vineyards and showed us
the different kinds of grapes. I tasted one that was
awful, really sour. But then, they aren't ripe yet.

"And then he took us into the place where they mash
the grapes in these huge crusher things, and then the
fermentation place where juice rots and turns into wine
and then the barrel room where there's a million barrels . . . and the place where they bottle it all and put la-
bels on it and . . .

"Gee, I had no idea there was so much to making
wine. All these things can go wrong, and then the whole
batch is ruined. Mr. Villa says it's an art, making good

wine. You could tell he's really into it. Believe it or not, but some of us girls think he's kinda sexy . . . you know . . . for an old fart."

"And old fart? He's in his forties. Believe me, when you get there, you won't think it's all that old."

"But he's got gray hair."

Savannah thought of the bottle of Midnight Brown—Color That Gray hair solution under her bathroom sink at home. "So, silver hair doesn't make a person old or a fart, so watch your mouth."

"Touchy, touchy."

For a moment neither of them spoke as Savannah considered the best words she could use to gently break the news about Barbie's demise. Atlanta was a very emotional, sensitive girl; Savannah didn't want this experience to scar her soul.

"Ah, 'Lanta, there's something I need to tell you. About Barbie Matthews, she—"

"Yeah, I heard. That really sucks . . . her going off a cliff like that. You guys were up all night looking for her, and there she was hanging from a bush, like, who knew? Too weird."

Savannah blinked and shook her head. Okay, so much for her little sister's delicate psyche. Maybe there was something to this "desensitized new generation" thing after all. Too much television and not enough trips behind the woodshed . . . that was Granny Reid's opinion on the matter.

"Were the other girls as . . . traumatized . . . as you were over the news?" Savannah asked.

"No, I was more upset than most of them, you know, since she was my roommate and all. One of the girls, Desiree Porter, was even jazzed about it. She said one of us had a chance now that the Barbie doll was out of the picture."

Savannah stood, ran her fingers through her hair, and slipped her aching feet back into her loafers. "Well," she said, "if the rest of the girls are taking this as hard as you are, it's a darn good thing we've got those counselors coming from Mental Health. We'd wanna head off any mass suicides."

"Huh?"

"Never mind." She strapped on her holster and gun, then went to her suitcase and got a fresh jacket. For some reason, the other one seemed to smell of death.

"You're right," Savannah said. "It . . . sucks. And I've got to get back to work. Throw the dead bolt after me."

"Yeah, yeah, you don't have to keep telling me. I—"

"Dammit, 'Lanta, for once will you just do something I ask you to do and not give me any lip?"

Savannah stomped out of the room and slammed the door behind her. Pausing, listening for the bolt to shoot home, she heard her sister say, "Boy, oh, boy . . . she's such a *grouch* when she wakes up!"

But there was someone who was upset about Barbie Matthews's death. Terribly upset. And Savannah heard her crying, even before she saw her. On a patch of lawn behind the guest lodge, Francie Gorton was sitting beneath a trio of palm trees on a white, wrought-iron park bench that overlooked the sweeping vista of Villa Rosa's oceans of vines. Her face was buried in a handful of tissues, and her shoulders were shaking with racking sobs.

Savannah walked over to her and sat down on the bench beside her.

The warm, late-summer sun was almost directly overhead, and the girl's long, glossy black hair shone iridescent, like a raven's wing.

Savannah wasn't sure Francie was even aware of her presence, until she heard her say, "It's my fault Barbie's dead. And I could have stopped it."

Trying to keep the eagerness out of her voice, Savannah said, "What do you mean, Francie? How could you have kept her from dying?"

The girl wiped her eyes with the tissues and blew her nose. Then she turned to Savannah, her young face full of grief. "Last night, when you asked me what was going on, I should have told you about it. Or maybe I should have called her parents and talked to them. I don't know if it would have done any good; and now I'll never know."

Savannah reached over and pushed the girl's tear-wet hair back from her face. "Francie, did you hurt Barbie?"

"No, she was my friend. I know a lot of people didn't like her, but she was pretty nice to me most of the time, and I liked her."

"Do you know who hurt her?"

A look of raw fear flickered in the girl's eyes, and she glanced away. "No."

"Are you sure?"

Francie nodded, but continued to stare at the far horizon.

"You have any idea who might have done it?"

Francie twisted the tissues between her fingers. "No."

Having no luck opening the front door of the conversation, Savannah decided to try the back door. "Last night," she said, "outside your room, I heard you warning Barbie to be careful. You told her that you were afraid she was going to get hurt. What was that about, Francie?"

The girl began to cry again, and Savannah could almost feel her fear—suffocating, paralyzing, until she could hardly breathe.

"I can't tell you. Please don't ask me."

"You can't tell me because you don't know, or because you're afraid? Which is it, Francie?"

"I'm . . . I'm afraid. If I tell you, if I tell anybody, I'll be next."

Savannah's heart ached for the girl; she was so like some of her sisters back in Georgia—old enough to get into trouble but too young to find her way out.

She stroked the girl's sun-warm hair, trying to comfort her. "Francie, sweetie, if you think your life is in danger, that makes it even more important that you talk to me about it. You can trust me. I'll help you, if you'll just let me."

Francie blew her nose again, then glanced at her watch. "I have to go and get ready for lunch. I have to act like everything is okay, you know what I mean?"

"No, I don't know what you mean. I wish I did. Is there *anything* I can do to help you, Francie?"

The girl shook her head and stood. "I really need to go. But thank you, Ms. Reid. It was very nice of you to stop and talk with me. I'm sorry I . . ."

When the rest of her words didn't come, Savannah patted her shoulder. "That's okay, dear. If you change your mind and want to talk, I'm in room 2G or you can call me. Here's my cell-phone number and my beeper, too. Anytime, night or day. Okay?"

She scribbled the numbers on a slip of paper and pressed it into the girl's palm.

"Okay. Thanks."

"I'll walk you back to your room, if you like."

Francie glanced around—the furtive, suspicious look of the hunted. "No, that's all right. I think it would be better if nobody . . . you know, if I wasn't seen talking to you."

"I understand."

But as she watched the girl walk away with the grace and bearing of a queen, Savannah cursed herself for not understanding. And for not knocking on that bedroom door last night and demanding answers. If she had, Barbie Matthews might be alive . . . and Francie Gorton might be thinking about winning beauty pageants instead of fearing for her life.

Chapter
15

"What is this crap?" Dirk pointed to the dish of food that had been set before him—half a pineapple, scooped out and filled with chicken salad, decorated with a sprig of mint and a paper umbrella.

"It's called lunch," Savannah told him. "Stick a forkful into your mouth. It'll keep you quiet . . . at least in theory."

"But it's sissy food. I don't eat girlie junk like this."

Savannah picked a walnut and a piece of fresh pineapple out of the salad, tasted it, and closed her eyes in ecstasy. "I realize," she said, "that if your grub hasn't moo-o-oed in the past twenty-four hours you don't consider it food. But this really is good. Besides, it's free."

Dirk reconsidered. "That's true."

He picked up his fork and began to shovel it in. She didn't understand why he made such an issue of what he was eating; he never took the time to taste it anyway.

A soft breeze rippled the edges of the umbrella over their table, a blue-and-white-striped affair, like a dozen others that had been set around the Villa Rosa swimming pool. Luncheon was being served to the pageant judges, hostesses, sponsors, members of the local press, and a number of society mucky-mucks, who seldom missed the opportunity to make appearances at this sort of thing.

The contestants were walking among the tables, modeling the latest swimwear fashions, furnished by a beachfront boutique. Savannah was relieved to see that her own sister was wearing a modest one-piece maillot instead of one of the skimpy bikinis that some of the other girls were wearing.

She spotted Frank Addison sitting at the end of the judges' table. His chicken salad was being badly neglected, as he ogled each young body that passed his way.

However, when Atlanta walked by him, Savannah was gratified to see him avert his eyes, suddenly interested in the conversation at his table. Her talk with him had made an impression on him after all.

"That Addison creep," she said. "I'd like to nail him for Barbie's murder. Just thinking about hearing you read him his rights does me a world of good."

Dirk shoved his mouthful of food to the side of his jaw, and said, "Yeah, I've been thinkin' about him. I told Jake McMurtry to check 'im out. Wouldn't it be fun if he had a rap sheet with some sexual assaults on it?"

"Don't toy with me. Only in my dreams." She took a sip of the wine that had been served to the adults at the luncheon. One of Villa Rosa's blush wines, it had a beautiful coral color and a surprisingly delicate, dry taste for a blush.

"Since when are you drinking on the job, Van?" Dirk asked, reaching for his own glass of iced tea.

"Yeah, right . . . like you wouldn't be guzzling beer this minute if they'd offered it to you. Besides, I'm only having half a glass. If I drank the whole thing I'd go right to sleep, sitting here in my chair."

"By the way"—he stuffed another forkful into his mouth—"Dr. Liu told me she examined that muck that was on the Matthews kid's bed. It was chicken guts, all right."

Savannah glanced down at her salad and silently cursed Dirk for his lack of timing. "Gee, thanks for letting me know."

"No problem."

"How did it go with informing the Matthews family?"

"Rotten, just like always. Dad cried, Mom cussed me out, then she cried, too. There just ain't no easy way to inform next of kin."

Savannah nodded. "It's the worst. I don't mind leaving that part of the job behind. Did they give you any ideas who might have had it in for her?"

"Mom said she's sure it's the boyfriend, a kid from the east end. And Dad said, 'No way. He's a good boy . . . even if he *is* from the east end.' "

"Yeah, when I interviewed them earlier, Mrs. Matthews didn't strike me as very liberal when it comes to embracing those of another economic status."

"No joke. She's ready to jab the needle in him herself, right now, trial be damned."

"Did you run the boy?"

"Yeap, a couple of misdemeanors, nothing major. I dropped by his place, but his mom said he was gone for the day. I'll try again tonight. It's not exactly APB time

. . . until Dr. Liu's done with the autopsy and we know for sure she was murdered."

"When is she doing it?"

"Tomorrow afternoon, I think."

"That's quick."

"Yeah, only one other stiff in the morgue. Lucky for us, it's a slow weekend."

"And even luckier for the would-be stiffs who ain't."

"Huh?'

"Never mind."

Dirk settled into serious eating, which meant he had no time for mundane conversation, as he polished off his first plate and sweet-talked a waitress out of a second.

Savannah finished her lunch and used the remaining minutes of the meal to relax and watch the crowd. Catherine and Anthony Villa were moving among their guests, the perfect host and hostess, cool and calm, with no hint of trouble. No one would have guessed that only hours ago, someone had been murdered on their property.

Savannah also kept an eye on the press members, who had been given a prominent table in the center of the room. While the pageant was hardly the most newsworthy event of the season, several of the local papers had sent reporters, and Savannah recognized the anchorwoman of the local cable channel.

She wondered if any of them knew about Barbie Matthews. From their casual demeanor, she assumed not. But no sooner had she come to that conclusion than she saw Rosemary Hulse, a newspaper reporter for the *San Carmelita Star,* talking on her cell phone. She had listened to her caller only a few seconds when her expression changed from laid-back to serious. Rosemary's forte was crime reporting, and she always seemed to show up when Savannah least wanted a public informer on the scene.

The moment Rosemary put her phone away, she stood and excused herself.

Elbowing Dirk, Savannah said, "Hey, buddy. Rosemary Hulse just got a phone call. She knows."

"Dandy."

"How long do you suppose it'll take her to corner Catherine or Anthony Villa?"

"About two seconds."

His prediction was dead center; Catherine had left her table and walked to the back of the room to speak to the headwaiter, and that was where Rosemary nailed her.

Watching the two women converse, Savannah saw Catherine Villa's struggle to remain the poised politician's wife. And she had to give the lady major points for "cool." As she answered Rosemary's questions, she wore the appropriate, sad, terribly concerned expression, although Savannah could imagine her agitation.

Rosemary had pulled a small tape recorder out of her purse and was holding it under Catherine's nose, taking the "quote," no doubt that would be on the headline of tomorrow morning's edition of the *Star*. Any homicide was big news in the small, quiet community of San Carmelita. But one involving a beautiful young woman, on the posh estate of Villa Rosa, whose owner just happened to be running for senator? That was too juicy for second-page news.

The conversation didn't last long; Catherine Villa was pretty good at wriggling out of an unpleasant situation, Savannah observed. She seemed to notice some urgent situation on the opposite side of the room that demanded her immediate attention. In a wink, Rosemary was standing alone, recorder in her hand and a frustrated look on her face.

The reporter glanced around the room, and her eyes met Savannah's. "Uh-oh." Savannah tossed her napkin onto the table and stood. "I'm outta here before she snags me, too."

"Me, three." Dirk gulped down the last of his tea and followed Savannah as they made their escape from the pool area and through a door that led back into the courtyard.

Catherine Villa was there, and so was Marion Lippincott. Savannah and Dirk could hear them arguing even before they saw them.

"That's it. This beauty contest is over. We can't take responsibility for your young ladies' safety," Catherine was saying. "You have to send them all home immediately."

"But, Mrs. Villa, we mustn't interrupt the pageant. The girls have been preparing for this for months. It's very important to them . . . the scholarship and—"

"We'll set up some sort of scholarship, whatever you like, but we have to end this pageant and get the girls out of here before something else awful happens."

Catherine glanced over and saw Savannah and Dirk. "You! Come here!"

"Us?" Dirk said.

"Yes, you. Please tell Mrs. Lippincott how important it is that we send the young ladies home right away. You of all people should know that. You saw that poor girl and . . ."

Catherine's façade of composure cracked, and she began to cry. Savannah walked over to her and put her arm around her shoulders. "There, there. Do you have an office, Catherine?"

"Yes."

"Does it have a lock on the door?"

She sniffed and nodded.

"Then I would suggest that we go there right away, because Rosemary Hulse is right on our heels, and I don't want a picture of you in tears to appear in the paper . . . and I'm sure you don't either."

Catherine wiped her eyes with the back of her hand, lifted her chin, and patted her French twist. "Follow me."

As Savannah, Dirk, and Marion Lippincott left Catherine Whitestone-Villa's office, "The Lip" was having a difficult time hiding her glee. "I can't believe you talked her into allowing us to continue!" she told them. "You were wonderful in there . . . both of you. Though I'm a little confused. To be honest, I'm surprised that you were on my side."

They paused at the end of the hallway, at the door leading to the gallery. "It isn't a matter of taking sides," Savannah told her. "It's an issue of keeping the status quo."

"What do you mean?"

"Easy," Dirk replied. "If we have everybody here in one place, it's easier to keep an eye on them. And chances are, we'll keep the murderer here, too."

The unflappable Mrs. Lippincott gave him a startled look. "Are you telling me that you think the killer is here at the pageant?"

"Better than even odds."

Mrs. Lippincott turned to Savannah. "Do you think so, too?"

"Whatever he says. He's the dude with the badge."

Marion thought that one over for a moment, then nodded. "I guess that makes sense. You will let me know as soon as you have a suspect, won't you?"

"Absolutely," Dirk assured her.

As she walked away, Savannah said, "You're not going to tell her squat."

"I know."

"So, you shouldn't lie to people. Your nose will grow longer."

"My nose? That's not what I heard. I thought it was—"

"Oh, shut up. What'd you do, rent one of those stupid, X-rated cartoons again?"

"Lie to me, Blue Fairy . . . lie to me."

"Eh . . ."

Chapter
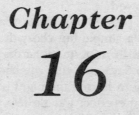
16

The girls were gorgeous; Savannah had to admit it as she watched them glide, as graceful as princesses at a coronation, past the judges' table in their evening gowns.

The lawns behind the Villa Rosa guest center had been converted into a fantasyland with a million white sparkling lights winking in the olive trees and rose topiaries lining the path where the contestants passed, while their admirers watched in rows of chairs that had been assembled for the event.

A Maypole had been raised in the center of a makeshift stage, its ribbons stretching to the ground, the pole itself wreathed in garlands of roses and twining vines heavy with grapes.

The girls were dressed in every hue, from the most delicate pastel to deep, intense jewel tones. And they all sparkled . . . with either rhinestones or sequins, as their budgets had allowed.

Savannah was pleased to see that Atlanta had made a lovely selection, a simple but classy dress of dark blue satin, accented with rhinestones across the bodice. She had admitted to Savannah that she had stuck them on with a hot-glue gun herself the night before coming to California, but the effect was no less stunning in the subdued, romantic lighting.

No one would have guessed that Atlanta Reid wasn't a pampered Southern socialite, but the daughter of a sometimes-truck stop waitress who was also known as the town's "loose woman."

But Atlanta was also Granny Reid's granddaughter. She had been taught to sit, walk, and talk like a lady since she was old enough to do all three. And as Savannah watched her cross the stage with the bearing of a queen, she wished that Gran were there to see her. She would have been busting with pride.

"Your sister looks lovely tonight," Ryan said. He stood at her shoulder, watching, as she was, from the sidelines. "I've seen you wear that color . . . sapphire blue, isn't it? It complements your eyes and hers, too."

Savannah batted her lashes at him. "Why, sir . . . I didn't think you'd noticed."

"Of course I've noticed. John and I were just saying the other day how beautiful you looked the last time we took you to dinner at Chez Antoine."

"You're only saying that because you're 'safe,' immune to my feminine wiles. Straight guys never say cool things like that."

"Some do. Just not that barbarian you spend most of your time with."

"No, but I like him anyway."

Ryan laughed. "I understand."

"You do?"

"No, but I'll take your word for it."

They watched a while longer as the remainder of the contestants made their appearances. The number of participants had dwindled since the noon swimsuit showing. Some of the parents had gotten wind of Barbie Matthews's demise and had come to collect their daughters. A few of the girls had been frightened and eager to leave, but most chose to remain and finish the competition.

Savannah's threats to send Atlanta packing had fallen by the wayside. Everyone seemed convinced that Barbie's bad luck had been of her own making and was unlikely to be repeated with anyone else.

Except Francie.

Savannah had been keeping a close eye on her, and the girl seemed just as troubled and nervous as she had that morning, maybe more. She tripped on the hem of her gown while walking up onto the stage, and when it was her turn to speak a few words at the microphone, she stammered and choked on her own words.

"I wish I'd been able to get her to open up to me," she told Ryan. "I'm sure she knows exactly what happened to Barbie and why. But she's too scared to talk."

"I know. I tried, too, but she was terrified to even have anyone see her speaking to me."

"Did you hear from John? Did he check her out?"

"Yes, he says she's had it rough, been in and out of foster homes her entire life, through no fault of her own. She's a good kid, no drugs, no record, very good grades. She's living at home now. Apparently, mom's got it together for the moment. Her last foster parents want to adopt her."

"Why don't they?"

"There's some problem with the mom giving up complete custody. Dad isn't on the scene."

"Any brothers or sisters?"

Ryan gave her a quizzical look. "Yes, I thought you knew."

"Knew what?"

"She's Trent's sister."

"Trent Gorton? The east end boy that Barbie dated?"

"The very one. That's how Trent and Barbie met. He was dropping his sister off at a pageant."

Savannah thought that one over as Mrs. Lippincott went to the microphone, thanked everyone for coming, and wished them a safe trip home.

Trent's sister, huh?

Now, that was a horse of a different feather.

Back in her room for the night, Savannah took a two-minute shower—a cleaning that Gran would have called, "a lick and a promise."

She didn't want to waste a moment on bathing that could be spent sleeping. Having agreed to meet Ryan for breakfast at 7:00 A.M., she was already dreading the prospect of hauling her weary bones out of bed. It would come all too soon.

Besides, Atlanta was pacing in the bedroom, impatient to begin her "beauty bath," which she said would include special moisturizers and exfoliates, the mixture being her own carefully guarded secret.

She had halfheartedly apologized to Savannah for refusing to share her "fountain of youth," until Savannah told her bluntly, "'Lanta, don't take this wrong, but I don't give a tinker's damn about beauty treatments right now. I don't have to look good to catch bad guys. Just don't stand between me and the shower or the bed."

In less than five minutes she had completed all the minimalist toiletries and was blissfully horizontal. And ninety seconds later, she was drifting in a pea green, dreamland boat with Winken, Blinken, and Nod.

But then, a bony hand reached out and rocked the boat. It was the Wicked Witch of the East . . . or was she from the South? She had a really heavy Southern accent and—

"Savannah, wake up."

"No, go away."

"Really, Van, wake up," Witchy Poo said. "It's important."

"I swear, if you touch me again, I'll hurt you."

More shaking, the bony fingers biting into her shoulder. "You've gotta hear this. Wake up."

Savannah came fully conscious and realized that Atlanta was serious . . . not like this morning. Whatever the reason for her waking her, it wasn't something as frivolous as snoring.

"The girls in the room next to us," Atlanta whispered. "You should come in here and listen. I was taking my bath when I heard them, and I thought I should wake you up."

Savannah squinted up at her sister and realized she was wet and shivering, a towel twisted around her torso, her sudsy hair dripping on the floor.

"Okay, okay." Savannah swung her legs out of bed and sat up. Her head spun, as though both tablespoons of her blood had raced to her feet, giving her a blood pressure of minus zero.

She followed Atlanta into the bathroom where she,

too, could hear a conversation going on in the next room. Apparently the plumbing provided an excellent conduit for eavesdropping.

Atlanta stood to one side of the toilet and pressed her ear to the tiled wall. Savannah took a position on the other side.

"You never liked Barbie anyway," one of their neighbors said. "I wouldn't be surprised if you were the one who pushed her off that cliff."

"Yeah, well, I don't like you either, Eileen, but I haven't done anything to you . . . yet."

"Don't threaten me. I'll go straight to Mrs. Lippincott and tell her how you ripped Barbie's evening gown and put drain cleaner in her shampoo."

Savannah looked at Atlanta and waggled her right eyebrow. Atlanta stifled a giggle.

"I don't know what you're talking about," came the reply.

"Okay, then you won't mind if they check her gown and her shampoo bottle, right?"

"I don't care what you say or what they do. I'm glad that Barbie Matthews is dead. She was a bitch, and I hated her guts. I hope somebody *did* murder her. It would serve her right."

"I think you killed her, because you were tired of her beating you in contests. Everybody knows you threatened to hurt her after she took the Miss California Sunshine crown and you were first runner-up."

"She fixed that pageant! She slept with two of the judges. That's the only reason she won."

"And you only slept with one of them, right, Desiree?"

Both Savannah and Atlanta cringed, expecting to

hear some indication of physical violence. Instead, they heard the voice, identified as "Desiree," reply with deadly calm, "I'll bet I won the evening gown tonight, and if I did, it's because I'm the only pro here. The rest of you are stupid little girls who couldn't win a pageant if you slept with every judge on the panel. And as far as whether I hurt Barbie or not . . ."

Savannah shoved her ear as tight against the wall as she could and held her breath.

". . . that's for me to know and you to think about. Think about it anytime you're going to say something stupid to me . . . or about me. You'd better think hard, Eileen. Your life might depend on it."

The sisters stood, plastered to the bathroom tiles, straining to hear more, but that was all. Apparently, Eileen had wisely decided to keep any further opinions to herself.

Finally, Savannah moved away from the wall and motioned for Atlanta to follow her back into the bedroom. They closed the bathroom door behind them.

"So . . . was that worth getting out of bed for?" Atlanta asked, a satisfied smirk on her face.

"Well worth it. And if you promise not to wake me up again—benevolent, forgiving woman that I am—I just might let you live to see the morning light."

But Savannah couldn't go back to sleep. Long after Atlanta was making z-z-z's in the bed next to hers, Savannah was cursing herself for wasting these precious hours tossing and turning. But images kept running through her head, disturbing pictures of a young woman falling off a cliff, of someone pushing an enor-

mous rock down on her, trying to crush her, of someone leaning through a window and pouring blood and
gore onto a beautiful, rose damask bedspread.

And those scenes were anything but soothing.

Finally, she rolled out of bed and walked over to the
window. Pulling back the curtain, she looked out and
savored the view. Directly below were the lawns where
the evening-gown competition had been held earlier.
And beyond the dark grass was a silver sea—the moonlit vineyards.

Only a few hours ago, the estate had been bustling
with activity. Now it seemed almost ghostly in its tran-
quillity. Apparently, everyone was asleep, except her.

The realization made Savannah bitter. Damned job,
anyway. She should have pursued her childhood dream—
becoming a caged go-go dancer in white boots and a
leopard minidress.

But another look out the window told Savannah that
she was not the only one awake after all. Right ahead, at
the edge of the vineyard, she saw someone walking
among the rows, a person whose white hair glimmered
in the moonshine.

Why was Anthony Villa wandering in his own vineyard so late at night? she wondered. So far, she had
dealt solely with Catherine, as the lady had requested.
But her curiosity was piqued by this man who wanted to
be a state senator, yet hated speaking to a crowd. A man
who wandered his land, alone in the moonlight.

Quietly, so that she wouldn't wake Atlanta, she
slipped off her pajama bottoms and donned a pair of
jeans. After pulling a sweater on over her top, she
stood, looking down at her Beretta in its holster. Her
system rebelled against the thought of strapping it on
again . . . but . . .

She took the pistol out of the leather, tucked it in the rear waistband of her jeans, and tiptoed out of the room.

Anthony Villa didn't see Savannah until she was only a few yards from him. But he didn't seem surprised that she, too, was walking the grounds.

"Good evening, Ms. Reid," he said as she approached. "Fancy meeting you out here. Are you making your rounds or something official like that?"

"No, actually, I'm suffering from insomnia," she replied. "And you?"

He grinned sheepishly, like a kid caught running around the house at night when he was supposed to be in bed. In his jeans and UCLA sweatshirt, he looked quite different from the formal host she had observed at the luncheon or the judge in a tuxedo, who had been evaluating the pageant beauties in their gowns that evening.

"Would you believe," he said, "I'm conversing with the vines?"

She smiled. "And are they good listeners?"

"The best. They hear every word I say, but they never give me unwanted advice." He laughed. "I used to sing opera to them, but it made the wine sour, so I've settled for moonlight heart-to-hearts."

Savannah nodded thoughtfully as she studied the vines with their clusters of plump berries. "They don't listen so good in the daytime?"

"Sure, they're here for me anytime. The problem is: I'm so busy these days that I don't have time to come out and commune like I used to."

"That's a shame."

"You've no idea." He reached down, picked up a way-ward vine, and gently coaxed it upward, twining it around the trellis. "These vines are dear old friends. My grandfather planted them himself, long before I was born. These particular ones are nearly seventy years old."

"I had no idea they would produce so long."

"They will if you take very good care of them. I'm afraid that if I win the senate seat, I won't have the time I need to nurture . . . Well, you don't want to hear my problems, Ms. Reid, when you have troubles of your own right now."

Savannah ran her fingers along a vine and could al-most feel the vitality flowing through it. She placed her hand under one of the clusters and was surprised how heavy it was. The dew-damp grapes felt cool and smooth against her fingers.

"They're starting to get ripe," he said. "Pretty soon we'll have to spread the nets over them to keep the birds away."

He knelt in the dirt and fingered a dark tube that lay half-buried in the soil. "Those damned coyotes," he said. "They're chewing through my irrigation lines again. They've discovered it's a great place to get a fresh drink of water. They eat the grapes, too. So do the deer and the raccoons. Half of this business is keeping the varmints in check. But then, you know all about varmint control."

"Yes, I'm afraid I do. But my varmints have two legs, and they aren't nearly so cute." She cleared her throat and changed the subject. "Your wife is very concerned," she said, "that my . . . problem . . . will become your problem, with the bad publicity and all."

He nodded and smiled, a tender expression on his face. "Ah, my Catie. She's always worrying about something. She's good at a lot of things, but worrying is what she's best at."

"She's very supportive of your campaign."

"Catherine *is* my campaign. We're partners in everything. She's my perfect complement."

"How nice to hear a husband speak so well of his wife. That's rare these days."

"Wives like Catherine are rare. Let me tell you a story, Ms. Reid . . . about grapevines . . . and about a true partnership."

He led her to the end of a row and pointed to a vine that was clearly illuminated in the moonlight. "This vine is a product of grafting. The roots are from vines that are native to America. The rest of the plant is a European variety.

"You see, until the mid 1800s there were grapevines here in the Americas, and others in Europe. The American vines were sturdy, hardy, but the European vines yielded the best wine. Then someone transported some vines from America to Europe, and, unfortunately, a nasty little bug along with them. The result was an infestation that destroyed most of Europe's vineyards by attacking the roots of their vines.

"But some bright person . . . or maybe his bright wife . . . got the idea of grafting the European vines onto the resistant American roots. The results were so spectacular that the practice continued, long after the European vineyards were out of danger. It was the perfect partnership, like my wife and me."

Savannah considered his story and his metaphor. She looked out across the vista of hills and valleys filled with fog and felt the cool, moist breezes on her face, and she wondered how he could cherish any partnership that would take him away from this magic place.

"So, which are you, the vine that produces wonderful fruit or the sturdy root?" she asked.

"I'm definitely the root. These are my roots, all around you. From the olive trees that I played in as a kid, to the rosebushes my grandmother Rosa planted, to the wine you drank at lunch . . . this ground gave birth to it all. We're dirt people, we Villas."

"And Catherine Whitestone?"

"She's the reason why the winery has grown by leaps and bounds these past ten years. It's her marketing genius that expanded the complex, built the guest lodge and put in the pool, added gourmet meals to the tasting-room menu. Really, before she arrived, all we did here was make wine."

"And that wasn't enough?"

He looked a bit confused . . . but only for a moment. "No. After all, a person should always try to better himself in life, don't you think?"

"Not necessarily." She shrugged. "I mean, if you're already happy doing what you're doing—and you seem very happy raising your grapes and making your wines—you're luckier than most. Maybe that's enough. Maybe it's a good life that doesn't need to be improved . . . just enjoyed."

He smiled, but it was a bittersweet expression. "I don't think my wife would agree with you."

"That's okay. I don't think many ambitious people would."

Suddenly, Savannah realized that she liked Anthony Villa much more than she liked his wife. And when she thought back on what Atlanta had said about him—

"kinda sexy for an old silver-haired fart"—she realized that she agreed with her younger sister. There was, indeed, something sexy about this earthy but intelligent man who felt passionate about his wife—whether she deserved it or not—his land, his wine, and his heritage. And he did look very good in a sweatshirt and jeans by moonlight.

Savannah decided then and there, it was time to leave the vineyard. *Just turn around and walk away, girl,* she told herself. *And make it snappy.*

"I've got to get back," she said. "Thank you for the history lesson . . . and for reaffirming my faith in happy marriages."

"Anytime, Ms. Reid. Anytime you suffer from insomnia, I'll probably be out here somewhere. And I'd love to tell you what the ancient Greeks and Romans thought of wine."

She didn't reply, just gave him a dismissive wave as she made a speedy retreat.

No, she wouldn't be returning for any more wine lessons in the moonlight with Anthony Villa. She was a well-trained, so-called decent Southern girl, and Granny Reid had told her more than once, "Savannah, darlin', if you ever feel yourself takin' a likin' to a married man . . . you just turn tail and run . . . run . . . run! 'Cause ain't no good gonna come of it. Only a heap o' tears and sorrow."

"Don't you worry, Gran," she whispered into the moonlit night as she increased her stride to a jog. "My tail is turned, and I'm a- runnin'."

Chapter
17

Breakfast, in all of its fresh fruit, yogurt, and bran-muffin glory, was served on the poolside tables beneath the blue-and-white-striped umbrellas. The coffee wasn't nearly strong enough to raise Savannah's blood pressure to even minimal levels. But she downed it, uncertain of when she might ever see food or a caffeine source again.

Afterward, she chased Marion Lippincott around the complex for over half an hour, trying to get a private moment with her. This beauty-pageant business was a lot more work than private detecting, she decided. And, as far as she was concerned, "The Lip" was welcome to it. She would just stick with chasing down the perverts and the robbers, murderers and wayward husbands who fooled around with the gals who groomed their wives' poodles. This pageant routine was far too stressful.

Finally, she nabbed Mrs. Lippincott inside the gift shop, buying a handful of 35mm film for one of the pageant photographers who was running low.

"You would think," she was saying to the woman behind the counter, "that a professional photographer would bring enough film to do the job. I can guarantee you, he will never work one of my pageants again."

The clerk didn't seem to care that Mrs. Lippincott was upset . . . or about anything else for that matter. Perhaps the coffee hadn't been strong enough for her, either, Savannah thought, as she watched her not even bother to stifle a leisurely yawn.

But it gave Savannah the opportunity to be sympathetic. She stepped up to the counter and plopped down a few dollars for some overpriced French crackers. "I can't believe you have to take care of something as trivial as film," she said.

"Oh, no. Film isn't trivial," she replied. "In this business, hairpins aren't trivial. With teenage girls, absolutely *everything* is monumental . . . especially at a beauty pageant."

Both women took their purchases, bagged in classy gold sacks with the Villa Rosa logo, and walked out of the shop.

"Before we go back into the center," Savannah said, pausing outside the gallery, "I need to ask you a few questions about a couple of your girls."

Marion hesitated, glancing over Savannah's shoulder at the door. Duty was calling, but she acquiesced. "Okay, but—"

"I'll make it brief. What can you tell me about a girl named Desiree who is staying in the room next to mine?"

"Desiree Porter is an odious child, who makes my life

miserable anytime she shows up at one of my pageants. She's spoiled, selfish, and not half as intelligent or attractive as her nitwit mother has led her to believe she is."

"Oh." Somehow, Savannah hadn't expected such candor from a professional like Mrs. Lippincott. Desiree must have really made an impression. "Is she highly competitive?"

"She will do *anything* to win. I daresay, she has done everything she can think of . . . and although she isn't at all wise, she's quite cunning. I would imagine she's thought of a lot of ways."

"Have you ever known her to hurt another girl at a pageant?"

"Nothing I can prove, but I've had my suspicions."

"How did she feel about Barbie Matthews?"

"More than once, they've been the winner and first runner-up for important crowns. Desiree hated her, and I'm sure the feeling was mutual."

Savannah gave a quick look around, but—other than some people in the parking lot, who were well out of earshot—they were alone. "Do you think Desiree is capable of killing another girl . . . like Barbie?"

"I wouldn't put anything past Desiree. Most of the girls I see in the pageants are delightful, lovely young women—the best of our society. But Desiree is the worst. I've only known one other girl who was more cruel, more manipulative and devious."

Savannah had a feeling that she knew what she was going to hear. "Yes . . . ?"

"Barbara Matthews. *She* was the worst." Marion Lippincott gave Savannah a little smile that sent a chill over her, in spite of the warm, morning sunshine that was chasing away the previous night's fog. "But she's dead now, isn't she?" said Marion. "And whatever happened to her . . . I can honestly say, I believe it couldn't have happened to a more deserving brat."

"I see."

"Now, I really must get this film back to the photographer. He's taking pictures of the girls in their interview suits."

She turned to leave, then reconsidered. "By the way . . . another one of the girls left today. She was afraid to stay after what happened yesterday, so she went back home."

"Who was that?"

"Francie Gorton."

Savannah sighed as she watched Marion Lippincott walk away with her determined stride, and she felt a bit relieved that the girl was no longer on the scene. It was probably better that way.

She'd feel much better once they were all home, safe and sound. And especially one little lady from Georgia.

Savannah found Dirk hanging around the now-empty breakfast tables. He was shoving a banana into his mouth with one hand and poking muffins inside his jacket with the other.

"You better watch that excess fiber, boy," she told him. "You know what it does to your digestive system, and you're going to be in the genteel company of ladies all day."

"Oh, yeah, you know all about it."

"Unfortunately, I do. I've sat on all-night stakeouts with you. I know you far too well."

"And familiarity has bred contempt?"

She grinned at him. "Naw, not contempt . . . maybe momentary disgust, but—"

"What have you got for me? Have you been layin' around in bed, eatin' bonbons, or have you been workin'?"

"Bonbons, I wish. You'll want to check out Barbie's shampoo, the bottle there in her room. Word has it, it's spiked with drain cleaner. The bottle probably has prints on it that belong to a sweet little darlin' named Desiree Porter. And she may have slashed Barbie's evening gown, too."

"Mmm . . . do you suppose she did more than that?"

"It's a possibility. But then, at this point, there are so many possibilities."

"How's that precious sister of yours this morning?"

"The one I'd like to hog-tie and send back to Georgia in a burlap bag?"

"That's the one."

"She's getting her picture taken with the rest of the girls. They are getting ready for the interview judging this afternoon, and then the talent show and the awards tonight."

"So you figure they'll be heading out of here tomorrow morning?"

"There's some sort of good-bye breakfast, and they're supposed to be gone by noon."

Savannah felt the cell phone in her purse buzz. She took it out, looked at the caller ID, but didn't recognize the number.

"Hello. Yes, this is Savannah."

She glanced over at Dirk, who was all ears.

"Yes, Francie, I'm glad you called. How can I help you?" She nodded. "Of course. I'd be glad to. I'll be right there."

Dirk tried to lean closer and listen, but Savannah nudged him away.

"All right. I understand. I'll wait until after eleven. Yes, I'll see you then, and thank you for calling."

"Well? What did she want?" Dirk was practically dancing. "Did she say anything about her brother? Did she say he was there at the house?"

"No, she didn't mention Trent, but she did say that she's decided to talk to me, to tell me what was going on just before Barbie disappeared."

"Hey, that's great! But she doesn't want you to show up until after eleven, huh?"

"That's right. Her mom will be going to work then, and she said she wants to talk to me alone."

Dirk's face fell. "I guess that answers my next question."

"That's right, big boy. You don't get to go this time. It's a girl thing."

"After hanging around here, I'm gonna have to watch football games, chew tobacco, and belch for a week to get all this estrogen out of my system."

Savannah patted him . . . hard . . . on the chest, right about where she figured one of his stashed muffins was. She felt it mash very nicely.

"I'm going to go tell Atlanta that I'm leaving the winery for a while. I'll have Ryan keep an eye on her for me while I'm gone."

"Yeah, and I will, too. Let me know right away if the Gorton gal tells you anything good."

"I will, sugar. I surely will."

As Savannah turned to leave, she thought she saw a movement among some oleander bushes only a few feet away. But the brush was extremely thick, and she couldn't see if it was a person or maybe a bird or—

No, she knew it wasn't a bird, or a gopher, or a stiff breeze; that was wishful thinking. It had been a person. Someone had been standing there. The question was: How much had they heard?

And the other question that nagged at Savannah long after she had left the pool area was: If they heard everything—would it matter?

She had an uneasy, almost sick feeling, deep in her guts that it would. She just wasn't sure how.

Savannah didn't need to see the graffiti on the walls of almost every building on Via Norte to know that she was in the bad end of town. The bars on every window and door were proof enough.

Having served her time on a beat in that neighborhood as an SCPD officer, she had memories . . . most of them unpleasant . . . of events that had gone down on nearly every street corner and in almost every alley. And the occupants of many of the houses were known to her, as she had seen some of them at the worst moments of their lives. She and Dirk had sometimes been the reason those were bad moments, as they had arrested them for everything from domestic abuse to public intoxication and sometimes much worse.

But she could also recall the good times, when she had returned a runaway five-year-old and his dog to his frantic mother, when she had arrived just in time to deliver a premature baby and managed to coax breath into the infant's tiny lungs, when she had talked a young woman into leaving her violent boyfriend and starting a new life for herself and her children in a safe house.

She had made a difference on these streets and inside these houses that were miniature fortresses, although that might not be obvious, looking at the neighborhood now.

Turning the Mustang down the road where the Gorton family lived, she noticed that this street was better than some. The yards were small but well-kept, with the patches of grass watered and mowed, flower beds blooming with geraniums, nasturtiums, and marigolds.

Savannah parked in front of 337, noting that there were no cars sitting in the narrow, gravel driveway. Francie's mother would have left by now, and although Savannah preferred to interview a minor with a parent's permission, the girl had been adamant about waiting until they could be alone.

Savannah also kept her eyes open for any sign of Trent. The boy stood a good chance of becoming their number one suspect, and the sooner they located him and started keeping tabs on him, the better.

Dirk had told her that he drove an old, restored Dodge Charger, but there was no sign of either the boy or his car.

As Savannah walked up the sidewalk to the front door, she heard a whining, coming from the other side of the fence that bordered their property. It sounded like a dog in some sort of minor distress. She made a mental note to check on it later.

No one came to the door when she knocked the first time, or the second, third, or fourth.

That's what I was afraid of, she thought. *The kid got scared and decided not to talk after all.*

She walked around the side of the house to the backyard and could hear the dog next door whimpering as he followed along the opposite side of the high, wooden fence.

To enter the rear of the property, she had to pass

through a gate. The backyard had been enclosed with a hurricane fence, and she saw a small henhouse at the rear of the property. A dozen or so chickens pecked at some grain that had been strewn on the ground, and an enormous red rooster sat atop a fence post, proudly surveying his domain.

"Chickens . . . Hm-m-m," Savannah said to herself. "Not a good sign for Master Trent."

No one came to the back door either when she knocked. *Double damn,* she thought.

"Francie," she called out. "Francie, it's Savannah Reid. Are you inside, honey? If you are, open up."

After another pounding on the door, and rapping on a couple of windows produced no response, Savannah had to admit she was licked. Either the girl had left the house, or she was inside and had no intention of showing her face.

The trip was a write-off.

The whining next door got even louder, and when Savannah turned around to look, she saw the source . . . and why he was upset.

A gorgeous animal stood on the other side of what was a wire fence farther back on the property, beyond the wooden planking. At first, she thought he was a purebred wolf, by his long, lean legs, big feet and lush fur. But as she walked closer to him, she saw that he had pale blue eyes and the markings of a husky.

"Well, hello, you handsome fella," Savannah told him as she stepped up to the fence. "Aren't you a beauty!"

The dog whimpered and shook his head, as though beckoning her to come over to his side of the fence.

"Yes, I would love to take you home with me," she said, "but I'm pretty sure you would have Cleopatra and Diamante for lunch. Or, at least you'd try, and you'd wind up with scratches all over that pretty long muzzle of yours."

She grimaced, looking at the mangled, half-chewed poultry carcass that someone had tied with pieces of rough twine around his neck. A sprinkling of white feathers littered the dog's yard. "Looks like you're already in trouble for trying to make lunch out of the neighbor's chicken."

Having been raised in the rural South, Savannah had heard of the practice of tying a dead bird around a dog's neck and allowing it to stay on him until it literally rotted off. A disgusting method, but supposedly an effective one for putting the animal off the idea of chickens. And certainly, this fellow looked as though he hated his situation.

"Maybe you should just stick with phoning the Colonel the next time you get a hankerin' for a drumstick, darlin'," she told him.

He mumbled something in wolf-dog that sounded like a pathetic denial.

"What's that?" she said, sticking her finger through the fence and stroking his moist black nose. "You say you didn't do it? You were framed? That's what all the bad guys say. Why should I believe you?"

The big eyes rolled, and he shook his head, fluffing out the magnificent ruff of fur around his neck where his gruesome burden was tied.

"Well, that's true. You've never lied to me before, but . . ."

Savannah stood there, thinking, wondering, evaluating her options. "Hang in there, handsome," she said. "I'll be right back."

And she was, a couple of minutes later with her Swiss Army knife in hand. "I'll tell you what," she said. "If you come back here to the gate . . . that's it . . . right back here, where I can reach you."

She leaned over the locked gate that connected the two yards. "Now don't bite me, okay?" Stretching as far as she could, she could almost reach the animal, but not quite.

"If you want me to help you, you'll have to stick those big clodhoppers of yours up here on the fence. That's a good boy . . . wolf . . . dog . . . or whatever you are."

He reared up and lifted his huge front feet onto the gate. She was shocked to see that he was nearly as tall as she was. Images from Jack London's stories and the Grimm brothers' fairy tales flashed through her mind.

"Hm-m-m . . . what big teeth you have, my dear," she told him. "Ah, but you're just a big baby, aren't you?"

Again, more eye rolling and whining.

"Okay, okay. Hold still." Reaching across the gate, she slid her knife blade beneath the twine and quickly sliced through it. She grabbed the end of the cut string and hauled the carcass over the gate to her side of the fence.

"But you can't tell anyone that I cut this off," she told him. "It'll just be our little secret. And if anybody asks, it fell off of you and right here into this yard, which, by the way, I was invited to come into by one of the house's occupants. Got that? I just found this foul fowl lyin' back here on this side of the gate."

Relieved of his albatross, the ancient mariner began to prance about, shaking himself, and grinning a big, toothy, wolfy grin.

"Feel better now?" she asked, as she leaned over and coaxed him back onto the gate so that she could pet him. Looking at the brass tag that dangled from his heavy leather collar, she said, "Nanook. That's your name, huh? Well, I've done you a favor, which means you owe me. If I ever find myself plagued by a kid in a red cloak or a trio of bothersome pigs, I'm gonna call on you, okay?"

The blue eyes looked into hers with a depth of intelligence and understanding that took her aback, and the quiet dignity of the creature touched her heart.

"You're welcome," she said softly. "It was my pleasure."

Moments later, as she was placing the dead chicken into a plastic bag she had dug out of her trunk, she heard Nanook pacing on the other side of the fence. At least he wasn't whining anymore.

But as she drove away, an ambulance siren sounded a few blocks away, and she laughed to hear her new friend answer with a comical parody of the siren's howl.

Now she had another memory for this neighborhood . . . the profound experience of looking into a wolf's eyes and, for a moment, touching a far more noble soul than her own.

Chapter
18

Like many California coast towns, San Carmelita had begun its life as a mission, established by Franciscan fathers who had traveled from San Diego to the San Francisco Bay Area, building churches and converting the Native Americans along the way . . . whether they wanted to be or not.

And the San Carmelita Mission stood—as it had since it was built by those new, reluctant converts in the late 1700s—on a hilltop, overlooking the town and beyond it, the ocean. The panoramic view became more magnificent with every hairpin turn of the road that zigzagged up the steep hill, giving a traveler the light-hearted feeling of truly being "above it all."

But Francie Gorton had no appreciation for the sweeping vista as she guided her brother's Charger up the hill toward the old mission. She was wondering why

Savannah Reid had changed their plans and asked someone to phone and switch the location.

"Behind the mission just after eleven," the caller had said. "And she won't have much time, so don't be late."

Francie had hoped that Savannah would keep their meeting confidential, but she seemed like a smart, nice lady, and if she had needed to change their meeting place and tell someone else about it . . . Francie would trust her judgment.

In a few minutes, she would be trusting her with a lot more. Her very life, in fact. But, remembering how kind and concerned the lady had been when they had talked there on the bench, overlooking the vineyards, Francie relaxed a bit.

Francie considered herself a good judge of character, and her instincts told her that Savannah Reid had a good heart. Someone had told Francie that she had been a cop for years, so if anyone would know how to handle this situation, she would.

Francie pulled the Charger into a parking lot that had been laid behind the mission for visitors, who were welcome to tour the place on weekends. In the seventh grade, her history teacher had brought the class here for a field trip. She recalled getting an A- on the report she had written about the visit, and Francie had been distressed. She wasn't accustomed to getting an A-, and she resented the reason the teacher gave for marking her down—her statement that she had felt the place was haunted.

But she had.

Francie had always been sensitive about certain things, feeling things that no one else was aware of. And she had been most aware of an uneasiness about the old place. Within those thick, adobe walls, she sensed them

. . . the spirits of the men, women, and children who had died of disease and abuse, while being forced to build those walls and worship a god who was a stranger to them.

Local legend said that there were literally hundreds of the Chumash tribe buried on the property in mass graves. But Francie didn't feel them in the ground. She felt them in those thick, white, adobe walls.

As she got out of the car and walked toward the mission, Francie wished that Savannah had chosen anywhere, anywhere at all, other than this place to meet. It was private, to be sure; no one was in sight, and hers was the only car in the parking lot. Nobody would overhear their conversation.

At least, no one who had been alive for the past two hundred years.

A breeze swept up the hill, a hot wind that whipped sand into her eyes, making them tear. She could smell the wild scents of the sage and margaritas blooming on the hills around her, their aromas rich in the heat of the midday sun. A mockingbird sang somewhere, repeating his song several times, then changing his tune, and a pair of doves cooed to each other in the nearby brush. Francie liked birds. She liked chickens. But it made her sad to think of her chickens right now.

She glanced at her watch. It was only a few minutes past eleven, so it wasn't surprising that Savannah hadn't arrived yet. But Francie was sure she would soon. Savannah seemed like a punctual person, and she had sounded eager to meet with her.

Thank goodness she had Savannah. She wasn't sure what step to take next, but Savannah would direct her. Savannah would protect her. For the first time since Barbie had told her that ugly secret, Francie felt safe.

But the feeling was short-lived. With every step she took closer to the mission, she found it more and more difficult to breathe. At first she thought it was the dust blowing around her, irritating her asthma. Then she decided it was the heat. The sun beat down on her, heating her dark hair until it felt like it was burning the top of her head.

And the air was thicker, harder to pull in and out of her lungs.

The wind caught the bell in the tower and caused it to chime, once, twice, three times. "For whom the bells tolls," she whispered. "It tolls for me."

Then she shook her head, trying to reorient herself to reality. This was no time to let her imagination take over. She needed to stay calm and grounded, and not think about the restless spirits within the adobe walls.

"Francie."

She heard it. She was sure she heard it . . . coming from the mission. Someone was calling her. The spirits, they were—

"No," she told herself. "It's Savannah. She *is* here. I don't know where her car is, but she got here before me."

"Francie."

There it was again, louder than before. It was coming from the side of the mission, from a stairwell that led down into some sort of dark cellar beneath the building. She recalled the guide taking her and the other students down there. It had been dark and damp, spooky and gloomy, and she hoped that wasn't where Savannah was waiting.

"Francie."

"Yes? I'm here. Where are you?"

She walked to the side of the building and stood,

squinting up at the whitewashed walls that were so bright in the sunlight that just looking at them caused spots to form in front of her eyes.

Feeling a bit dizzy, she walked to the top of the narrow stone staircase. About fifteen steps down was a small landing, where the steps turned and proceeded down to the cellar. She really didn't want to go there. If Savannah was in the cellar, she should come up here into the sunshine. Why stay down in the dark?

"Savannah? Is that you? Are you in the cellar?" she called. "If you are, please come out. I don't want to come down there. Savannah?"

Standing on the top step, she strained to hear any sound from below, but all was silent.

A seagull screeched overhead, frightening her. She jumped and leaned one hand against the wall to regain her balance. Leaning forward, she peered into the darkness below, and called, "Savannah, please answer me. I'm up here. Come out. Okay?"

She felt it again . . . just as she had on the field trip . . . that uneasy conviction that she wasn't alone. Something, someone was there with her. She felt their grief, their rage, their—

A blinding white light, a lightning bolt of pain flashed through her head, obliterating every other sensation.

She was flying. Falling forward into the darkness.

She hit hard. And she heard, rather than felt, some of her bones break.

Lying on the cold stone, she was dimly aware of someone standing over her.

"Are you dead?" she heard a voice ask. "Well . . ." The nudge of a foot in her broken ribs. ". . . are you?"

"No," she whispered. "I don't think so."

"I don't think so either. You're not making this easy, you know."

She felt hands reach beneath her . . . lift . . . and shove.

Over and over she tumbled, farther down into the musty darkness. She landed even harder than before.

"Are you dying?" asked a voice, but it wasn't the hateful, angry voice on the stairs. This was a soft, gentle voice . . . maybe that of a Chumash Indian child . . . or a saint . . . or an angel.

"Yes," she whispered. "I believe I am."

"Then, come with me."

"Where?"

"With me. You're one of us now."

Francie felt a hand slip into hers . . . and tug. "But who are you?" she asked.

"You know."

After a few minutes, there were footfalls on the stone stairs, going up, out of the darkness and into the sunlight. Hurried steps, the steps of the living, not the dead.

The dead remained behind with all the others who had died violently, unjustly, within the thick, adobe walls of Mission de San Carmelita.

With her black garbage bag in her hand and a grim smile on her face, Savannah walked up the sidewalk to a building that held hardly any good memories for her at all. It was the medical examiner's complex—a drab blue-gray cement-block structure that would never be confused with anything more cheerful, like a discotheque or even a funeral parlor.

Savannah had spent some of her worst moments as a

cop inside that building, bringing people to identify the physical remains of their loved ones. Another part of the job she had hated and didn't miss.

This time the victim was a dead chicken, and as much compassion as she had for barnyard poultry, it wasn't as bad.

Inside, sitting at the reception desk with his finger in his nose was the repulsive Officer Kenny Bates, another reason why Savannah avoided this place like a bad case of PMS.

"Savannah, baby! It's about time you dropped in to see me!" he exclaimed as she walked through the door.

"Drop dead, Bates."

He grinned as though she had just propositioned him. Judging from the peanut butter between his teeth and the white bread guck stuck to his gums, she assumed he had just finished his lunch. "You miss me, don't you, baby? Been havin' hot dreams about me?"

"I assure you, Bates, I don't. I might miss an infected hangnail, an abscessed tooth, an enormous pimple on my chin . . . but I don't miss you."

She walked up to the desk, grabbed the sign-in clipboard, and scrawled her name across it. Not wanting the police department brass to know she was there, she usually signed a fictitious name. This time it was "Minnie Mouse." Nobody, especially the worthless Officer Kenny Bates, actually checked.

"Give me a call sometime, honey," he said as she walked away, "and I'll take you out. Wednesday is ladies' night at Hooter Hollow. You can drink all you want for free, and we'll watch the strippers. They can . . . ah, load my gun, and then we can go to my place and I'll let you pull my trigger, if you know what I mean. What'dya say?"

"I say that you are a wart on the buttocks of humanity, Bates."

"But you like me."

"I despise you."

"You want me."

"I loathe you. All women do, Bates. Haven't you noticed that even nice ladies spit on you when you walk by?"

"They don't spit on me. Nobody spits on me."

"Check out the back of your jacket sometime."

She chuckled as she walked down the hall, knowing that at that very moment, he would be twisting his spine out of alignment trying to see behind him. What a moron.

Ahead, at the bend of the hall, was a pair of double stainless-steel doors. Dr. Liu's autopsy suite. The M.E.'s office was around the corner to the right, but she was seldom there. Jennifer spent most of her time in the field or performing her examinations.

Savannah swung the door open a crack and peeked in. Dr. Liu was standing at a steel table, scalpel in hand, wearing surgical gloves, greens, cap, and disposable paper booties over her sneakers. Her long, black hair was tied with a brilliant pink-and-purple silk scarf.

A corpse was on the table, its chest open, major organs removed. Dr. Liu had Barbara Matthews's heart on a scale and was dictating the numbers into a microphone that was suspended over the table.

When she turned and saw Savannah, she tapped a pedal beneath the table with the toe of her shoe, turning off the microphone.

"Hey, lady!" she said, "Did you bring me some chocolate goodies?"

Savannah laughed. "No, sorry." She held up the black plastic bag. "This definitely isn't a delicacy."

"I thought you were stopping by to get the results of the Matthews examination."

"Well . . . since I'm here, I'd be very interested in anything you have."

She peeled off her gloves and tossed them into a biohazard waste can. "First, let me see what you have there."

Savannah handed her the bag. "Actually, for the record, it's Dirk—not me—dropping this off . . . in an evidence bag."

She reached out and took it, giving Savannah a suspicious look. "And does Dirk know that he's dropping this off to me?"

"He will."

"Okay."

She glanced into the bag and made a face. "What is this mess?"

"I suspect it's the rest of the chicken. Would you take a quick look at it . . . when you get a chance, of course . . . and let me know if it died from natural causes?"

"And what would you consider a natural way for a chicken to croak?"

"If a wolf bit it."

"I see. And where did you find this mangled, half-rotten, disgusting . . . treasure?"

"Tied to a wolf's neck with a piece of twine."

Jennifer stared at her for a long moment, then shook her head. "Okay, I won't ask. And I'll check to see if it's missing a gizzard. But you owe me so-o-o-o big for this one."

"Dirk will settle up with you."

"No way. His idea of payment is a Hershey's Kiss. And, while I like them, this dead chicken thing is a Godiva job."

"I hear you. What have you got on Barbie?"

Dr. Liu glanced at the table and a sadness crossed her face. "A perfectly healthy young woman who died a very unpleasant death."

"I'm sure falling off that cliff wasn't very pleasant."

"She was dead before she went over the edge. There's lividity along her left side. She was lying on it a while before the body was moved."

"Then what was the cause of death?"

"Her sinus cavities, esophagus, bronchial tubes and lungs were chemically burned. She inhaled something highly caustic."

"Like what?"

"I don't know yet. We'll have to wait for the lab results. But I'm sure it wasn't anything she was sniffing recreationally. If she had been physically able to escape that poison, she would have."

"You said before that you think she was bound."

"Yes, and I'm sure of it now. There was even a shred of tape still on one of her wrists. It looks like standard duct tape, but we'll run tests on it, too. I'll see if we can identify a brand for you, but I wouldn't bet on it. There wasn't much."

"Any hair or fibers?"

"Hairs were all hers. We have some dark fibers. I think they're carpet threads. Maybe from an automobile. I'll get that for you, too."

Savannah walked over to the table and looked down at the earthly remains of Barbara Matthews, Beauty Queen, and felt bad that she didn't feel worse.

Not only was the young woman dead, but so few

people seemed to be sorry. Everyone deserved to be grieved. Even unpopular, bratty girls like Barbie.

And, although Savannah couldn't summon an enormous amount of grief from her heart, she would do everything she could to supply justice for Barbara Matthews. Even unliked, ungrieved victims of murder deserved justice.

"Yes," Jennifer said as she walked up to stand next to Savannah by the table, "a perfectly healthy young woman. A perfectly healthy, pregnant young lady."

Savannah gave her a quick sideways glance. "Really?"

"Really. About eight weeks."

"Mm-m-m." She silently reaffirmed her promise. Now there were two victims who required justice, and that doubled her burden of responsibility.

Chapter
19

When Savannah returned to Villa Rosa that afternoon, she found the pageant activities centered,
once again, on the patio surrounding the swimming
pool. At one end of the area, on a stage decorated with
gold-and-silver-mylar balloons, the interview portion of
the pageant was being conducted.

On a set designed to look like a talk-show stage, the
young ladies were taking turns sitting in the guest's
chair, chatting with the pseudo-host, a very debonair-
looking Anthony Villa. But Savannah could tell that in
this case, looks were deceiving. Although he was playing
his role well, she got the distinct feeling Tony would
have much preferred to be walking in his vineyard.

She spotted Dirk at the edge of the crowd, showing
half a dozen snapshots to first one, then another, of the
girls. But as each one took a look, she shook her head,
then walked away. He had his "I'm Discouraged—I

Hate My Job" look on his face. Savannah wondered if
what she was going to tell him would cheer him up or
plunge him further down into the "I Hate the Whole
World—Life Ain't Worth Diddly" mode.

"Hey there, good-lookin'," she told him with her best
Mae West impression, one hand on her hip, the other
patting her hair. "If you're not getting anywhere with
those youngsters, show a *real* woman what you've got."

But he was in too lousy a mood even for Mae's double entendres. "I got squat, that's what I got." He wiped
the sweat off his forehead, and Savannah noticed that
he was flushed all the way up to the receding hairline
he denied he had.

"Why don't you come over here and sit in the shade
a spell," she told him. "Take a load off and all that."

She led him over to an umbrella-covered table and
sat him down. Dirk wasn't able to go all day long at
breakneck speed the way he had when she'd first met
him. The old fella was getting some mileage on him.
While she, on the other hand, felt fresh out of the show-
room.

She sat down on the chair beside him and groaned
with relief as she propped her feet in the crook of the
table legs. Okay, so her odometer had rolled over a few
times, too. They were still an awesome twosome . . . at
least in her estimation.

"Whose picture are you showing there?" she asked.

He fanned the photos out on the table like a Las
Vegas card dealer and pointed to the one in the middle,
a gangly, teenage boy with stringy long hair and a sullen
expression that looked more like a mug shot than the
school picture that it was. "That's Trent, the boyfriend,"
he told her. "I was hoping that maybe somebody saw

him come back later in the evening, after Ryan pitched him off the property."

"Any luck?"

"Nope. Nobody saw *nada*. They were all at that dinner thing."

"Have you found him yet?"

"No. But once I got the word from Dr. Jennifer this afternoon that it was murder for sure, I put an APB out on him and his dark blue Charger. By the way, she says you dropped something off to her and told her it was from me."

"Did she tell you what it was?"

"Something stupid that didn't make sense. She said to tell you not to bring her any more cowardly poultry. What the hell does that mean?"

Savannah chuckled and shook her head. "Our Dr. Liu has a weird sense of humor. I suspect that's her way of telling me that she did the examination and it was, indeed, a gutless chicken. I had a feeling it would be."

Dirk scowled. "Do you wanna fill me in here, or do I have to just wonder what you whacko broads are talking about?"

Briefly, she told him about her new canine friend, his strange burden, and how she had relieved him of it.

With every word, Dirk brightened. "All right!" he said. "And we've got the kid's fingerprints on the windowsill and the flower dish."

"Where did you get his prints?"

"He was in Juvie once for malicious mischief and another time for smacking a kid in the head with a skateboard."

Savannah studied the face in the picture, the eyes, looking for something that would tell her whether or not this young person was capable of murder. But she seldom saw anything like that in any suspect's eyes. It was amazing what people could hide.

"I suppose Dr. Liu told you that Barbie was pregnant."

"Yeah, she mentioned it. Do you suppose this guy's the dad?"

"When you find him, you can ask him."

Dirk growled. "When I find him . . . I'm gonna have a who-o-ole bunch of questions for him."

"Hey, look," Savannah said, pointing to the opposite side of the pool. "It's Ryan and John."

The two walked over to their table, pulled up chairs, and sat down. Ryan took a stack of folded papers from his pocket and handed it to Dirk. "Here are the cell phone records you wanted," he told him.

"That was fast." Dirk unfolded the wad and glanced over the pages.

John smiled, causing the ends of his silver mustache to curl upward. "Life is much simpler, old chap, when you no longer have to concern yourselves with such frivolities as court orders. Friends in high places work much more quickly than the justice system."

"Is that Barbie Matthews's record?" Savannah asked, trying to see over Dirk's shoulder.

"It sure is," Ryan replied. "She must have had her phone surgically attached to her ear. I've never seen such a phone bill."

"Including the day she died," Dirk said, studying the columns of numbers before him. "Calls coming in, calls going out. It's gonna take me a month just to run down these numbers."

"Is the call there from her mom?" Savannah asked.

"Mrs. Matthews said she called Barbie to ask why she hadn't shown up for dinner."

"It doesn't give you the numbers of the incoming calls, just the times," Dirk said. "This one at 7:21 P.M. is the last one that came in. I'll bet you she was on her way out to the parking lot then. She probably got nabbed right where we found her phone."

"Yeah," Savannah added. "They grabbed her, she dropped her phone, and when they pulled out, they ran over it and crunched it."

Ryan leaned over and pointed to the bottom of the last page. "I think that's the one you'd be most interested in. The last one she called . . . at 7:05 P.M."

Dirk nodded thoughtfully. "True. She could've been setting up a meeting, agreeing to meet somebody there in the lot. We'll have to check with the phone company and find out whose number that is."

"Or . . . you could just ask us," John said.

Dirk half grinned, half grimaced. Savannah chuckled to herself. She knew he was torn between being pleased to have information so close at hand and irked that the other two guys had something that he needed.

"Well?"

That was as gracious as Dirk ever got under such circumstances.

"It's a pay phone."

"Great. That's just friggin' peachy." Dirk shook his head, disgusted, sliding into the old "My Job Sucks" mode. "Where?"

Ryan smiled. "In that little alcove right between the men's and women's rest rooms behind the potted palms."

"Here?"

"That's right, my friend. Barbara Matthews was calling the public phone right here in Villa Rosa, minutes before somebody killed her. And, now that we've done the hard part . . . all you have to do is figure out who was on the other end and . . . crime solved."

Dirk looked at Savannah. She grinned, and said, "Easy got as a wet foot on a rainy April morn."

He just grunted.

Leaving the men to look over telephone bills and formulate the psychological profile on the sort of person who would give a girl a bouquet of flowers and chicken entrails on the same night, Savannah made her way over to the stage where the interviews were taking place.

She looked around for Atlanta, hoping to catch hers, then realized that the entire process had ended.

But the trip over wasn't a total waste of time. Hearing one girl address another as Desiree, Savannah decided to get acquainted.

Up close and in person the girl was very simply stunning. Savannah wasn't surprised that she had won numerous beauty contents. With her golden blond hair, perfect skin, and classic features, she reminded Savannah of a young Grace Kelly.

Savannah tried to reconcile that pretty face with the cruel, sarcastic voice she had heard on the other side of the bathroom wall. It was a difficult fit.

"Hello," Savannah said. "I'm looking for Atlanta Reid. Would you have any idea where she is?"

The blue eyes that met hers were a rare and lovely shade of teal, the color of the Pacific on a crisp October morning. But somehow, they seemed devoid of life, eerily empty.

"Who? The hick with the drawl?" came the reply.

Savannah gave her a tight smile. "No . . . ," she said carefully, "the pretty one with the Southern accent . . . the one who looks a bit like me—seeing as how we're sisters and all."

Desiree didn't even bother to pretend that she was embarrassed for her faux pas. "Nope, haven't seen her."

The teenager gave Savannah one of those quick, evaluating, glance-overs that some females give to other women, females who consider all others to be competition in some sort of ridiculous game that exists only in their own limited minds.

When the girl lifted her nose two notches, turned her back on Savannah, and prissed away, Savannah watched her go, wondering if she had any idea what a sad cliché she was.

Any woman who only saw other females as competitors would never know the joys of sisterhood, of having another woman standing by her when she really needed her, offering that unique maternal love and support that only a woman could give.

And that deprivation alone was just punishment for her egotism.

Another girl, whom Savannah didn't recognize, stepped up to her. "Hi, I'm Lynette. I overheard you asking about your sister, Atlanta. She said she was going to her room to practice her guitar for a while."

"Thank you very much," Savannah told her.

"No problem. I like Atlanta; she's cool. She did really good on her interview."

"When I see her, I'll tell that you said so. Thanks again."

As Savannah walked away, heading back to their room, she thought of what Marion Lippincott had said about most of the girls being gems. She could see that was true.

Too bad the rotten ones seemed to be getting the most attention.

As soon as Savannah started down the hallway, before she even reached their door, she could hear a clear, sweet voice singing an old gospel tune that she hadn't heard for at least fifteen years.

The last time she had heard that song, Granny Reid had been singing it, and she had been rocking Atlanta to sleep in the old bench swing that hung from chains on the front porch. Gran's only accompaniment had been the creaking of those rusty chains as she swung back and forth and fanned herself and the baby on that sultry summer night.

But Atlanta was playing along on her guitar, simple but lovely chords that provided a harmony for her solo.

Savannah stood outside the door, enjoying the song until it ended. Reluctant to break the spell, she unlocked the door and slowly, quietly, pushed it open.

"Where were you?" Little Sister demanded, pissed again. "You missed my interview, and I did good, too. I looked all over for you, and you weren't there!"

Well, so much for sultry summer nights and all that sentimental crapola. The kid's lip was stuck out again.

"I'm sorry. The guys and I were comparing notes on this case, and by the time I got over there the interviews were finished. But I heard you did very well."

"Yeah, sure."

"No, it's true. This nice girl named Lynette said so. And she said you were cool, too. So, there."

Savannah stuck out her tongue at her, and they both giggled.

"I heard you singing. It sounded great. I didn't realize you've gotten so good."

"There's a lot of things you don't know about me. You aren't the only one in the family who can do stuff, you know."

"Of course, I know that. You're a unique person, Atlanta, with talents all your own. I've always known that, and I'm very proud of you."

Atlanta glanced away and laid the guitar on the bed beside her. "So, how is the case going? Have you guys figured out who killed Barbie yet?"

"No, not yet. We just found out for sure this afternoon that she was murdered. But we're working on it."

Savannah sat down on the other bed, took her loafers off, and wriggled her toes. "I think that Barbie was killed by someone who specifically wanted *her* dead. But I don't want you and the rest of the girls to let your guard down. Remember what I said about always being in groups and keeping the door locked at all times."

Atlanta gave her an exasperated look. "Can't you stop being a big sister even for minute?"

"A whole minute? That's a lot to ask. I've been a big sister since I can remember."

Atlanta reached down and trailed her fingers over the guitar's strings and mumbled something under her breath.

"I didn't quite catch that," Savannah said.

"That's probably a good thing," Atlanta replied. "What did you come up here for anyway? To check and see if the door was locked?"

Savannah drew a deep breath, knowing she was swimming into shark-infested waters. "Mrs. Lippincott and Catherine Villa have asked some counselors from Mental Health Services to drop by this afternoon and talk to anyone who might be upset about this thing with Barbie and—"

"I'm not that upset."

"I know. You're handling it very well. But I was thinking that maybe you and I could speak to one of the counselors about, you know, what I found under the bathroom sink."

The look on Atlanta's face was even worse than Savannah had expected. Savannah had seen the same expression on the mugs of guys who had just been zapped with a stun-gun.

"Are you kidding?! You've *got* to be kidding! Like I'm going to discuss something like that with a complete stranger! Forget about it. It ain't happening."

"'Lanta, I'm worried about you. Very worried. So, I'm going to speak to a counselor about you."

"Not without me there, you aren't. You're not going to talk about me behind my back."

Savannah slipped her shoes back on, stood, and walked to the door. "I'm so glad you changed your mind. I'll make the appointment for later this afternoon."

She quickly stepped out of the room and closed the door behind her. It was only a couple of seconds until she heard something hit the other side. *Mmm*, she thought, *too small to be a guitar . . . must have been a hairbrush or sneaker.*

It was definitely time to make tracks in the opposite direction.

* * *

A few minutes later, she was standing at the pay phone near the rest rooms downstairs, her calling card in her hand. After punching in the required 7,053 numbers she heard a soft voice on the other end.

"Hi, Gran," she said. "Have you got a minute for me?"

"For you, my darlin', I have two. And from the tone of your voice, I'd say you might need three or four."

Savannah glanced around, making sure she was alone, and then she leaned back against the wall, sighed, and began, "It's 'Lanta, Gran. I'm worried about her. I noticed that she's lost a lot of weight since I saw her last, and then I found these . . ."

Chapter
20

Savannah had been told that Angela Herriot, one of the counselors from Mental Health Services, was in the courtyard. So she was there, looking for her, when her purse buzzed. It was Dr. Liu, calling with her latest lab results.

"The fibers *are* from an automobile carpet," Jennifer said, "just as I thought. Sorry, I can't tell you the year and model of the car, but the carpet is black . . . and new. This type of nylon blend has only been in commercial use for the past two years."

"Okay, black and new. That should help."

"And the shampoo did have drain cleaner in it. A standard brand available in any grocery store. There were several prints on the bottle that were the victim's and two that matched the sample Dirk sent over."

"Dirk sent you a print?"

"Yes, a thumbprint from a driver's license . . . just a minute and I'll tell you the name. . . ."

Savannah heard her shuffling papers. She adored Dr. Jen, such a fount of knowledge. What would they do without her?

"Desiree Porter."

Savannah grinned. "That's what I was hoping to hear."

"Then you'll probably be delighted to hear that the evening gown was cut."

"Cut? Not just torn?"

"Nope. Scissors were definitely used. It had to be deliberate."

"Ah, ha! You're right; I'm delighted. Thank you, Sweet Stuff. I'm so-o-o grateful."

"Hey, that's *Doctor* Sweet Stuff to you!"

"Forgive me, oh Lettered One."

"You don't have to kiss up. Just bring chocolate. I'm having a vicious attack of PMS."

"Then I'll bring potato chips, too."

As Savannah replaced the phone in her purse, she saw a vision of color walking across the courtyard, a handsome black woman of generous proportions, dressed in a colorful caftan and head wrap. The garment billowed around her as she moved among the potted palms and patio furniture.

Savannah had dealt with Angela Herriot several times before and was impressed with her: a no-nonsense, down-to-earth shrink who told it like it was. And Savannah knew she was particularly adept at dealing with young people, having served a three-year sentence as a middle-school counselor.

She took off after her, feeling better already. With

Dr. Liu's latest report and professional help within reach for Atlanta, things were definitely looking up.

Things were in the crapper.

Although Atlanta was sitting across the room, officially attending the meeting that Savannah had arranged between them and Angela Herriot, she hadn't spoken a single word. So, it had been a fairly tense and unproductive thirty-one minutes thus far.

Thirty-two.

Savannah watched the digital clock on Catherine Villa's desk change. She was sure that if it had been a windup timepiece, she would have been able to hear it ticking.

Catherine had volunteered her office as a private place for Angela to council the traumatized girls. With its picture window that looked directly into the winery's massive fermentation room and its old gentleman's club décor, the room was cozy enough.

But, so far, Savannah was the only one who had set an appointment. The girls had other, more important, things on their minds; the talent show and final judging were that evening.

So, they had Angela all to themselves.

The psychologist had pulled Catherine's chair out from behind her desk and dragged it around so that she could sit facing both sisters. She sat with one ankle propped on the opposite knee, the full skirt of her caftan flowing about her. Around her neck and dripping from her earlobes were ornate, handmade beads of the same brilliant reds, greens, and oranges as her dress and turban. Eight of her ten fingers were adorned with at least one ring; some had two or three. If nothing else, Angela was fun to look at.

"So, if you don't want to talk, Atlanta, why are we here?" she asked. There was nothing subtle—in dress or demeanor—about Angela Herriot.

Finally, the statue spoke. "I don't know why *she's* here." She jabbed a thumb in Savannah's direction. "I'm here so that she doesn't talk trash about me behind my back."

"And what sort of trash do you think she's going to say about you?" Angela asked.

Atlanta hummed and hawed for a moment, then shrugged. "I don't know. She's just making a big deal outta some stuff that's not a big deal. She's always done that, and I hate it."

"Making a big deal out of something . . . ," Angela thought for a moment. "Do you mean the laxatives that you've been taking to lose weight?"

Atlanta shot Savannah a hateful look. "Yes. She was poking around in *my* stuff and then she started asking questions that were very personal."

"And why do you suppose she did that?"

"Because she's a nosy, controlling busybody who doesn't trust me to run my own life."

Savannah bit her tongue and listened while Angela continued. "Do you suppose your sister might have had any other reason for confronting you the way she did, for insisting that you talk to a professional?"

Atlanta shuffled her feet and stared down at the ornate pattern of the Oriental rug on the floor. "I guess she's worried. But she doesn't need to be."

"Are you using laxatives to lose weight, Atlanta?"

Atlanta gazed out the window for a long time before giving a slight nod.

"Do you induce vomiting?"

"No. I hate to puke."

Angela smiled. "I'm glad to hear that. Most of us do. And do you binge eat?"

"Sometimes . . . if I've been dieting for a long time really strict, I get hungry and I pig out, like a whole pint of ice cream and half a package of cookies."

Savannah gulped, thinking of her own extravagances. Bingeing? Wasn't a pint of Chunky Monkey and a package of Oreos just your run-of-the-mill dessert? An entire peanut butter chocolate-dipped cheesecake along with the Chunky Monkey, the Oreos, and a dozen Winchell's donuts . . . now *that* would be a binge.

Not that she had actually ever done that herself, of course.

"Do you weigh yourself every day, Atlanta?" Angela asked.

She nodded.

"And if your weight is down, do you feel good about it all day? And if it's up, it bums you out?"

Another yes.

"Have you ever fasted to lose weight?"

"Yeah."

"And do you think about your weight a lot . . . like off and on all day?"

"Yeah, it's important to me to look good."

Angela fingered the beads of her earring thoughtfully. "And do you think you look good? Are you happy with the way you look?"

"I'm still heavy in my hips and right here." She grabbed half an inch of skin on her bare midriff and pinched it distastefully. "No matter how much I diet, I can't get rid of that."

"Do you exercise a lot?"

"I should do a lot more."

Angela said nothing for a long, tense few moments as she studied Atlanta, who sat, squirming, in her chair.

Finally, Angela spoke. "I want to thank you for talking to me about this, Atlanta," she said. "I know it wasn't easy for you. Your sister did the right thing, asking you to speak to a professional about your problem."

"I don't *have* a problem. That's what I'm trying to tell you."

"You do have a problem, potentially a very serious, possibly fatal eating disorder."

"No way! I've read the lists of symptoms on the Internet, and I'm not bulimic or anorexic. I'm not!"

"I didn't say that you are either of those things. I said that you have an eating disorder. Millions of people do. Thousands die from theirs. If you don't get some help, you might be one of them."

"That's so lame. No way."

"Atlanta, you don't have to have *all* the symptoms on those lists. Even a few of the signs are reason enough for concern."

Angela turned to Savannah. "I'm going to give you some phone numbers of professionals in Atlanta's area who specialize in eating disorders. It's very important that she get help and that it be from someone who is experienced in this field."

"Thank you. I'll take care of it."

"No! I'm not going to see no shrink!" Atlanta began to cry. "I'm not crazy, and I'm not helpless. I don't want my big sister to do that; she's always taking care of me, and I *hate* that!"

"I don't believe you're crazy or helpless," Angela told her as she reached over and placed her hand on the girl's arm. "But these first few steps are very difficult for a person to take on her own, and finding a professional and setting up appointments are actions that loved ones can take for someone in your position. Let her do this for you, Atlanta. Savannah may be bossy sometimes, but I assure you that she loves you very much. Let her help."

Savannah rose from her chair, walked over to Atlanta, and knelt beside her. "Please, sweetie . . . trust me," she said. "I'll find someone who's good, someone you like and can relate to. The right person will make this situation better for you, not worse, I promise."

When Atlanta didn't answer, Savannah took her hands and folded them between her own. "Let me do this for you. Someday when I'm old and senile and can't remember where I left my dentures, I'll need you to make some calls and set up some appointments for me . . . okay? We'll take turns taking care of each other."

When Atlanta gave a small, curt nod, Savannah felt better.

But when Atlanta threw her arms around Savannah's neck, buried her face on her shoulder, and sobbed, Savannah found that her own tears were flowing as freely as her little sister's.

Good tears.

Soul-cleansing tears.

A few minutes later, when Savannah and Atlanta came out of the office, bidding Angela a grateful good-bye, Dirk came rushing up to them, an excited look on his face.

"I've been looking for you all over the place," he told Savannah. "I . . ."

He looked from Savannah to Atlanta and back. Both were wiping their eyes and noses with tissues and sniffing.

"I'm sorry," he said. "Is everything all . . . are you gals all . . . are you okay?"

"We're fine," Savannah said, her arm around Atlanta's shoulders. "What's up, doc?"

"We've got the Gorton kid."

"Francie?" Atlanta asked.

"No, her brother, Trent."

"Where did you find him?" Savannah said.

"In the arcade at the mall. Figures, huh?" He chuckled. "In the old days, when we were looking for a local punk, we checked out the pool halls. Now it's the mall arcade . . . where all the mommies send their little kids when they're shopping. Scary, huh?"

"Very." Savannah tucked the tissue into her pocket. "So what's next?"

"A lineup. I've got Mrs. Lippincott coming down to the station in an hour to see if he's the one who dropped off those flowers. Wanna come and watch?"

Savannah turned to Atlanta.

Atlanta blew her nose soundly and gave Savannah a weak smile. "I'm all right. I've gotta practice my guitar anyway, get ready for the talent competition tonight. You go ahead."

"Okay," Savannah said, "but—"

"I know . . . I know. Keep the door locked! Ugh!"

Chapter
21

"Marion Lippincott must love you," Savannah said, "you pulling her away on the last day . . . the big day . . . of her pageant."

"Actually, she hates me," Dirk replied. "In fact, she called me a few names that I'm pretty sure aren't supposed to be uttered at an All-American function like a beauty contest. But she don't have to like me. She just has to show for the lineup."

With Dirk at the wheel, the battered old Skylark rounded the curves, heading out of wine country and entering lemon-grove country. In another ten minutes they would be "in town," not that San Carmelita was a metropolis by anyone's definition.

Savannah was enjoying just sitting in the passenger's seat, kicking back, savoring the view and a few responsibility-free minutes. And she had to admit she was actually glad to have some downtime with Dirk. Although she usually considered him a nuisance, he was a habit. And even an aggravation, if it was habitual, could be dear to the heart.

"If Lippincott picks the Gorton boy out of the lineup, are you gonna hold him?" she asked.

"I haven't decided yet. But if she does ID him, it'll give me a little more torque to squeeze him with."

"So, you haven't questioned him yet?'

"Nope. But I'm gonna right after the lineup. Wanna watch?"

"Are you gonna use the rack and the pendulum?"

"Naw . . . they're at the repair shop. But I got this cool new contraption called an Iron Maiden. It's this casket sorta thing with spikes inside. You stick the inter-viewee in it and slam the door closed."

"A la Edgar Allan Poe and Vincent Price?"

"Exactly."

"Cool. I definitely wanna watch."

"What is this, man? I been treated with nothin' but disrespect all day long, man. You know what I'm sayin', man?"

Trent Gorton walked with that cocky bee-bop stride that made Savannah wish she had an enormous fly-swatter so that she could whack him across the butt with it. As she watched Dirk lead him down the hall from the temporary lockup to the room where they would do the lineup, she wondered how this scraggly, moronic gangster could be from the same gene pool as his lovely, intelligent, sensitive sister.

"What's up?" he asked for the tenth time in three minutes. "Where we goin'? Whatcha'll doin' with me

here? I didn't do nothin' and nobody's told me nothin'."

"You're gonna stand in a lineup, pal," Dirk told him.
"We've got the lady who saw you delivering that batch of
flowers to Barbara Matthews the night you killed her."

"I didn't kill nobody. I was through with her, man.
We was broke up, and I'm on to another old lady. You
know what I mean, man?"

"For right now, let's just see if we can get a positive
ID. Then we'll take it from there."

"Can I leave, man? I mean, if you get that positive ID
you want, can I leave?"

Dirk stopped, spun him around, and began to re-
move his handcuffs. "We'll see. One thing at a time, my
friend. I'm gonna take these cuffs off for the moment,
'cause we don't want you to be only one standin' there
wearin' bracelets. But you try to pull somethin', and I'll
be all over you . . . you know what I mean, *man?*"

"I hear ya."

"Good."

At that moment, Savannah heard a door open to the
right and, to her dismay, Marion Lippincott walked
through it. There was nothing quite like lack of organi-
zation to spoil a perfectly good lineup.

"Shit," Dirk muttered. "What's she doin' back here?
. . . ruins everything."

Trent looked around him, a definite haziness in his
eyes that spoke of too many nights spent partying and
not enough studying. "What?" he said, equally concerned. He spotted Marion Lippincott. "Oh, all you
need is a positive ID, right?" he asked Dirk.

Dirk froze. He gave Savannah a quick, I-Can't-
Believe-It glance, and said. "Ye-e-e-es."

"Okay, then . . . I recognize her," Trent said, happy to comply if it meant this ordeal might be over. "That old gal there . . . she's the one who was at that wine place when I dropped off the flowers. I recognize her. Okay?"

Dirk and Savannah stared at each other, then back at Trent.

"Well, what're you waitin' for?" Having performed his civic duty, Trent was getting antsy. "You got your positive ID. Now I'm outta here, right?"

Dirk shook his head, still incredulous. "Boy, you gotta lay off sniffin' that paint or whatever you're doin'. You ain't got much left upstairs."

Dirk replaced the cuffs, then walked over to Marion Lippincott who looked equally impatient. "I believe you can go back to your pageant now, Mrs. Lippincott. Thanks to Mr. Gorton, we've got all we need here."

Savannah stood behind the glass and watched Trent Gorton squirm in what was called the "sweat tank," but politely known to the public as the interrogation room. And Dirk was one of the best when it came to making a suspect sweat.

"So, why did you kill her? Was it because she broke up with you?" Dirk paced up and down behind the kid's chair, the action designed to raise his anxiety level as much as to work off Dirk's nervous energy.

"She didn't break up with me; I broke up with her. I've done told you that."

Dirk laughed. "Oh, yeah, a gorgeous gal like that . . . a scumbucket like you just up and dumps her. I'm supposed to believe that, huh?"

Trent shrugged his skinny shoulders and toyed with the enormous skull ring on his middle finger. "You can believe it, or don't believe it. It don't matter to me what you believe, you know what I'm sayin', man? That's what happened, I swear it on my mama's grave."

Dirk reached over and gave him swat on the back of the head. "Your mama ain't dead, peabrain, so you swearin' on her grave don't mean dick. Now you better start telling me the truth or I'm gonna start showin' you some serious disrespect. We found your fingerprints on the flowerpot, so we know you were at Villa Rosa that night. And even better, we've got more of your prints on the windowsill. You left them there when you leaned in and poured the chicken blood on the bed."

"Okay, okay! So I did the chicken thing. I'll admit that. But I didn't kill Barbie. I didn't even see her there that night. I just did that business with the chicken to get back at her, and then I left. That's all I did."

"You didn't figure you'd knock off the mother of your baby to make your life a whole lot simpler?"

Savannah watched the kid carefully and saw genuine surprise dawn in his eyes. He hadn't known. Barbie hadn't told him.

"Barb was pregnant?" he asked. "She was gonna have a baby?"

"You didn't know that, huh?"

"No. She didn't say nothin' about it. But, come to think of it, maybe that's why she was actin' weird."

"Weird?"

"You know, man, wantin' to break up with me and all that."

"So, now *she's* the one who wanted to break it off with you? Make up your mind. Usually, a girl who's knocked up ain't the one callin' it off. Usually it's the guy who wants out. Whose kid do you figure it was?"

Trent jumped up from the seat, but Dirk pushed him

right back down. "If Barbie was pregnant, it was my kid," he said, slamming his fist on the table. "You understand me, man?"

"I think you're tellin' me that you were so special that she wasn't doin' nobody else but you. That's what you're sayin', right?"

"Right! That's exactly right. She didn't need nobody but Trent. I was more than enough for that bitch."

Dirk walked around the table and sat down across from him. "Tell me something, Trent. What color is the carpet in that Charger of yours?"

The kid's eyes narrowed. "Why do you want to know?"

"I'm planning to recarpet my Buick, and I thought I'd ask your decorating advice. You seem like such a discriminating kinda guy."

"It's black. But what's that got to do with anything?"

Dirk nodded thoughtfully. "I've heard your Charger is cherry; you rebuilt everything on it yourself."

"Everything but the paint job. My cousin did that."

"So, when did you put the new carpet in?"

"Last summer. Why?"

Dirk grinned. "Just askin'. I'm the sorta guy who's curious about a lot of things. Like I'm wondering right now, where is that Charger of yours? They say you weren't driving it when they picked you up at the mall today."

"That's right, my stupid sister took off with it, and we haven't seen her since. When she gets home, she's in big trouble with me. She knows better than to drive my wheels."

Listening on the other side of the mirror, Savannah felt a small chill of premonition. His sister took off with his car . . . and she hasn't been seen since?

That felt bad.

It felt really bad.

And Savannah had learned through painful experience, that when something felt that bad, it usually was. Sometimes it was even worse.

Half an hour later, Savannah and Dirk were getting into his Buick, intending to head back to Villa Rosa, when Dirk got a call.

Digging the phone out of his jacket pocket, he flipped it open. "Yeah?"

In the passenger's seat, Savannah grinned. Dirk wasted precious little energy on such frivolities as courtesy or diplomacy. Being bridled with a Southern upbringing which requires an exhausting degree of gentility, she vowed to be exactly like Dirk when she grew up someday. How deliciously liberating it would be.

"Okay," he said. Turning to Savannah, he said, "They found the Charger."

"Good, where is it?"

"Where is it?" he barked into the phone. "What's it doin' there?"

He listened again and scowled. "All right. I'm on my way."

As he refolded the phone and tossed it onto the dash, he sighed.

"What's up?" she asked, afraid of the answer.

"The car is at the old mission. It's sitting in the parking lot."

"All right. Anybody in it?"

He shook his head. "No, it's empty. The keys are still in the ignition."

"So, what's the matter?"

"Trent's kid sister is there, too."

"Francie? What's she doing at the old mission?"

It took Dirk a long time to answer. "Nothin'. Dammit, she ain't doin' nothin' at all."

When Dirk and Savannah pulled into the mission's parking lot, they saw the dark blue Charger, sitting empty, as they had been told it was. A patrol car was next to it, and inside the unit sat Officer Mike Farnon. On a routine round through the parking lot, he had spotted the Charger. And with the help of the mission curator, he had found Francie.

He looked shook-up. His door was open, and his feet were on the ground. He had his hands over his face, and he was rubbing his eyes.

Savannah felt sorry for him. She knew the gesture. She also knew that it wouldn't help. Whatever vision he was trying to wipe away would remain with him for the rest of his life. In this business, you saw sights that scarred your soul and made you old before your time.

Savannah figured she was about ninety-eight.

Dirk parked his car next to the cruiser, and when she crawled out of the Buick, she felt like someone had poured her body full of liquid cement.

That beautiful girl. Dead. Yes, she felt very, very old today.

"Where is she?" Dirk asked Mike.

He nodded toward the back of the mission. "Down those stairs."

"Where's the curator?" Savannah asked.

"That's her over there," Mike replied, pointing to an elderly woman who was kneeling at the edge of the parking lot. "The one puking into the weeds."

"Is she okay?" Savannah said.

"About as okay as I am." Mike shook his head and let

out a long, shuddering breath. "She got here right after I did. I asked her if she'd look around and she did. At first, we didn't think anybody was here, but then she went downstairs and . . . Sorry, but it kinda got to me, the kid being so young and all."

Dirk slapped him on the back. "Just sit here and get yourself together, Mike. We'll go down on our own."

Savannah was already on her way to the stairwell at the back of the building. Going down those steps was the last thing on earth she wanted to do. But she had to have answers, and they lay down there in the darkness.

The moment she began to descend the stairs, she felt the coolness of the old adobe structure surround her, sheltering her from the afternoon sun. Her eyes took a while to adjust to the darkness and when they did, she saw a sharp turn halfway down the narrow staircase.

It was when she reached that landing and turned to the right that she saw her. A pitiful, crumpled heap at the bottom of the stairs.

Savannah was only faintly aware that Dirk had caught up to her and was standing on the step above her.

"Shit," she heard him say, quietly . . . a lot of pain expressed in one word.

"Yeah," she replied. "Yeah."

"Here," he said, shoving a flashlight into her hand.

"Thanks."

"Watch where you're steppin'."

"Okay." Normally, she wouldn't have needed to be reminded about crime-scene protection. But at the moment, she wasn't thinking; she was feeling.

"Oh, sweetie," she said, the words catching in her throat as she hurried on down the steps and knelt beside the girl. As she reached out her hand to touch the body, she knew that Mike Farnon was right. Francie

Gorton was dead. But until Savannah actually touched her, she wouldn't allow herself to believe it.

Behind her, Dirk wasn't saying anything. He knew, too. But he asked anyway, and she understood why. Hope. Until you absolutely, positively knew for sure . . . there was always hope.

"She's gone," Savannah said. "No pulse, no breathing. No rigor yet. It hasn't been long." She reached down and stroked the long, glossy hair that spilled across the girl's face and onto the floor. "Poor baby, no wonder she stood me up. While I was there at her house, she was . . ."

Savannah felt Dirk's hand, big, warm and comforting on her shoulder. "Come on, Van. We'll call Dr. Liu. Why don't I walk you up and outta here."

The professional deep in Savannah's mind told her that they should be searching the floor and every inch of this stuffy, dark, spooky little room for evidence.

But a louder voice that was speaking from her heart told her, "To hell with evidence. What does it matter now? You can catch and execute a dozen killers for this, and this sweet, young girl will still be dead."

"I'm sorry, Francie," she said. "I told you I'd look out for you, and . . . I'm so sorry."

Dirk's hands were under her arms, lifting her. "That's enough. Let's go."

He pulled her to her feet and turned her back toward the stairs. On rubber legs she climbed the steps into the sunlight. As if she were a feeble, newly released hospital patient, he guided her to the Buick, opened the door, and seated her inside.

After getting her settled, he walked over to the cruiser and shared a few words with Mike Farnon. Then he returned to the car and got in.

He didn't say anything as they drove away, out of the parking lot and onto the highway, heading back toward Villa Rosa.

It was when they reached the citrus groves that Savannah lost it. The grief came crashing in on her, so intense that she began to shake all over. Her hands covering her face, she leaned forward in her seat and began to sob.

Immediately, Dirk pulled the Buick off the road and parked it between two rows of lemon trees, where he cut the engine.

He reached over the back of the seat and fumbled around in the rear floorboard.

"Here, Van," he said, shoving a handful of yellow Wendy's napkins at her. They smelled of ketchup and onions, but she took them anyway and continued to cry into them.

She felt his arms go around her, pulling her to him. Giving in to a rare and luxurious moment of complete neediness, she sagged against him and buried her face in his warm, solid chest.

"It's okay, honey," he said. "Go ahead and bawl your face off if you wanna. I won't tell nobody." He patted her head like she was a distressed golden retriever. Then he began to slowly run his fingers through her hair, from the nape of her neck and out. It was deliciously soothing.

"That's why I got you outta there right away," he said. "You looked like you were gonna start blubbering any minute."

"Th-th-thanks," she said, hiccuping.

"No sweat. It ain't nothin' you wouldn't do for me. Except, of course, I wouldn't actually be cryin', but you bein' a broad and all, you can do that sorta thing and—"

"Dirk . . ."

"Yeah?"

"You're ruining the moment. Just shut up and hug me."

"Oh . . . okay."

His arms tightened around her until she could hardly breathe. But she liked it. She felt that same, sweet, protected feeling that she had experienced as a kid when Gran would allow her to crawl into bed beside her in the middle of a big, scary lightning storm.

She felt safe. She felt loved.

"I liked that thing you were doing . . . you know . . . with my hair," she said, her face still against his chest.

He hesitated, then reached up, laced his fingers into her curls and combed them through. "You mean this?" His voice sounded husky, a little breathless.

"Yeah, just like that. Thanks."

"You're welcome, honey." He pressed his lips to her forehead and gave her a long, sweet kiss, then put another, quicker one, on her cheek. "Sh-h-h . . . be quiet now," he said. "You're ruinin' the moment."

Chapter

22

Savannah could feel the electricity in the air. It was the final night, talent contest, final judging, the awarding of the Miss Gold Coast crown, and the girls were almost hysterical with excitement.

But there wasn't enough energy in a nuclear power plant to recharge her depleted batteries. The only force driving her was sheer anger . . . channeled into determination to catch the son of a bitch that had turned a lovely girl into a heap of garbage at the bottom of a musty, old stairwell.

Not that she knew for sure that anyone was responsible for Francie's death. During Dr. Liu's initial examination, the only injuries she found were consistent with taking an accidental tumble down a flight of stone steps.

But Savannah knew she had been pushed. And she was going to find the person who did it and throw them off a cliff or out a window or whatever was handy at the time . . . if she didn't fall down dead in her tracks from sheer emotional exhaustion and sleep deprivation first.

The evening's festivities were being held, once again, in the tasting room. And Villa Rosa was living up to its name with multicolored bouquets of roses on every table, roses that had been cut from bushes on the property. The heavenly scent filled the room and spilled out into the gallery, even to the courtyard.

Teenage girls, wearing every sort of garb imaginable, were scurrying about. Ten minutes 'til talent-show time.

Standing in the doorway separating the tasting room and gallery, Savannah watched them and tried to guess what their talent might be. Some were obvious: the majorette with her baton, the one in the formal black gown carrying a flute, the cowgirl with a rope, another dressed in a tunic and tights, carrying a skull and reciting, "To be, or not to be . . ." under her breath.

She had left a tense Atlanta upstairs, strumming her guitar and making strange sounds that she called, "warming-up exercises." Savannah hoped that she would at least place somewhere in the top five. If she didn't, she was going to be difficult to get along with . . . even more difficult than usual. And if one of the Reid gals got to be cranky tonight and tomorrow, Savannah had already decided that she was the one. After the day she'd had, she deserved it.

On second thought . . . it had been a pretty rotten *week*. The whole month hadn't been that great.

But before she plunged headfirst into the deep end of the self-pity pool, she reminded herself of Francie's mother—her daughter in the morgue and her son in Juvenile Hall for malicious mischief, suspected of murder. No matter what was going on, somebody else always had it worse.

"Is it true?"

Savannah turned around to see Marion Lippincott, her perpetual notebook in her hand, her tortoiseshell glasses perched on the end of her nose, a worried look on her face.

"You mean about Francie?" Savannah asked.

"Yes. I just heard that—"

"It's true. But it may have been an accident."

Marion's eyes searched hers, and Savannah knew she was taking into account her tear-swollen lids and red nose that a generous dusting of powder hadn't remedied.

She also knew that the All-Seeing Mrs. Lippincott didn't believe it had been an accident either.

Marion glanced around, then took Savannah's arm. "Come with me," she said.

She led her out into the courtyard where they found a private spot beside the fountain, which was lit with pink floodlights in honor of the final night of competition.

"I wasn't going to mention this," Marion said, "because I didn't think it was important. But this morning, when I was at breakfast, I left my notebook on the table and walked away for a few minutes to attend to something. When I came back, it was open."

Savannah tried to think what value this information might be. But it wasn't readily apparent.

"So?"

"It was open to a particular page."

Marion moved closer to a lantern that hung from an ivy-entwined wrought-iron pole and held her notebook up to the light for Savannah to see.

She looked over the page which had a list of names with columns of numbers next to them. Other than recognizing some of the names as the contestants', it made no sense to her.

"I'm sorry. I don't see your point," she told her.

"This is a summary of the judges' tally sheets . . . so far, that is. It shows how they scored the girls in their evening gowns."

Savannah was tempted to sneak a peek at Atlanta's marks, but resisted. "Okay. And?"

"And, as of this morning, before she left, Francie was ahead. She was winning the Miss Gold Coast crown."

A lightbulb switched on in Savannah's tired brain. "I see. And whoever was looking at that page at breakfast, they would have known she was ahead."

"That's right. This was my first pageant with Francie, but she was a lovely, poised, intelligent girl, and they say she played the violin beautifully. She had an excellent shot at winning this one, or any other pageant she chose to enter."

"Hmm." Savannah stood, thinking, watching the fountain for a moment, as its water tumbled from one tier to the next, sparkling like myriad tiny pink sapphires in the rosy light.

She thought of the dark stairwell at the old mission.

"This morning, according to your book, who was in second place?" she asked.

"Take a guess," Marion Lippincott replied.

"Desiree Porter?"

"Desiree Porter."

Savannah was so proud that she was very simply about to bust. Rather than risk another bout of "You

Never Support Me in Anything I Do" with Atlanta, she had staked out a seat, front and center, for her sister's talent presentation. She had wanted to make sure that Atlanta couldn't miss her when she looked out over the audience.

But now that she was sitting there, looking up at a talented young woman who also just happened to be her sibling, Savannah was thrilled to her toes.

With all the confidence and talent of an experienced professional, Atlanta was belting out an energetic version of the old country classic "Silver Threads and Golden Needles," and her California audience was enthralled. Most were clapping and some were even singing along on the chorus. She was receiving a far more enthusiastic response than the flute player or the baton twirler.

Savannah watched, mentally recording every detail to relate to Gran later on the phone. She knew that it was a memory she would replay herself many times, just for the sheer joy of it. This picture was one of those that would hang in her own special "Atlanta Gallery" for the rest of her life.

When the song was finished and the applause roared through the tasting room, Savannah felt her eyes fill with tears. Again. For the third time that day.

It had to be a record for a non-PMS week.

And, as usual, she had no tissues.

Since Dirk wasn't around with a handful of fast-food-joint napkins, she decided to run to the ladies' room and get something to wipe away the sniffles. As soon as Atlanta exited the stage, bowing all the while, Savannah left her seat and made her way through the side door and into the hallway.

As she approached the rest rooms, she was surprised

to see Anthony Villa, who was coming out of the men's room.

Wasn't he supposed to be in there judging the competition? She hated to think he had missed that marvelous Reid performance.

He looked preoccupied, even worried, and didn't seem to notice her.

Just as he passed the pay phone on the wall, it rang. He jumped as though the thing had shot a string of bullets at him, and the color drained out of his face.

Savannah watched, fascinated, as he stood there, first reaching out to touch the receiver, then pulling his hand back—a man torn with indecision.

It's just a phone, she thought. *Pick it up for heaven's sake.*

But he didn't. He stood there, hand outstretched, fingers trembling, but he didn't.

Instead, he began to walk away, so fast that he nearly ran headlong into Savannah.

"Oh," he said. "Ms. Reid. I didn't know you were . . . I didn't see you and . . ."

The phone rang again. And again.

Savannah stared at Anthony Villa, watching as his anxiety seemed to grow by the second. "Are you going to answer that?" she asked.

He shook his head. "No, it's probably nothing. And I have to get in there for the judging."

"Okay. Then I'll answer it," she said. "It might be important."

Savannah strolled over to the telephone, feeling his eyes on her, feeling the tension radiate out of him in almost palpable waves.

She picked up the receiver. "Hello?" She listened for a moment, then said, "No, this isn't Henry's Pizza. I'm afraid you have the wrong number. This is a pay phone."

Hanging up, she turned to Anthony, who looked like he was going to melt into a big puddle right there on the floor. She had never seen anyone look so relieved.

What the hell had he been expecting? A call from the grave?

"I . . . I . . . really should get back now," he muttered.

"Yes," she said smoothly. "You really should, you being a judge and all."

For a few seconds their eyes locked, and Savannah knew.

She saw his guilt, she saw his fear, and she knew.

And Anthony Villa knew that she knew.

Turning on his heel, he hurried to the door and disappeared into the tasting room.

Savannah glanced back at the phone. "Well, I'll be damned," she whispered.

"Now let me get this straight: You want me to lock up a guy who may be our next state senator because you say he looked at a phone funny. That is what you're telling me, isn't it?" Dirk was staring at Savannah as if she were one queen of hearts short of royal flush.

"I know it sounds stupid," she said. "You had to have been there. Really. He looked like a ghost from the past was trying to reach through the phone and grab him around the throat. He was white, I mean, the guy turned blanc de blanc right there in front of me."

She and Dirk were standing, nose to nose, in the middle of the room that Barbie and Atlanta had shared. Dirk had been searching it yet another time when Savannah had marched in to give him her news.

He was less than impressed.

Considerably less.

"Well, I think I've already got the guy who did it," he said. "He's locked up right now in juvie, and it's going to take a heck of a lot more to convince me that he ain't the one than some nonsense about Villa lookin' at a phone."

"But that's the phone she called him on. We know from the records that she called that particular pay phone right before she went out to the parking lot and got nabbed."

Dirk shook his head. "We don't know that he was the one who answered that night. We don't even know if her making that phone call had anything to do with her getting killed. Besides, Villa's got phones at his house, in his office, probably in his car. Why would she call him on a pay phone?"

"Because she had a cell phone, and there's a record of every call she makes. And Anthony Villa is a married man."

"So, what are you saying? That little Miss Barbie and future senator were doing the grizzly-bear hump?"

"Well, he wouldn't be the first politician to screw up his life that way. Besides, he's a judge here at the pageant. She's been known to drop her knickers for judges before."

Dirk thought that over for a moment, then shook his head. "Naw, it's the kid. Don't ask me how I know, but I know. That's it."

"Er-r-r-r. You're as stubborn as a mule's behind, you know that?"

He grinned. "You've mentioned that . . . several times in fact. I don't know what it means, but . . . Now, if you don't mind, I need to get to work here."

He turned away from her, walked into the bathroom, and began searching under the sink.

Savannah left, grumbling beneath her breath, ". . . men . . . won't listen . . . think they know everything . . . pee-pee heads . . . baboon butts."

Surveying the acres of cars in the dark lot, Savannah had no idea which vehicle belonged to the Villas. She had searched the rows for the green Jeep that she had seen Catherine driving previously, but it wasn't there. She had seen the height of Catherine's heels tonight and she was sure that she had driven, not walked down from the house on the hill. Apparently, they had driven another car. But which one?

Savannah stepped back into the center and grabbed the first waitress she could find.

"Hi, would you do me a big favor?"

The waitress smiled, eager to please. "Sure, if I can."

"Please tell Mr. or Mrs. Villa that the left front tire of their car is flat. They might want to have it taken care of now, rather than later this evening when they're ready to leave."

"Of course. I'll let them know right now."

The waitress hurried away, and Savannah returned to the parking lot, where she found a nice dark place to hide in the shadow of some tall oleanders. She grinned, savoring the anticipation.

It didn't take long. In less than three minutes, Catherine rushed out the front door and made a bee-line for the back of the lot and a BMW that was approximately the same size as Savannah's house.

In her ankle-length evening dress and her high, high heels, she tiptoed around the car . . . once . . . then again . . . and a third time. Finally, shaking her head, she walked back to the center and through the front door.

From her hiding place Savannah could see the confused look on her face. She felt only the slightest bit of guilt. Just as food—when eaten standing or off someone else's plate—didn't contain calories, lies told on the job didn't exactly blacken your soul. Catching one really bad guy would provide absolution for at least one hundred fibs. She was sure it was a rule that was written somewhere in the cosmos.

Once she was fairly sure that the Villas weren't coming back out, and that no one was around to observe her, she headed straight for the BMW.

It was black, she noted with a sad kind of satisfaction. And it was a pretty good bet that the carpeting inside would be black, too.

Standing beside the driver's door, she looked inside for any tiny red light that might indicate an alarm was employed. But she didn't see anything.

After glancing around once more and affirming that she was alone, she tried the door handle. But no such luck; it was locked. Even out here in the country, the Villas had secured their Beamer.

She flashed her penlight through the back window and verified that yes, indeed, the carpeting was black.

From her purse she took her handy-dandy, all-purpose lockpick and stuck it into the door. But once again, she was up the proverbial creek paddleless. The newer locks were more advanced than the old ones, and it was getting harder and harder to break into things these days. No amount of jiggling and twisting would do the trick.

She walked around to the back of the car and repeated the process with the trunk lock. Just when she was about to give up . . . bingo! It snapped open. So, the old girl hadn't lost her touch after all, she noted with satisfaction.

One more look around, then she raised the lid and looked inside.

Other than the black carpeting . . . which as Dr. Liu had said, would be less than two years old in the trunk of a late-model car, she didn't see anything particularly incriminating. It was just your standard, spotless, yuppie family trunk with tennis rackets, a kid's skateboard, a roadside emergency kit, and an empty bag with a designer label on it.

And it smelled good. In fact, it smelled great . . . springtime fresh like clothesline-dried laundry. Several detergent commercials and their catchy jingles danced through Savannah's mind.

It had just been cleaned. Scrubbed from stem to stern. There wasn't one smidgen of sand, dirt, or lint in the entire trunk. She placed her palm flat on the floor and could feel a slight dampness.

And when she leaned back and played her light over the side of the car, the wheels, and bumpers, she realized that the entire vehicle was spotless. Nobody's car, not even Catherine Villa's, was this clean, unless it had just been professionally detailed.

Turning back to the trunk, she pushed the tennis racket and skateboard aside. Even the carpet beneath those items was damp and immaculate . . . or was it?

What were these? Six little black things that were almost invisible against the rug. Leaning inside and shining her light directly on them, Savannah could see what they were—six flies, quite dead, lying on their backs, their tiny feet sticking straight up in surrender.

Why would flies be in a perfectly clean trunk? And why would they be dead in that immaculate trunk? Savannah could hazard a guess. But a guess—a feeble one—was all it would be.

She could see herself going to Dirk and saying, "The flies were there because they were attracted to the smell of death that was present in the trunk even after Barbie's body had been removed. And the flies died because some caustic chemical . . . like insecticide residue was there, even though it's been cleaned."

She could just see him presenting that to the DA, along with Anthony Villa's suspicious reaction to the telephone. And if that weren't enough concrete evidence, they had Savannah's equally useless gut feeling that he was a guilt-ridden, fearful man.

Okay, so she needed more. But what?

Closing the trunk, she stepped back from the car and looked it over one more time. Shining her light on the rear left tire, she noted that it was well worn, not new. So, Anthony hadn't had them replaced when he had the car detailed.

Maybe they could get a match from the plaster mold of the track up by the cliff.

She shone her light on the front left tire, and saw that it, too, was well worn. But something caught her eye. It was different. The two tires on this side of the car were different makes, even different sizes.

"Hmm," she said, as she walked around to the other side. The rear tire matched the one on the left, but the front right was yet a third make, and it wasn't even a whitewall.

Three brands, three sizes on one car.

Savannah mulled that one over. She was far less vain about such things than Catherine Villa, but she had insisted that Dirk replace her shredded wheels with matching tires. This mishmash seemed completely out of character for the persnickety lady.

As Savannah left the car and walked across the parking lot back to the center and the evening's festivities, she could feel the adrenaline hit her tired bloodstream.

Contrary to popular opinion, a private detective's life involves a lot of boring, solitary work and few moments of true drama. But now she was getting close. Like a bloodhound with her nose to the ground, she knew she was on a fresh track, and her prey wasn't far away.

For just a moment she wished that it was almost anyone other than Anthony Villa. But she thought of Francie, lying crumpled like a broken doll at the bottom of the staircase, and she didn't give a damn who the killer was. She just wanted to get her teeth into him.

Chapter
23

"I sang good tonight."

"You sang great."

"And I looked good, too."

"You looked fantastic."

"So . . . so . . . so, why didn't I win . . . *anything!*"

Savannah sat on the edge of the bed, holding her hysterical sister in her arms, rocking her as she had years ago when she had fallen down and skinned her knees. But this was much worse than a boo-boo that would respond to a kiss and a Donald Duck bandage.

"I'm not kidding, 'Lanta," she told her, wiping her cheeks with a wad of tissues that was getting more soggy by the moment. "I thought you were amazing! I had no idea that you could work an audience like that! They were behind you all the way."

"But . . . but . . ." She hiccuped. "But the judges liked that stupid girl with the skull. What was that 'To be or not to be' crap? That doesn't even make sense."

"Well, actually, it's Shakespeare, and it's a really cool speech but—"

Okay, so that wasn't the right thing to say, Savannah decided as Atlanta's sobbing reached new levels of volume.

"It isn't fair!" She hit the mattress with her fist and kicked her foot. "That girl wasn't even *cute,* let alone pretty. Did you see how fat she is?"

Savannah figured it wouldn't be wise to mention that she thought the winner had a beautiful figure, or that she was especially poised and seemed like a very nice person. No, she thought she'd just keep that two-bit opinion to herself.

"Life isn't fair, 'Lanta," she said, rubbing her back and continuing to rock. "I hate to say it, but it's so true. Rotten things happen to great people and wonderful things happen to crummy people, and that's just the way it is. The sooner you stop expecting things to be fair, the sooner you'll be a happy camper. Or at least, not so miserable."

"Oh, shut up!" She pushed her away. "I just lost the most important thing in my life. I'm devastated, and I don't want to hear any of your Chinese proverbs."

It had been a long, hard day. Savannah snapped.

"The most important thing in your life? Get real! And get over it already!"

Her face screwed up again. "You don't understand!"

"No, Atlanta Reid. It's *you* who's clueless. In a world where little babies get burned with cigarettes, and nuns get raped, and good cops with families at home get shot dead in dark alleys . . . you losing a beauty pageant just ain't high drama. Sorry if I'm not impressed."

"This was more than a beauty pageant. It was my career. My dream!"

Savannah sighed. "Oh, yes . . . I forgot. You were going to be discovered."

"I was. But there weren't even any talent agents there, like they said on the website. I looked around and didn't see a single one."

"Really? What exactly does a talent agent look like?"

Atlanta thought for a moment, then shrugged. "Well, I don't know, but if I'd seen one, I would have known it."

"That's where you're wrong, Twerp. There was an agent, of sorts, there."

She perked up and blew her nose. "What do you mean?"

"I mean, someone who knew that you're my sister approached me and told me they were very impressed with your performance."

From tears to a radiant smile in less than two seconds—the transformation was astounding.

"Really? Really, really?"

"Really, really. In fact, he suggested a gig for you next Saturday, if you aren't too busy."

She jumped up off the bed. "No way! Where? When? How? What?"

"In Hollywood at a recording studio, singing backup for Dixie Lynn. She's cutting a new record, or CD, or whatever they're cutting these days, and she could use another singer."

"Dixie Lynn? Dixie Lynn? Are you kidding me? Are you making this up? I mean, Dixie's won Grammys, and she sang at the Oscars last year, and she's been on the cover of *Rolling Stone* and—"

"I know. She's very hot right now. Are you up to it?"

She bounced off the bed and around the room. She couldn't have achieved more height with a pogo stick.

"Am I up to it? Am I up to it? I've been practicing for this my who-o-ole life. This is too cool! I can't believe it!"

Since the tide had turned, Savannah decided to crawl into bed and catch a few hours sleep if the human yo-yo would settle down. Morning was going to come early, and she already had a mental list a mile long of "to do's".

Besides, any minute now, Atlanta might think to ask the name of this high-powered, wheeler-dealer, Hollywood agent. All too soon she would find out that her agent was none other than John Gibson, who knew absolutely everyone who was anyone in most of the continental United States, and even more in Europe. He had set the whole thing up, bless his heart, and Savannah would love him forever for doing it.

But Atlanta didn't need to know that just yet.

"Good night, sweetie," she told her sister as she climbed beneath the covers. "This is our last night here, and I am going to sleep an entire night in this lovely, free bed. So lights out."

Moments later, she could hear Atlanta wiggling around in her bed, giggling, still ecstatic. How nice, to be so young and full of hope for the future. Marion Lippincott was right: All that energy and beauty, it was wasted on the young.

Nearly every town had an industrial section, and San Carmelita—graceful seaside village that it was—was no exception. And while most people wouldn't chose to live in that area of town, they were thankful for it when they needed some of the more basic things of life done, like their car lubed, their tires rotated, or a fresh coat of paint sprayed on the old jalopy.

Savannah had brought her Mustang down here so many times that almost every shop owner knew her by name and reputation. Californians loved their restored classics, and the Ford Mustang was one of the most popular. Savannah liked to think that her baby was the prettiest "pony" in town.

So, as she drove down one street after another, checking every detail shop she passed, she was heartily greeted and had to fend off a multitude of offers, most of which weren't worth beans.

When it came to buying classics, a lot of car lovers made empty promises . . . sort of like drunks at a bar at closing time.

She had already tried at least six or seven places, showing a snapshot of the BMW, and a photo she had cut out of a Villa Rosa brochure she had snagged from the reception desk. It was of Anthony Villa pouring a glass of wine. But she had cut off his name and the part of the picture with the wine, just to make sure they didn't make the connection.

With only two more places to check, she was beginning to wonder if maybe Dirk wasn't right when he told her she was ditzy. This morning, when she and Atlanta and the rest of the girls had cleared out of Villa Rosa, he had reiterated his opinion to her. Once again, she had told him where to file his opinions, using his hemorrhoid medication applicator for convenience.

But long ago, she had observed that, if you actually found what you were looking for, it was *always* in the last place you looked. Another one of those cosmic rules. And she reminded herself of that profound truism anytime she was searching for anything, be it her keys, a pair of panty hose without a run, that package of Little Debbie cinnamon rolls she had hidden in the back of the pantry, or a detail shop that had recently processed a BMW owned by a guy who looked like Anthony Villa.

As she pulled into Rory's Car Wash, she saw the Irishman standing next to a purple Corvette, his sleeves rolled up to show off the biceps that he had earned buffing cars from dawn to dusk. His hands were the same shade of purple as the car, which was covered with some sort of chalky compound. Purple dust had landed in the reddish blond curls that hung down to his collar. He was polishing, muscles rippling, and Savannah didn't mind at all stopping for a chat and a look-see.

"Ah, Savannah, me darlin'!" he called out in his delightful Irish brogue as she approached. "'Tis a sight for these sore eyes, ye are, love."

Ah . . . that accent of his. She swore the man could have simply "talked" her into an orgasm if she listened long enough. And he wouldn't even have to say anything dirty. With a voice like that, he could read the weather report and she would swoon.

"You're a cheerful sight yourself, lad," she replied, giving him her best Southern sashay as she walked up to him.

"Don't tell me you've brought that little red car of yours about for my attentions. She's still looking fine from the last buffin' I gave her."

"She is, Rory. She is, indeed. So, that's not why I'm here."

His eyes, greener than ol' Ireland, sparkled as he glanced appreciatively up and down her figure. He had informed her long ago that he considered her a "well-balanced lass." No anorexic models for this red-blooded son of old Erin.

"Could it be that Lady Luck herself has smiled upon me," he said, shoving a rag, stained as purple as his hands, into the back pocket of his jeans. "Is it me own handsome self ye've come to see?"

"It is . . . and I'd like to ask you if you've seen this car lately." She shoved the snapshot under his nose. "Or this fellow." She handed him the clipping.

His face fell, but only a little. Rory was an optimistic chap, if nothing else.

"Ah, 'tis information she's after," he said with a cluck of his tongue. "She wants me for me brain and not me body. What a bitter disappointment, but I'll bear up."

He took the pictures from her and looked from one to the other. "And why is it you're askin', lass? Did this fellow do a wrong deed by you? If he did, you give your friend Rory his address, and I'll be settlin' that score straightaway."

"Thank you for your chivalry, but it's nothing like that. I just need to know if you've cleaned his car recently."

"I did. Let's see . . . only a couple of days ago, I believe. He tipped me handsomely, told me to do an extra good job for him. I told him I always do a fine job . . . but I took the tip anyway. No point in insultin' the lad."

"Exactly." She savored the thrill of victory for a second, then said, "Tell me, Rory. Did you notice anything . . . unusual about the car?"

"Anything out of the ordinary, you mean?"

"Yes."

"Like what?"

"I'd rather not say. Just think back if you would."

He gazed into the distance and rubbed his nose, leaving a purple streak across his face. "Let me see now. I recall thinkin' two things, I did. First, I thought the car wasn't that dirty. Didn't really need a deep cleaning. Asked me to shampoo the trunk twice, the fella did. And second, I thought the trunk smelled a bit strange. Like some sort of chemical . . . like ant poison or some class of medicine . . . had been spilled in there. But I saw no stain on the carpet. Maybe that smell was why he wanted it shampooed a second time."

"Maybe." Savannah had to control herself to keep from doing an Irish jig right then and there. "One more thing, Rory . . . you vacuum thoroughly before you shampoo a carpet, don't you?"

"I do, indeed."

"And that big commercial vacuum of yours . . . how often do you clean out the bag?"

"Bag? Oh, it has no bag. The refuse goes into a big metal drum, and I don't have to empty it but once in a great while."

"Have you cleaned it since you vacuumed that car?"

"No. I had cleaned it just the day before."

She beamed, giving him her deepest dimpled grin. "You, Rory, are a jewel, a credit to the mother that bore you. Will you do me an enormous favor and not clean that drum until later this afternoon when a guy by the name of Dirk will be coming around with his tail tucked between his legs to collect what's in it for evidence?"

"I'd be glad to refrain from work, but only because such a comely lass as yourself asked. And also because I'm going to be rubbing out this monstrosity of a vehicle for the next two days anyway."

Savannah couldn't resist; she stood on tiptoes and

gave him a peck on the cheek. He laughed and the sound was deep and throaty, reaching parts of her anatomy that, for far too long, had gone undisturbed.

"Thank you, Rory. I owe you a pint of Guinness."

"And I'd be glad to share it with you, Savannah, me love. Drop by sometime and I'll buff yer fenders for ye."

"Yes," she murmured as she walked away. "I'll just bet you would. Ah-h-h . . . you cheeky lad."

Savannah thought there was a plethora of detail shops in the industrial area of San Carmelita, but to her dismay, she discovered there were far more junkyards selling used tires.

She and Tammy had agreed to start at opposite ends of the Junkyard Jungle and work their way to the middle, giving each other a buzz if either found what they were looking for.

So far, she had questioned a dozen dealers who were happy to see her, until they realized that she wanted information, not a used radiator or a replacement hood ornament. She had risked life and limb, fending off testosterone-ridden mongrels who guarded their yards, their rusted heaps of metal and piles of tires as though these assets constituted the National Treasury.

But she hadn't found anything yet, and, so far, her purse hadn't buzzed, so, neither had Tammy.

It was as she was crawling back into the Mustang, feeling a bit down as the "detail victory" began to wear off like a previous sugar fix going downhill, that she heard it. Her purse . . . specifically, the phone in her purse.

"Hallelujah," she said, though silently warning herself not to get too excited. Tammy could be calling to suggest that they meet somewhere for some afternoon donuts and coffee.

But then . . . it was Miss No-Donut, Health Conscious Tammy, not Dirk, so . . .

"Whatcha got?" Savannah asked.

"Todd's Tires, Four ninety-eight East Maple."

"I'm on my way."

Three minutes later, Savannah pulled onto Maple Street, which must have been named by a homesick, displaced native of Vermont, because there wasn't a maple . . . or any other kind of tree in sight. She spotted Tammy's hot pink Volkswagen Bug parked under a hand-painted sign that identified that particular lot as Todd's Tire Emporium. A lofty name indeed for what was basically a mountain of rubber.

The canine protector of this fortune was an ancient golden retriever, who looked like the type who would open the gate for an after-hours burglar and show him the cash box. His white muzzle, arthritic limp, and wagging tail hardly inspired fear as Savannah walked up to him and patted his head. "Hey, old man," she said, stroking the silky ears, "have you seen a dingy blond running around here? Okay, how about Todd? Where's your master, eh?"

At that moment, Tammy and a young man in overalls emerged from a ramshackle shed that bore the ambitious sign OFFICE on its door. Tammy's eyes were glistening, her face an ear-to-ear grin.

"This is Todd," she announced proudly. "He sold a BMW some new tires, I mean, old tires a couple of days ago. And he identified the picture of . . . you know."

Savannah's pulse rate shot up along with her spirit and her basic will to live. Yes! Yes!

But along with the elation that she had been right came the strange, sad feeling she got when she realized that someone she liked had done something terrible. It wasn't a good feeling. Before this was over, so many lives would be destroyed. Even the serene, beautiful world that was Villa Rosa would be changed forever. But, as always, she reminded herself that she hadn't caused this situation. Someone else had begun the avalanche of catastrophic events. She was simply putting an end to it.

"Hello, Todd," she said. "I'm so happy to meet you." She shook his grease-stained hand and gave him a warm smile that made the young man blush with pleasure. "What can you tell me about this transaction that took place between you and the fellow in the picture Tammy showed you?"

Todd wiped the sweat off his face with a red rag, then stuck it back into his pocket. "I remember it so well because it was weird," he said. "This guy in this gorgeous Beamer came in here and said he wanted to swap out his tires. I tried to talk him into some good recaps, but he said, 'No, they've gotta be used. The more used the better.' Now, that's weird. I've been selling tires here with my dad, Todd Sr. for years, and nobody ever said, 'The more used the better.' And folks don't buy old tires when the ones they've got are in great shape."

Savannah mentally crossed her fingers for luck, and said, "Tell me that you still have the tires, Todd, that you haven't sold them yet."

Tammy wriggled all over with delight. "He's got them! I already asked."

"Yeah," Todd replied. "They're so nice that I saved them for myself. They're out in the yard."

"Fantastic!" Savannah slapped them both on the back. "That's just friggin' fan-tastic! Let's see 'em."

Savannah found it embedded in the tread of the third tire that she examined. Within seconds she had Dirk on the phone.

"Get over here right now, Todd's Tire Emporium on East Maple. There ain't no West Maple. Haul butt, will ya?" She glanced over at Tammy, who could hardly contain her glee. They loved getting one over on Dirk. "Let's just say . . . I'm looking at four tires off a certain person's BMW. And from the pattern, I'd say they're a dead ringer for that plaster cast of yours . . . and . . . on one of the four tires, we found a wedge of gray plastic stuck between the treads."

She replaced the phone in her purse and grinned. "Needless to say, he's on his way. It's about a twenty-minute drive." She snickered and gave Tammy a high five. "He'll be here in ten."

Chapter
24

Savannah felt his presence, even before she saw Anthony Villa standing near the center of the cavernous aging room, surrounded by endless wooden barrels and stainless-steel tanks, holding the fruits of his artistry. Unaware of her entrance, he swirled a glass beaker in his hand and gazed into the contents that were a beautiful golden coral. His face had the look of tragedy, an expression Savannah had seen on too many people, when they were going through one of life's worst cycles.

On the Wheel of Fortune, she knew that Anthony Villa was right there at the bottom of the rotation. And, considering that he seemed to have aged a decade in the past twenty-four hours, she was sure that he knew it, too.

She didn't know what he was looking for in the beaker, but he seemed to find it. A slight smile softened some of the dark concern on his face, as he lifted it to his lips and took a sip. Holding it in his mouth for a long time, he finally swallowed, and she saw the contentment, the pride on his face. Apparently, the master winemaker of Villa Rosa had done it again.

The underground room was chilly, and she was grateful for the thick, oversize Aran sweater she was wearing. Or maybe it was what she was about to do that gave her the shivers. She couldn't recall when she had experienced so many conflicting emotions when cornering a criminal. It just wasn't nearly as much fun when you liked the person.

As she walked closer, he saw her and gave her a casual nod hello. She watched for any sign of surprise, but there was none. If she didn't know better, she would say that Anthony Villa had been expecting her.

"Good evening, Savannah," he said, then took another sip from the beaker. "How nice to see you."

She doubted that, but replied, "How kind of you to say so. What are you doing, tasting your wares?"

"I am. I knew this white zin wasn't ready, but I had to see how it was coming along. That's the hard part, you know, the waiting. We wait for the grapes to grow, we wait for them to ripen, we wait during the fermentation, we wait during the aging."

"It sounds like you have to have a lot of patience in your business."

"Or like me, you may not have it in the beginning, but you learn, just like you learn everything else." He held out the beaker to her. "Would you like to sample it, tell me what you think?"

She walked over to him and took the beaker. His hand brushed hers as they made the exchange. It was warm, large. Even that brief touch conveyed his masculinity, his vitality. Savannah had always found it a bit unsettling—how normal a killer's hands could look.

She took a sip of the wine and found that it was very good, even better than what had been served to them at the luncheon. Looking into its vibrant color, she said, "They must be pretty, the grapes that you make this from."

He looked momentarily confused. "I beg your pardon?"

"The white zinfandel that isn't really white. It's this gorgeous, peachy color. I mean . . . you make white wine from green grapes and red from red, right?"

"Yes, but . . ." Comprehension dawned on his face. "Oh, I understand what you're saying. But white zinfandel is also made from red grapes. You see, when we make white wine, we separate the skins and stems from the juice as soon as the grapes are crushed. With red, we leave them in there and the skins enhance the red color. With white zinfandel, we use red grapes, but separate the skins from the juice right away, as we do with white. Some of the color is still there, but not so much. Do you understand?"

"I do," she said, "and I feel like a dope."

"Don't. I know wine, you know private detecting. . . . We all have our realms of knowledge. That's why we have to ask questions and learn from one another."

She handed the beaker back to him, and there was an awkward silence as they stood there, looking into each other's eyes. She was thinking about his reaction with the pay phone the night before, and she knew he was remembering, too.

"So, what would you like to ask me about private detection, Mr. Villa?" she asked, her tone heavy with subtext.

He turned his side to her and set the container on the nearest barrel. As he placed a large stopper back into the hole in the barrel's top, he said, "I would like to know how you intend to apprehend this person who . . . who killed those girls."

"Okay," she said. "I'll tell you. I think I should check around at detail shops and find out who took his car in recently to be cleaned . . . someone whose trunk smelled strongly of chemicals. I believe I'll start with my Irish friend, a fine lad named Rory, who has a shop out in the industrial area."

Although his side was to her, she could see his profile well enough to tell when her verbal arrow found its mark. His entire body visibly sagged. But he didn't look scared or distressed. He looked deeply tired, a fatigue, not of the body, but of the soul.

"I see," he said so softly that she hardly heard him.

"And then," she continued, "I would check out all the used tire places in that same area, to see if someone traded in their nearly new tires—the ones that would, undoubtedly, match that plaster cast we took by the cliff—for some old used tires. And, of course, I'd make sure that the junkyard guy and my detail friend could identify the suspect from a photo."

He leaned forward, resting his elbows on the barrel top and hung his head. "And?"

"And we would check the vacuum at the detail shop for any long red hairs that matched the first victim. I'm sure there would be a few. All we need is one or two."

"I see."

"And then, Detective Coulter would get a warrant to have the crime technicians check the inside of the suspect's trunk for chemical residue. I've done some research, and I understand that something like, say a bug bomb, lingers long after it's released . . . no matter how good a job the detailer did of cleaning it."

Anthony laced his fingers together and studied them thoughtfully, as though seeing them for the first time. It occurred to Savannah that maybe he, too, was surprised at what his hands had done. "And do you think . . . if you did all that," he said, "it would be enough to convict your suspect of murder?"

"I think that once the DNA results come back from the lab on the fetus that Barbara Matthews was carrying, and it's compared with our suspect's DNA, we'll know for sure that he's the father. And if he happens to be a married man and someone who's in the public eye and quite concerned about negative publicity . . . I'm sure Detective Coulter will have enough."

This time the silence that stretched between them was painfully long. She saw the battle on his face and knew he wanted to tell her. It was building inside him, and he wanted to speak and let it out. They always wanted to talk, but especially the ones who hadn't led a habitual life of crime, people who had—other than one or two extremely foolish or cruel things—committed mostly decent deeds in their lives. They just couldn't bear the burden alone.

"If that phone hadn't rung last night," he said, twisting his hands in front of him so hard that his knuckles were turning white, "at that very moment when you and I were both walking by it. If that person on the other end had dialed correctly . . ."

"Or if you hadn't decided that murder was the best way to handle this problem."

When he didn't reply, she decided to nudge him a

little more. "Why didn't you just let her win the beauty pageant, or pay her the money, or whatever she was wanting from you?"

"Pay her? Fix the contest? If only that had been all she was asking for. Demanding. No, she wouldn't let me pay for a quiet abortion, or send her away to Europe for a luxury 'vacation' and then find a good home for the baby. Not Barbie. She expected me to divorce Catherine and marry her. Winning a crown wasn't enough for her; she wanted to be a senator's wife. She wouldn't settle for anything less."

"And you didn't feel you had any other choice."

His eyes met Savannah's; they were haunted, full of pain. "I did something very stupid, Savannah. I'd been faithful to my wife from the moment I met her, and then, this little twit comes along, shaking it under my nose, telling me what a strong, smart, sexy older guy I was, telling me how much she'd like to win this contest. She caught me at a lonely moment, and I went for it. Not once, but twice. Two times and she was pregnant. Can you believe it? The sex wasn't even any good."

Savannah shook her head. "Such a big price to pay— those two girls' lives, yours, your wife's, your children's, all destroyed—for some bad sex."

"Yeah, we sign these blank checks, buying something we want, without thinking what's going to be written on the line. Someone my age should've known better."

"And you should have known that killing those girls would make it worse."

Anthony pulled back his fist and hit the barrel so hard that she heard the wood crack. "Don't tell me what I should have known, what I should have done," he shouted. "You don't know what you would have done in my shoes. I had hurt my family with my stupidity, and I had to protect them any way I could from the repercussions of what I'd done. I did what I did for them . . . and this." He waved his arm, encompassing the vast room and its bounty.

Then his anger dissolved as quickly as it had appeared. He sagged against the barrel and began to weep.

"I'm so glad that my father is dead," he said, "and my mother and my grandparents. They were such proud people. They would have been so ashamed . . . so ashamed."

Savannah would have walked over to almost anyone who was sobbing, broken like that, and tried to comfort them. But the thought of Francie's cold skin stopped her. She just stood there, watching, until she heard the footsteps behind her.

Dirk and Jake McMurtry were entering the aging room, and behind them came Ryan, John, and Tammy. Dirk had a pair of cuffs in his hand.

"Did you get it all?" Savannah asked Ryan.

"Yes, every word," he replied.

Anthony Villa continued to cry as Dirk put the cuffs on him and Jake read him his rights. He was still weeping when they left the room with him, the rest of the entourage following close behind.

"Thanks for the loan of that new high-tech equipment," she told Ryan, lacing her arm through his. "Dirk's old department-issued wires don't work worth beans, and I wanted to get everything."

"Well, they got it all," Tammy said proudly. "I was sitting right there in the van with them while they were taping it. You came through loud and clear, and best of all, so did he. Congratulations."

Savanna watched as Dirk and Jake loaded Anthony

Villa, husband, father, winemaker, and senate candidate into a waiting cruiser. "Yeah," she said, subdued. "Thanks."

When Savannah crawled into her own bed that night, she couldn't believe how comforting it felt to be home. Her old flannel nightgown, her familiar pillow, the moonlight streaming through her lace curtains and painting lovely shadows on the pink comforter that she had treated herself to last Christmas.

Life was hard, work was brutal, her daily grind anything but feminine. So, Savannah made up for it in her own bedroom with all the "girlie" things her heart desired but didn't get during waking hours. Within these four walls, she was all woman, with lavender-scented sachets under her pillow, silk, satin, and velvet everywhere she touched, and a bouquet of fresh flowers in the vase on the dresser.

Romance novels stacked on the nightstand chased the harsh realities of the day away when read by the light of a pink, Victorian lamp, complete with a three-inch fringe.

Having a crystal dish brimming with Mon Cheri chocolates close at hand didn't hurt either.

This was her sanctuary. And tonight, she was thrilled to be back inside its cozy confines to renew her tired spirit.

But when she turned out the lights and snuggled beneath the covers, she kept seeing Anthony Villa's face, and she imagined what Catherine must be doing at that moment. Maybe she was in bed, too, but crying, holding her two boys close to her. Or perhaps she was pacing the floor, making phone calls, trying to find the best attorney possible to defend her husband.

Whatever she was doing, Savannah didn't envy her. And she felt bad that she had been the catalyst to bring a family to ruin.

No, she thought, *not me.*

Anthony Villa had destroyed his family—with some help from a stupid, but seductive teenager, who was old enough to know that what she was doing was wrong, but far too young to understand the terrible consequences.

Not me.

Tomorrow morning she would wake up and continue with her life, doing things that had nothing in common with the Villas. And once the trial was over, they would become nothing more to her than a sad memory. They, on the other hand, would live in this nightmare for the rest of their lives.

With thoughts like those, she wasn't surprised that it took her a long time to go to sleep. And when she did, she found that the sweet familiarity of home wasn't enough to chase away the restless dreams.

She was standing in the old cemetery just outside her hometown, an ancient graveyard where the brave sons of the Confederacy had been laid to rest next to their wives and children who had died when Sherman had cut his deadly swath of destruction across Georgia.

Graceful drapings of moss hung from the trees, dipping down to the weathered marble stones, some so aged that their names and dates were barely visible. The grass was halfway up to her knee and tickled her calf as she walked along between the monuments, reading the names of families who had lived in the area for generations.

Savannah recognized the place and many of the names. She had played hide-and-seek here as a child, and being more courageous than some, she had even ventured here at night to speak to Grandpa Reid after a tractor accident had taken him from them when she was only six.

As she usually did when she visited this place, she carried a bouquet of flowers in her hand, bachelor buttons and snapdragons, picked from Gran's garden. She brought them for Gramps. He had always told her that bachelor buttons and snapdragons were "manly," unlike those sissy flowers like pansies, roses, and daisies.

She was trying to find Gramps's grave . . . but she couldn't remember where it was. All around her there were fresh mounds of earth, new graves recently dug. At least a dozen of them. And when she stepped in the soft soil, she sank in to her ankles.

Looking down, she saw a name on one of the new stones.

"Villa"

Her heart caught in her throat, and she looked at the next grave marker. It, too, was inscribed with that name. And the next and the next. An entire family. Dead. Gone.

Sherman had marched through Georgia again.

"It was you, Savannah. You did it."

In the darkness she couldn't see the face of her accuser, but she recognized the smooth, aristocratic voice.

"No, Catherine," she said, "it wasn't my fault. I'm sorry for your loss, but I didn't cause it."

"Everything would have been okay. But you couldn't leave it alone. You had to come after Tony."

"He killed two girls. He has to pay for that."

"Tony didn't kill anyone, you fool. *I* did."

Savannah sat upright in her bed, her pulse pounding in her ears, cold sweat pouring off her body and soaking her nightgown.

She was shaking all over and could hardly breathe. "No," she whispered. "That isn't true."

"Yes, it is," Catherine replied. "Tony couldn't kill anyone . . . not even when it was necessary. He's weak. All men are weak. We women have to take care of them."

It took Savannah's sleep-drugged mind two seconds to realize that she was no longer dreaming. And when she did, she lunged for her nightstand and yanked the drawer open. Inside was her Beretta.

"Don't!" Catherine said. "If you do, I'll shoot you dead right now. I swear I will."

Savannah saw the glint of the gun that was only a few feet from her head. The moonlight was bright enough for her to see the front end of the barrel and know it was high caliber.

She froze, as she had been ordered to do.

"If you do everything I tell you to do," Catherine was saying, "I'll let you live for a few more minutes. Because I want you to hear what I have to say to you. I want my words to be the last thing you hear on this earth."

Chapter

25

With a super charge of adrenaline coursing through her bloodstream, Savannah's mind raced, thinking of a hundred plans, but discarding each one. Catherine was close, but not close enough for her to grab the gun.

She couldn't possibly get her Beretta out of the nightstand drawer in time to use it without being shot herself.

No weapons were within reach, and she couldn't imagine defending herself with a pillow against a high-caliber pistol.

"Have you ever been married, Savannah?"

What the hell does that have to do with anything? she wondered.

But she said, "No, I haven't."

Catherine chuckled . . . a most unpleasant sound. "I

didn't think so. You aren't really the sort of woman that men want to marry, are you?"

Not sure how to answer that one, Savannah said nothing. She didn't want to give Catherine the satisfaction of her admitting that, indeed, no man had ever asked. But then, there was no one to whom she would have said yes, so maybe it was just as well.

"If you haven't been married," Catherine continued, "you can't know what it's like to have your husband betray you with another woman."

"I can imagine."

"No, you can't. Until you've experienced it, it's truly unimaginable. The rage that you feel, the incredible hurt, the images that play over and over and over again in your mind. You see her touching him. You see him touching her, doing all those special things with her that he's done with you. You think of sweet things he's told you, things you treasure, and you wonder if he said those things to her. And you lose those precious memories, because when you recall them, they don't give you pleasure anymore, because . . . you wonder . . ."

"You're right," Savannah said. "I've never suffered that particular pain. It must be terrible."

"You're damned right it is. And don't patronize me. Don't try to be my girlfriend here, because in a few minutes I'm going to kill you."

"Catherine," Savannah said as gently as she could, "I wasn't the one who slept with your husband."

"No, but you took him away from me and our boys. I had it all fixed. I had forgiven him, and we were going to go on from there. But tonight he's in jail instead of being home with us where he belongs. And that's your fault."

"If you kill me, Catherine, you'll get caught, and

then where will your boys be? With both of their parents in prison, what'll happen to them?"

"Both of us won't be in prison. After I shoot you, I'm going to turn myself in. I'm going to confess that I killed Barbara. I'll tell them that Anthony had nothing to do it. That isn't completely true; he's the one who threw that little whore over the cliff. I told him that if I could kill her and get her off our backs, the least he could do was get rid of the body. And he even screwed that up. I'm telling you, men are helpless."

"Did he know you were going to kill her . . . and the other girl, too?"

"Not until afterward, when I told him I had already done it . . . for us."

"So he had nothing to do with the actual murders?"

"That's what I said. You aren't listening."

"But when I questioned him this evening," Savannah said, "he confessed."

"He's protecting me, taking the blame so that I can stay free and be with the boys. And I can't let him do that. A man who's killed two teenage girls—he'd get a death sentence. But they'll go easier on me, a woman. I'll tell them everything, about that little slut coming after my husband. I'll tell them that I was temporarily insane, and if there's one woman on that jury, I'll be found not guilty."

"But what about Francie? What about me? How are you going to explain killing us?"

"Who needs to explain anything? There's no evidence saying that I killed either of you. I was very careful with the second girl, and I've been very careful tonight. No one will ever prove that I did the two of you. I'm going to get away with this. All of it. You just wait and see."

She laughed, and again the sound of it went straight through Savannah like a cold, wet wind.

"Oh, what am I saying?" Catherine added. "You won't be around to see it."

"Catherine, really, I don't believe you've thought this through. You believed you had all of the bases covered with Barbie, too, but you didn't. If you kill me in cold blood, there's no way you can chalk that up to temporary insanity. You won't get away with it."

"I think I will," Catherine said. "Let's see who's right."

Savannah saw her hand tighten around the gun as she took one step closer.

She was going to shoot. Savannah knew it.

She also knew that her only hope was to lunge for the gun. She would probably take a bullet. With any luck, it wouldn't be fatal.

What a miserable option. But it was her only one.

"Actually, you should thank me," Catherine said. "At least you're going to go quick, like the second kid. The little whore wasn't so lucky. I guarantee you that when she was sucking in that insecticide, she would have welcomed a bullet between the eyes . . . like I'm going to give you right now."

Savannah braced herself, ready to spring. But at that exact instant, there was a whooshing sound in the darkness behind Catherine, and then a loud crack and strange twang as the woman's right leg shot out from under her. She spun sharply to the left and fell backward.

Savannah had the gun before Catherine Villa hit the floor.

The light switch was thrown, and through squinted

eyes Savannah saw her baby sister Atlanta standing over
Catherine, her broken guitar in her hand and a satisfied look on her face.

"So, Big Sis," she said. "What's all the ruckus in here?
I'm tryin' to get some sleep down the hall there, and
you gals woke me up with all your chatterin'. Thought
you might need some help, Van."

Savannah looked down at Catherine, who was
writhing on the floor, holding her leg.

"That was a pretty good wallop you gave her," she
said appreciatively.

"Yeah, you owe me a new guitar. By the way, I heard
everything she said about killing those girls. Want me to
call Dirk?"

Savannah grinned. "Please, darlin'. I'd be most
grateful."

Casually, as though she had nothing else to do with
the rest of her night, Atlanta turned and walked out of
the room.

Savannah nudged the squirming Catherine with her
toe. "Hey, did you get a load of that?" she asked her.
"That was my little sister who knocked your leg out
from under you . . . a chip off the old family salt block.
Not bad, eh?"

Catherine muttered only inarticulate cries of pain.

"Stop your whining," Savannah told her. "I'll make
sure Dirk takes you by the hospital on the way to jail. It's
probably not broken. Although . . . it does look sorta
funny, sticking out sideways like that. . . ."

The entire Moonlight Magnolia clan was miserable.
Deliciously miserable. They sprawled on lounge chairs

in Savannah's backyard, buttons and belts loosened, holding their distended stomachs and vowing to never eat another bite of food for as long as they lived.

Savannah was ecstatic—a job well-done!

To celebrate the closing of the case and the fact that it was Saturday—persons of Southern heritage don't need much reason to celebrate—she had plied them with barbecued ribs, potato salad, baked beans, corn on the cob, homemade rocky road ice cream and beer. For some reason, nobody seemed to have an appetite for wine.

They were stuffed to the gills; her task was done.

Even the usually prim and proper John Gibson was flat on his back in her hammock, his eyes closed as though he were in a coma, his trouser button undone, his mustache sporting a kernel of corn, a blotch of barbecue sauce on the front of his polo shirt.

Dirk was cranking the next batch of rocky road in the old-fashioned ice-cream churn . . . just in case anyone got faint from hunger and needed a sugar boost.

Even Tammy had joined in the decadence. Although she had dismissed the idea of eating ribs, she had chowed down on the beans, corn, and salad. And, for the first time Savannah could almost see a tiny bit of a paunch going on beneath that middy blouse of hers.

"I'm in agony," Ryan said from his chaise. "Savannah, I've never eaten so much in my life. You're a delightful sadist."

"Sadomasochist, you mean," she said, holding her own tummy. "I put away more than any of you. Remember, I have to taste everything . . . several times . . . at each stage of cooking just to make sure I'm getting it right."

"You got it right," Dirk said. "You got it so right. You're my kind o' woman."

"One who gives you free food and does half of your work for you?"

"Exactly." He stopped cranking for a moment and looked over at her driveway. "By the way, where are those new wheels I bought you? I wanted the guys here to see 'em."

Savannah laughed and shook her head. She was never going to hear the end of the tire saga. The fine city fathers had decided they didn't owe her a new set, because she shouldn't have been "interfering" with a police pursuit at the time hers were ruined. She was lucky that *they* didn't sue or prosecute *her* . . . or so they said.

So, Dirk the Tightwad of the Ages had forked over the big bucks from his own pocket. Savannah didn't feel too guilty. Long ago she had decided that he was probably independently wealthy since he had a full-time job and seldom spent a single cent on anything. He could afford it.

And they were nice ones—a new set of radial red-walls, just like she had asked for.

"They're underneath my sister right now," she said. "Atlanta drove to Hollywood to do her backup singing gig for Dixie Lynn today. She left before I was even out of bed and should be home anytime. I can't wait to hear how it went. Thanks a million, John, for arranging it for her."

John groaned and nodded, but he kept his eyes closed. "You're welcome. It was my pleasure."

"And I have to thank you guys, too, for those refer-rals in Georgia," she said. "I'm setting up appointments for Atlanta to go to as soon as she gets home—a counselor who specializes in eating disorders and a support group, too."

"Do you think she'll stick with it?" Tammy asked.

"I hope so. She's seen Angela twice this week, and she's getting past the idea that it's a shameful thing to talk to a pro. One step at a time."

"She's lucky she has you for a sister," Tammy said, giving Savannah an affectionate smile.

"I'm lucky to have *her*. I have to tell you, guys, if it wasn't for my little sister smacking Catherine Villa with her guitar, I honestly don't think I'd be here right now. That gal was going to kill me . . . then and there . . . no doubt about it."

"Well, she's gonna get hers," Dirk said. "That busted leg ain't settin' right, I heard, and she's gonna have to have it operated on. Not to mention the charges against her."

"I understand," Ryan said, "that they're cutting a deal for Anthony Villa, that he'll probably receive a light sentence and be back with his sons and vineyard in a few years."

"That's right." Dirk lifted the lid of the churn and looked inside. "Did you hear? The results of the tests are back. The chemical used to kill Barbie *was* an insecticide, like we thought. A bug bomb called, Pests No More. Appropriate, huh?"

"Be nice," Savannah warned him. He dipped his finger in the ice cream and she swatted his hand.

"And here's the clincher," he added. "The baby wasn't even Anthony's after all. Trent Gorton was the father."

"So, Barbie had the Villas dancing on strings for nothing." Savannah shook her head. "Do you think we'll get Catherine for Francie's death?"

"Yeah, I think between you and Atlanta testifying to what she said when she came after you . . . it'll be enough. You Reid gals are pretty convincing with those big blue eyes and that sweet Southern drawl. You're so deceptively innocent-looking."

She batted her lashes and deepened her dimples. "Why, thank you, kind sir. Want some more ice cream?"

"Do bears—?"

"Here." She shoved a bowl at him.

The purr of a well-tuned motor caught their attention as Savannah's Mustang pulled into her driveway.

"Oh, good!" Savannah exclaimed as her sister climbed out of the car and walked over to the patio where they were. "Atlanta's back! She must be so excited . . . on cloud nine . . . her dream come true . . . a—"

"It sucked! It so-o-o sucked!" Atlanta plopped down on the grass, her legs crossed, her lip out. "I hated the whole thing! You wouldn't believe how *boring* it is to record a song! You sing it over and over and over again until you're just *sick* to death of hearin' it!"

Savannah stared at her, unable to comprehend this reversal. It was so abrupt. So . . . Atlanta.

"It ain't what it's cracked up to be, this singing thing," she said. "Dixie was downright cranky, and I don't really blame her. I had to be there at nine, but she'd been recording since seven in the morning. She hadn't even had time to do her hair and makeup. I'm tellin' ya, she looked like crap! Nothin' like she did at the Oscars."

Lying in his hammock, eyes still closed, John smiled, his mustache twitching.

Ryan and Tammy gave each other a sideways look. Dirk started dishing up a bowl of ice cream.

Savannah walked over to the barbecue grill. "Okay," she said. "So much for that. We saved you some ribs. The veggies are on the kitchen counter. Can I dish you up a plate?"

"Naw, I'm not really . . ." Atlanta paused. Her eyes met her sister's for a long moment. "Yeah, okay," she said. "I'll take some of that potato salad you made yesterday and a piece of corn."

As Savannah walked into the house, she heard her sister saying, "You know what? On the way here on the plane I was noticing that those flight attendants have got a pretty good job. I mean, they get to dress up in cute uniforms and meet lots of rich guys and travel all over the world. That would be cool, you know. I'm just thinkin' that maybe if I was a stewardess, I might meet some movie director in first-class, and . . . you know, a lot of actresses get discovered that way, because . . ."

Marion Lippincott was right, after all, Savannah decided as she put a double-sized scoop of potato salad on a paper plate; all that energy, all that optimism—it really was wasted on the young.

But at that moment, as she gazed out her kitchen window at her loved ones—those her own age and those younger—Savannah was extremely contented to be exactly where she was on life's road.

Right here . . . this spot where she was standing . . . it was the very best place in the world to be.

Please turn the page for
an exciting peek at the
newest Savannah Reid mystery

PEACHES AND SCREAMS

now on sale at bookstores everywhere!

Several hours later, having been plied with copious amounts of double Dutch chocolate fudge, popcorn, and the potables of their choice, Savannah's guests began to take their leave.

Tammy departed first, promising to return in the wee hours of the morning to take Savannah to the airport. Although Savannah returned home as seldom as possible to the tiny rural town in Georgia where she had been born and raised, this visit was unavoidable. The oldest of nine children, Savannah had been summoned to yet another wedding.

If there was anything worse than going home, it was to a wedding, not your own, without any sign of a ring on your finger, without even an escort on your arm.

Ryan and John were the next to leave, waving goodbye from their vintage Bentley as Savannah watched from her front porch. She could hardly see through the tangle of bougainvillea that was taking over the front porch of her Spanish-style bungalow.

"Have a safe trip to Georgia, dear," John called as they pulled out of her driveway, his silver hair glowing in the light of the streetlamp.

"Be sure to give us a ring if you need anything, okay? Ryan added, his head stuck out the window. "In fact, give us a call whether you need us or not. We're going to miss you."

"I'll miss you, too." She blew them a kiss.

"Eh, what're you wasting that on them for," said a grouchy voice behind her. She turned to see Dirk standing there, pulling on his battered bomber jacket. "Those two aren't into *girl* kisses."

"Stop," Savannah said. "Stop right now. Behave a little better, and I might blow you . . . a kiss . . . now and then."

His eyes twinkled. "Mmm, had my hopes up for a half a second there."

She scowled. "Get real, Nacho Chip Breath. Are you going home now, too?"

"Yeah. Some of us have to work tomorrow, while *other* people get to leave on vacation."

"Some vacation . . . watching one of my zillions of siblings get married, while I'm still. . . ."

"Yes?" His eyes searched hers; she quickly glanced away.

"Nevermind." Linking her arm through his, she began walking him toward his Buick, which was parked on the street in front of her house.

"Were you about to moan and groan about still being single?" he asked. "I could have sworn that was what you were going to say."

"No way. I like being single. No man's shoes to trip over . . . except your rotten old sneakers when you're here for Monday night football and the free pizza.

Having the toilet seat *down*, where it belongs, all the time . . . except when you visit and leave it up."

"So, with a guy like me around, you don't need a husband. Is that what you're saying?"

"Yeah, except for vehicle maintenance, lawn care, and the occasional plumbing job, I do okay."

"But then there's the old bada-bing, bada-boom." He prodded her with his elbow.

"Eh, if I can do without having my oil changed, my tires rotated, and my pipes roto-rooted I can give up the old binging and booming."

His smirk faded into a look of concern. "Speaking of . . . romance . . . are you going to be seeing any of your high school buddies there in Georgia?"

For a second, memories of adolescence flashed before her mind's eye: sultry nights in pecan groves, stolen kisses behind the athletic field bleachers, daring caresses at the drive-in movie, the back seat of Tommy Stafford's '56 Chevy.

Yes, she'd had a few "high school buddies." However, only one face came to mind. Tommy's.

But did she even want to see his face again?

"No. I don't think so," she said.

"Good."

Dirk looked so relieved that she didn't bother to set the record straight, to admit she had been answering her own question, not his.

It was her turn to nudge him. "Why, Detective Coulter, I do believe you're jealous."

He jerked his arm away from hers. "I'm not neither. I just don't want you getting into trouble. You bein' so far away, I won't be able to bail you out."

Before she could protest, she recalled that he had, in fact, bailed her out—both figuratively and literally—numerous times over the years.

She looked up at his face, street fight scars, perpetually mussed hair, and all, and felt a rush of affection for her best friend in the world. Standing on tiptoe, she gave him a kiss on the cheek.

His 'stakeout shave' rasped against her lips, but she had long ago decided that Dirk's rugged masculinity was perhaps his most appealing attribute . . . along with a rabidly protective streak toward those he cared for. The rest of the world could go to Hades in a pink Easter basket, as far as Dirk Coulter was concerned, but the handful of people he loved . . . he loved fiercely.

"I'll be fine," she told him. "I'll get Marietta married off . . . for the third time . . . and I'll be right back. You won't even know I'm gone."

To her surprise, he bent down and returned her kiss, his lips warm as they lingered just a bit longer than the usual "peck" on her cheek.

"Oh, I'll know you're gone," he said, clearing his throat. For once, he didn't add any smart aleck disclaimer to dilute the sentimentality of the moment. "Believe me, I'll know."

As she watched him drive away down her street, his taillights disappearing at the corner, Savannah realized she was going to miss him, too. A lot.

Whether she ran into Tommy Stafford or not.

"Thanks for bringing me to the airport," Savannah told Tammy as they pulled into the short-term parking lot of the mystery maze known as Los Angeles International Airport, "and for taking care of the kitties and the agency for me while I'm gone."

Tammy had a slight pout on her face as she swung her old, hot pink, Volkswagen bug into an empty spot and cut the engine. "And all I asked in return was one, little, itsy-bitsy peek at the dress."

"You're not looking at the dress. That's it; that's all. I don't even want to think about the damned thing, okay?"

They got out of the car, locked it, and headed for the trunk in front. Tammy opened it and helped Savannah haul out her suitcase, carryon, and one enormous garment bag.

"It can't be that bad," Tammy said, grabbing for the bag, which Savannah snatched out of her hand.

"It's revolting. Let's just say, it makes me look like an enormous, upside down tulip."

"What color?"

Savannah winced at the thought. "Florescent peach."

"Ouch."

"Yeah. I swear, Marietta picked that style just to make the rest of us look ridiculous. She's not above it, you know."

Tammy grabbed the suitcase, Savannah the carryon, and they headed for the departure terminal. "What color is the maid of honor wearing?"

"Mint green."

"That's not so bad . . . I guess."

"Yeah, Marietta was set on dusty rose, but we talked her out of it. Dusty rose and peach. That girl never has had a lick o' sense when it comes to colors, or dressing, or decorating . . . or men."

"This is her third time around, huh?"

They stood at the crosswalk, waiting for the constant flood of taxi cabs, limos, vans, and transport busses to come to a halt. Even in pre-dawn hours, LAX hustled and bustled. Savannah punched the signal control button several more times, although she knew that—like the panel on an elevator—repetition did no good. It only provided the illusion of control to the puncher.

"Yeah, this is Hubby Numero Tres. And she's got two children, one from each of her ex's. Impulse control isn't exactly Marietta's forte, either. She was asking everybody whether they thought it was silly for her to wear a white gown and veil. They said it was, but she's going for it anyway."

Finally, the light changed, and they started across. A nearby bus coughed out a cloud of acrid, diesel smoke, and Savannah tried to breathe momentarily through her ears. Ah . . . the luxury of travel.

The electronic doors slid open, ushering them into the terminal full of harried, mostly irritated, passengers. "When Marietta asked me what she should wear," Savannah continued, as they headed for the endless queues, "I suggested that she wear a football jersey with the number '3' on the back."

Tammy laughed. "You didn't! What did she say?"

"Nothing . . . for two whole weeks. Absolutely not a word. Clammed up tighter than Dirk's wallet."

"Only two weeks?"

Savannah shrugged. "Hey, that's a record for a Reid gal. The only thing we like more than eating, is talking."

"I wish I were coming with you," Tammy said as she set the suitcase on the floor at the end of the mile-long, twisting, turning, cordoned line. "All that family togetherness sounds like fun."

"It might be . . . for some other family." Savannah sighed, realizing that she didn't really mind the long, long line. It could even be longer, for all she cared. Although she hated to admit it, she was in no hurry at all to return to the bosom of her homeland. "For us," she said, "family togetherness tends to spell trouble."

"With a capital 'T'?"

"Oh, yes. Trouble . . . in all caps, bold, underlined, italicized. We Reids don't do anything halfway."

"If that Macon doesn't shape up real quick, I'm gonna slap him naked and hide his clothes," Waycross Reid said as he drove the old Ford pickup down the pothole-ridden road. Savannah sat next to her brother and wondered, with every bounce of the shock-shot truck, if one of the exposed seat coils was going to take intimate liberties with her backside. She looked wistfully at the truck's dash, wishing there was some sign of an air conditioner vent; she had forgotten how humid the South could be in mid-August, and she was melting inside her cotton suit.

But, while Waycross had a state-of-the-art stereo system, there was no hint of a temperature control device. As a young man, his priorities were notably different than those of a perimenopausal female.

The saga of the Reid family "troubles" had begun the moment Waycross has picked her up at the Atlanta airport two hours before. Twenty-nine years old, the only redhead in the batch, Waycross was the oldest of her two brothers. His relationship with his younger brother, Macon, had always been rocky, at best. And Savannah usually agreed with Waycross, the more hardworking, sensible, and responsible of the two. If he said Macon was being a pain, it was probably true.

"What's he doing?" she asked.

"I don't even know what he's doing. I'm afraid to ask," Waycross replied. "But I know who he's doing it with. Since he graduated from high school he's been hanging out with those Whitney boys, and you know what trailer trash they are . . . especially that Kenny Jr.

What a friggin' yahoo that one is. He's so lazy the dead lice wouldn't fall off him and stupider than a dirt clod."

"The Whitneys. Yeah, I remember their old man," Savannah said, searching her memory banks. "He drank like a skunk and practically lived in Sheriff Mahoney's rear cell. It's no wonder the kids turned sour."

As they drove through Savannah's hometown of McGill, she noted, with a twang of the heartstrings, some of her favorite haunts: the drugstore where she had enjoyed the occasional strawberry ice cream cone on a hot, Saturday afternoon, the library where she had discovered the joy of Nancy Drew mysteries, the elementary school where she, her mother, and even her grandmother had attended. All three generations had played tag among the giant oaks and hopscotch on the hard-packed earth, where the grass had been worn away by hundreds of small, energetic feet.

But the trip down memory lane didn't take long. When Savannah had been a child, McGill, Georgia had been only three blocks long.

Now it was four.

Urban sprawl.

"Have you given Macon a talking-to?" Savannah asked him.

"I've preached whole sermons to him . . . so has Gran . . . but it just rolls off him like rain off a duck's back. You can't tell Macon Reid nothing; he knows all there is to know about everything. If you don't believe it, just ask him."

"How's everybody else doing?"

"Gran's good, full o' piss and vinegar, as always. Alma helps her out a lot."

Savannah smiled, reminding herself that there would be a few blessings to this visit. Seeing Gran and Alma were two. Savannah liked to think she loved all her siblings equally, but she had to admit a favoritism toward Alma, who had always been the one to nurse a sick kitten, rescue a baby bird, or help Gran wax a kitchen floor or even scrub a toilet when necessary.

"Alma's a sweetheart," she said. "I wish she were the one getting married, instead of Marietta. She deserves to find a good husband."

"Yeah, but I don't see that happening any time soon. She's still pretty shy with the boys."

"And Cordele?"

"Still as uptight as ever. Goes around telling everybody what they oughta and oughtn't do. She reads those psychology books and has a label for everything everybody does. I called her a busybody the other day, and she told me I'm a passive-aggressive with severe parental abandonment issues. Whatever the hell that means."

Savannah chuckled. "That sounds like Cordele. And Vidalia?"

"Going crazy with those two sets of twins, and taking Butch along with her. He works with me at the service station about eighteen hours a day. Says it's to make ends meet, but I think he's just avoiding diaper duty."

Savannah felt another surge of mixed emotions as they left the asphalt highway at the edge of town and turned left onto a dirt road. She wondered how many times she had walked this road from Gran's house to the highway to catch a school bus, to check the mail box, or just to get away for a moment of blissful solitude, away from a house full of nine kids, perpetually runny noses, mountains of soiled laundry and dirty dishes.

With an absentee, truck-driving father, and a mother who spent more time in the local tavern than standing at a kitchen sink or in front of an ironing board, the duties of childrearing had fallen upon Granny Reid and Savannah, the oldest of the brood. Other than producing a child every year or two and naming them after Georgia towns, Shirley Reid had contributed little to her children's welfare.

Savannah and Gran hadn't complained, though. Not even in their most private moments. Watching the babies grow into children, and the children into adults, they had figured it was time and energy well spent.

Now, looking back on it with older, more experienced eyes, Savannah wondered that she hadn't been more resentful at the time. The injustice of the situation had been lost in the chaotic hustle of caring for the babies that just kept coming. Savannah had been too busy to consider whether or not she was being used. And now, she couldn't honestly say she would change anything. All in all, it had been a good childhood. And what her parents hadn't, or couldn't, give to their children, Gran had more than provided.

"You did good, Savannah. Real good." Waycross gave her a sweet, loving look that went straight to her heart. It was as though he had read her thoughts. He reached over and patted her on the knee with his work-roughened, grease-stained fingers. "You had your hands full back then, and don't think we don't appreciate what you did for us."

She placed her hand over his and squeezed. "I wouldn't have missed a minute of it."

He grinned. "Not even the afternoon I brought home that snake and . . . ?"

"Ah, yes . . . the snake in my lingerie drawer episode. *That* one I could have done without. The frog in the sugar bowl wasn't exactly a high point either, but all in all, it was pretty cool, raising you guys."

Waycross rounded a corner and the house came into view. As always, when she had been away for a long time, Savannah was shocked at how small and shabby it was. The simple wooden structure was commonly known as a "shotgun" house, the rooms lined up in a straight row, from the front of the house to the back—living room, dining room, kitchen, and bedrooms, one opening into the other. It was so named because if someone stood at the front of the house and shot a gun, the bullet could exit the back door without striking a wall.

The tiny house had probably been built for a family of four, maybe five. With ten people, three bedrooms and one bath, it had been extremely cozy, to say the least.

Desperately in need of a coat of paint, it wasn't as white as she remembered, several of the tar-paper tiles were missing from the roof, and the porch sagged on the left.

But it was home.

More importantly, it was where Gran lived. Feisty and wise, Granny Reid had walked the earth for more than eighty years and generously shared her collected wisdom with Savannah and the rest of her grandchildren. Some had embraced her teachings more than others, but all had been given the benefit of her counsel . . . whether they wanted it or not.

Suddenly, it was very important to Savannah to get out of the truck and into that house. As soon as the vehicle rolled to a stop, Savannah's door was open.

She was across the yard and onto the porch in a matter of seconds, replaying in her mind the memories of coming home to Gran, whose hands were always busy peeling potatoes, folding laundry, and bandaging skinned knees, but who always had time to listen, to hear how someone's day had been, to enjoy the latest bit of gossip, or to help with an arithmetic problem.

Year after year, Gran had been waiting, a smile on her face when Savannah came through the door.

But this time was different.

When Savannah barged inside, shouting, "Gran, it's me; I'm ho-o-me!" she found her grandmother sitting in her overstuffed armchair, quietly weeping. Savannah's sister, Alma, sat on the ottoman in front of her, holding a handful of tissues. She, too, was crying.

Savannah felt her heart do a few double beats, and time slowed, as it did in those fractions of a second just before you hear something you'll never forget.

"Oh, no . . ." she said, "who died?"

"Ma-ma-con," Alma replied between sobs.

Waycross had come into the house behind Savannah just in time to hear the news. "Macon's dead?" he said in a hoarse whisper.

"No, he's not dead," Gran said, wiping her eyes. Savannah was shocked to see that, for once, she actually looked her eighty-plus years. "But he might as well be. Deputy Stafford just came here and arrested him."

Savannah felt her knees go weak, from relief or fear she wasn't sure. Sinking onto the couch, she said, "What was he arrested for?"

Alma began to sob even harder, while Gran steeled herself to reply. "They say he killed Judge Patterson."

"Killed . . . ? Macon? That's ridiculous!" Savannah said. "He wouldn't—"

"Yeah, he might have," Waycross replied, shaking his head as though suddenly weary. He sat on the sofa beside Savannah.

"No! I don't believe that for a minute. Gran, do you—?"

The look of misery in her grandmother's eyes

chilled Savannah nearly as much as her words. "Well, Savannah," she said, "you see, Macon's changed. He ain't the boy we used to know no more . . . been into all sorts of meanness lately." She dabbed at her eyes, then wadded the tissue into a tight ball. "I'm sorry to say that Waycross is right. Macon just might have murdered that old geezer."